Stained Radiance

By the same Author

HANNO, OR THE FUTURE OF EXPLORATION

POLYCHROMATA, a story-cycle

Stained Radiance

A Fictionist's Prelude

J. Leslie Mitchell
(Lewis Grassic Gibbon)

Polygon
EDINBURGH

© (Typographical text only) Polygon 1993
© Introduction Brian Morton 1993

First published by Jarrolds (London) in 1930
This edition published by Polygon
22 George Square
Edinburgh

Printed and bound in Great Britain by
Hartnolls Limited. Bodmin. Cornwall

British Library Cataloguing In Publication Data is available.

ISBN 0 7486 6141 7

The Publisher acknowledges subsidy from the Scottish Arts
Council towards the publication of this volume.

Dedication of these Old Foes
with New Faces to the
laughter and pity of one who
has known them in other
guises:
My Wife,
RHEA MITCHELL

Life, like a dome of many-coloured glass,
Stains the white radiance of eternity.
                                    – SHELLEY

But before the Builders upbuild in Mu
Tollan, the City of the Sun, there shall
be war, and the breaking of altars, and
the rending of hearts.
            – *Ascribed to Ma-Uinic brother*
            of Kukulcan, the Maya Bud-
            dha, in Atlantis, c. *600 B.C.*

CONTENTS

INTRODUCTION

On March 30, 1927, Rhea (Ray) Mitchell wrote to a friend: 'My husband and I are not friends. He is writing a novel and his characters all want soaking in double strong disinfectant for a week, then they want scouring and hung out to get some good fresh air!' Exactly a year later, J. Leslie Mitchell saw the end in sight: 'I am novelling at a great rate out here in the wilds. By the end of the month I shall be looking around for some publisher on whom to unload *Stained Radiance*.' Mitchell's first novel was rejected by twenty publishers before being taken on – as diffidently as it was offered – by Jarrolds of Paternoster Row, St Pauls: 'We feel that *Stained Radiance* is not likely to make a great appeal to the average literary subscriber. It is interestingly done but the outlook is fundamentally ironical.'

It isn't clear whether publishers were put off more by that quality or by Mitchell's defiantly announced 'disposition to call a spade a sanguinary shovel', or whether Jarrolds merely wanted to shave even further a desperately needed advance, but it is a fact that *Stained Radiance* has never found favour even with those critics prepared to argue the importance of Mitchell's 'English' novels relative to his masterpiece as 'Lewis Grassic Gibbon', the trilogy *Sunset Song, Cloud Howe*, and *Grey Granite*. In their respective studies of Gibbon, Douglas Young[1] and Ian Campbell[2] pass over it with barely a comment. Valentine Cunningham[3] calls it an 'anti-novel', though he recognises that Mitchell's concerns are archetypally of their time. Certainly *Stained Radiance* is too savagely bitter, too self-consciously ironic, too determinedly unsentimental and 'without asterisks' to be entirely convincing or successful.

[1] Douglas F. Young, *Beyond the Sunset*, London, 1973.
[2] Ian Campbell, *Lewis Grassic Gibbon*, Edinburgh, 1983.
[3] Valentine Cunningham, *The British Novel in the 1930s*, London, 1987.

However, its very real merits have been overlooked. It contains better writing and is more carefully structured than work completed 'later' in Mitchell's astonishingly compressed and foreshortened career; as a transparently autobiographical work, it offers important insights into Mitchell's development as a writer and political thinker; and it contains in Thea Mayven the most obvious prefiguring of Chris Guthrie, heroine of the *Quair* trilogy.

Thea, a Scots girl from the Mearns, shares a London flat with the ruthlessly promiscuous Norah Casement and with a young milliner, Ellen Ledgworth. In so far as the novel has a plot, it concerns the relationships of the three young women and an older, wealthier woman, the dilettantishly political Mrs Gayford, with four men. Norah is involved, *inter alia*, with a former soldier, James Storman, now the secretary of the Anarchocommunist Party; Ellen with the chinless Edward Snooks; and Thea with a young Air Force clerk (and would-be writer) John Garland, a minister's son possessed of a 'nameless curiosity – a damnable, ceaseless, hopeless curiosity' – who, despite the red herring of a Wiltshire birth, is transparently Mitchell himself. On the fringes of the group is the mysterious Koupa, a romantic poet-revolutionist who, like every other character, abandons principle to self-interest and who, having wrested the Anarchocommunist secretaryship from Storman, becomes Mrs Gayford's gigolo-husband.

The characters' lives are interwoven in a chaotic urban landscape reminiscent of John Dos Passos in *Manhattan Transfer* (and in the later *U.S.A.* trilogy) and through Mitchell's device of short, jump-cut 'subchapters'. Garland's attempts at fiction-writing are clearly intended as a heavily ironic commentary on Mitchell's own: 'His characters, intended to collide and produce ironic mirth for their abrasion-rubbings and ingenious theorizings on the subject of collisions, were becoming unmanageable.' Garland seems dangerously detached from real life; his seduction of Thea is a technical problem, like having his heroine lose her virginity on schedule. While working at his desk at the RAF camp, Garland witnesses a plane crash and watches a young Flying Officer burn to death. Curiously turned on by the sight, he also experiences a literary breakthrough.

In the central chapters five and six, he and Thea pass a 'Bucolic Idyll' with her family in Aberdeenshire, an episode which dispenses with Thea's virginity and underlines her divided nature. It also adumbrates Mitchell's obsession with pre-history, atavism, and the destructiveness of desire; a knife, found in a Stone Age grave, becomes a jilted woman's instrument of revenge against her employer-lover. (The chapter also includes a first glimpse of Malcolm Maudslay and Domina Riddoch, central characters of Mitchell's next novel *The Thirteenth Disciple*, together with first versions of important characters to be developed in *Sunset Song*.)

As a result of their love-making, Thea falls pregnant. However, John is posted overseas, to Egypt and the Holy Land, where he experiences a powerfully negative epiphany of the nature of religious belief. Left behind, Thea is evicted by her policeman landlord because of her friendship with the Communist Storman. As her pregnancy advances, she falls victim to eclampsia and is put in a pauper's hospital, where she lies at death's door. Alerted to her plight by a letter, John engineers a discharge by mangling his hand in the breech of a gun. He arrives in time to see her delivered of a stillborn child. Against all odds, she recovers. As the novel ends, John has taken over the Anarchocommunist Party from Storman and Koupa, not out of conviction, but because it pays a wage.

Mitchell's socialism was, as Cunningham insists, never more than dyspeptically marginal. His 'realism', particularly in the portrayal of Thea Mayven (based on his wife Rhea Middleton), borders on squeamish misogyny, but she is nonetheless a remarkable attempt to capture 'a cramped, happy, disturbed life'.

Stained Radiance is, for all its faults, a very remarkable novel, and merits re-publication, both for its intrinsic qualities and for the light it casts on the future career of a major Scottish writer.

Brian Morton.

CHAPTER THE FIRST

Wherein Various Unclassifiable Female Characters, together with a Revolutionist, a Soldier and a Gentleman, are presented to the Reader, and some Account given of Heaven and the Giant Wars.

Subchapter i

"MIGGOD," said Norah Casement, "there's Billy!"

She halted in the sunlight of Kensington High Street. She was twenty-three years of age, her eyes blue, her hair black. She had a short nose and the pretty, contemptuous face of a sane, uneasy, cultured monkey. She loved words like Miggod and Biggod and Divvle, for they stamped her with Irishy, good-heartedness and irresponsibility. But behind their cover she regarded the world scaredly, and with a greedy pity.

"Which is there?" demanded Thea Mayven, stopping beside her without excitement.

She was younger than Norah. She had a little hollow in her throat. Her eyes were like the sea, green and grey and a changing spectra of colours. She had red-brown, winey-tipped hair, cut short in the modern style and older in fashion than the panel-sculptures of Palenque. Her ears lacked lobes. She was the result of five hundred thousand years travail and bloody endeavour. She jogged Norah impatiently.

"What?"

Norah, screened under the awning of a shop-window, pointed. Looking across the street, Thea saw a short young man wearing the tie of some appogiatose school. He hurried. His face was a greasy cleanliness. Absentminded, he thumped against an oncoming perambulator. The woman in charge asked him if he was a bleeding rhinoceros. He hurried.

Norah breathed on the glass of the shop-window. "Promised to

1

meet him this afternoon. 'D forgotten all about it. Is he looking?"

But the short young man, cleanly, greasy and intent, had by this time borne his tie far down the street. He expected to take Norah to a *thé-dansant* and theatre. Afterwards, perhaps, he would sleep with her. He was mistaken. Relieved of his nearness, she uncovered a gold wrist-watch.

"Four o'clock! Divvle take it, Thea! I've to meet a boy at Charing Cross in half an hour. Why didn't you tell me the time?"

"I'm not a damned clock," said Thea.

She swore often and readily, with an unconscious precision and delicacy of accent which shocked and astounded. Below her burnished kindliness was a stratum of irritability. It outcropped unreasonably and unexpectedly, while her eyes still smiled. For this reason all treated her warily. Young men, members of the Middle-Class Tennis Union Club, would hitch their slacks at sight of her and regard her knowingly, desirously, and with apprehension.

Norah's scaredness flickered her eyelids. She and another girl shared a flat with Thea.

"Don't be starchy. There's a dear. I'll have to rush like the very divvle. The boy'll be waiting for me. Extra special he is. Bringing him to the flat for tea."

"Oh. You'll have to hurry. Who is he?"

"Wait till you see. *Some* boy!"

"What about Billy?"

Norah was unexpectedly vicious. "He can go to the divvle. There's my bus. Shan't be long."

She scampered across the pavement. The bus slowed down. She boarded it. The conductor looked down from the top. Smart filly. He banged the bell. The bus went on.

Thea Mayven crossed the street and boarded another. High up, and on the front seat, she rode day-dreaming through London. The sunlight burned through her thin frock and, with the changing lights, obscuring and brightening in her eyes, she looked down upon the streets.

Scots, she had never ceased to feel foreign in London, and intrigued by it. Beyond the city and the central and south-western districts, she knew nothing of it. But east in Poplar and Limehouse were Chinamen and Negroes and forgers. In Soho were Bolsheviks and Italians. In the west were wealthy people living in Mr. Frankau's novels. Somewhere, in the streets and places she had never yet had time to visit, lived and flourished Romance.

Believing this, she loved London with the faith of a pilgrim denied the Holy Sepulchre in Jerusalem through the necessity of earning a living by carrying the luggage of wealthier pilgrims from the railway station to the hotels.

"But some day, when my sulky atheist is a bestseller, I'll also live in the west," said Thea.

Behind her gaiety, and her occasional irritability perhaps a projection of it, was the sad romantic realism of the peasant. In Scotland, on the little farm where she had been born, she had hated the peasant life. In London she remembered it with gladness and with tears, a thing of sunrises and rains and evening scents and the lowing of lone herds across the wine-red moors. Yearly she went to Scotland for a holiday, seeking the sunset and peewit's cry. Then she would find her days obsessed with talk of cattle disease and the smells of uncleaned byres and earwigs crawling down her back when she lay in a field. She would long for London as her spiritual home and as a haven of security. She came back from her holiday and her heritage of the earth, homing to London like a lost bird.

Then the old songs of the winds and skies of the grey northland would go whispering through her heart again. . . .

She led a cramped, happy, disturbed life. Sex was a remote, tamed, humorous thing; occasionally a disgusting thing, and so to be disregarded. Politics were remote personalities. She had a vague, indifferent republicanism, a vague, indifferent contempt of royalty, and all the peasant's dislike and distrust of the working-class. She read much, but guardedly, gaily, unconvincedly. She looked upon religious emotion as hysteria, and upon God and His existence as improbable unpleasantness.

She descended from the bus near the "Good Intent" in Chelsea. She nearly stepped on a beggar-woman selling matches. Matches, lidy. Pipe-cleaners. She stared at the woman with her heart contracting strangely; always at the sight of such people, her heart contracted strangely. Oh Christ. A shame. A damned shame. And with that burning, suffocating pain in her breast she would walk on, hating for a little the brightness and indifference and the calm cruelty of the London streets.

Within five minutes of leaving the bus she was deep in the heart of old Chelsea. Antique, unclean, weather-beaten, ancient houses brooded above deep-sunken basements. Children played and cried in the warm stench, spun tops, ran races, quarrelled with greedy, accusing eyes, teased one another with the ingenuous cruelty of the young. Once the houses of prosperous merchants, those long stretches had passed through an English Bohemian phase of unwashed underclothes, art-for-art's-sakeism, and unconnubial beddings in studios inadequately aerated. Strong young men in those houses had fried kippers above paraffin stoves, quoted Swinburne, and derided God. They had passed. Slumdom had encroached with the years, growing like a grave, intent cancer, stealing down towards the River. But here and there some street still held out, hiring rheumatic charwomen to scrub doorsteps and polish bellpushes. Typists, mannequins, journalists, sales-letter businessmen and middle-class prostitutes, reading the *Daily Mail* on weekdays and going out to Box Hill on Sundays, dwelt in those streets, with the ancient houses converted to three- or four-roomed flats. Lying abed in winter nights they could hear the sound of the rain on the distant River, and in early mornings would awake to find its exhalations, like those of a lung-diseased beast, blinding the streets yellowly and densely in a soft foam of fog.

Rosemount Avenue was one of those streets. When Thea turned into it that Saturday afternoon it lay smitten in a coma by the heavy sun warmth. Its cliffs of stonework towered like the reaches of a dead, gaunt face. A dog lay panting in the middle of the street. It wagged a languid tail at sight of Thea. A flea. It scratched with hysteric abandon. Thea passed. It resumed its panting. A gramophone was playing "Nearer My God to Thee".

Ascending the steps of No. 41, Thea whistled the tune of "Nearer My God to Thee". Slop. Banisters nearly red hot. Wonder if Ellen's in and made tea yet? Hope so. I'll die if I don't have an unofficial cup soon. Even though it be a cross. This heat's killing. Might be August almost. Sun, moon and stars divide, upwards I fly. Wish to God I could. Still, all my thoughts shall be. But not in these trousers, not in these . . . Shower-bath? No time. Ffuu, you're getting puffed and padded, my gel. Latchkey? Forgotten it? Well, I'm—No. Yes—damned.

She had reached a landing. A solitary door fronted her. Ceasing to search for the latchkey, she pressed the bell.

Thereat the door opened and a chinless, foreheadless, gentlemanly face was obligingly projected. . . . Overcome, she giggled. . . . *What* a name!

Subchapter ii

James Storman, the noted Communist who was an ex-captain of Artillery, came down to the River from Covent Garden and walked along the Embankment. The plane trees shook in a little wind. The muddy waters sparkled. A tramp slept on a bench. The Communist ex-captain walked with a swinging stride.

He was six feet in height, his complexion sallowly brown, his eyes a shade of brown, his hair brown. But his eyes denied the neutrality of their colour. They were the shining, humorous eyes of a man fundamentally unhumorous. He had a cleft chin and a small, closely-clipped moustache. Keen, calm, a mathematician, he was a mystic and religious, with Communism his religion. He looked at the world with the blind, clear eyes of faith.

Presently he ceased to walk, and leaning his arms on the stonework above the River, surveyed the dying capitalist system. Opposite him, in confusion and multitude, warehouses, wherries, and docks sprawled down to the water's edge. Their blue backgrounded signs jostled everywhere. They uplifted advertisements to Heaven. They flaunted an obscure, obscene, vulgar life. They did not look dead. Only ugly.

"It cannot last," said Storman.

He had been secretary of the Anarchocommunist Party for five years. In the days of the General Strike it had been the spearhead of the movement to transform sporadic revolt into active revolution. Storman and other officials had toured the home counties on motor-cycles at breakneck speeds, killing chickens, haranguing strikers, pleading for order and discipline, and leading attacks on tramcars and buses. Emerging from those May days of 1926 with an enhanced reputation and a dour éclat, the party had since devoted its energies to publishing portraits of the wives of Labour leaders wearing furs and diamonds, and to seeking affiliation with the Labour Party. Under Storman the Party membership, consisting originally of Morrisian Utopians, Kropotkine anarchists, and young men of the middle-classes attracted to the idea of a forcible revolution with barricades and machine-guns which said Ha-Ha, had changed complexion to a considerable extent. Shaken and disgusted by the tactics of one who planned revolution as an engineer plans a bridge, the young men of the middle-classes had deserted *en masse*, taking the anarchists with them. For they believed in Individual Liberty and the Righteous Soul of the Common People. Strengthened by these desertions, the Party had acquired a coarse vigour and an uncultured forcefulness. It was denounced and freely advertised by Socialists, rotary clubs, dissenting churches, Conservative newspapers and the Sultan of Muscat.

"Nothing succeeds like excess," said Storman.

Now, brown, tall, well-tailored, he stood looking across the Thames. He had no hat. His hair was short-cropped and smooth. He looked like the engineer he had been. The tramp snorted on the bench nearby. Pigeons, sun-winking, flittering, bright-eyed, circled down to the pavement and, chireeking, pecked around the boots of the tramp. In the air hung a strange, fugitive smell.

"It is the smell of Spring," said Storman.

And, because he never associated Spring with England, but with the Nile and the brown lands of Khartoum, his thoughts went back on that lost fragrance to a reservoir he had once helped to build in Sudan. Auricularly, memory of it returned to him—the thin, far chants of the gang-labourers, the beat of the steam cranes under the blue glassiness, the pappat of hammers upon the culverts. Immersed in a steel-smitten retrospect, he was only gradually aware that the hammertaps of memory were mimicked by actuality. He was listening to approaching feet shod in hobnailed boots.

He turned his head. A private in the uniform of the Air Force had crossed Hungerford Bridge and was now close at hand, walking towards Victoria. He was of middle height, his jacket gathered at the waist by a belt and steel buckle. His calves bulged under the folds of his puttees. From underneath the black felt of his hatpeak he glanced at Storman out of a ruddy, sulky, thick-lipped face. He had questioningly-assertive eyes. In his hand he swung a small stick ornamented with a steel bulb and some obscure decorations in birds and Latinity. His buttons winked in the sunlight.

His eyes and those of Storman met.

The Air Force private half-halted. His eyes, collected and curious, looked into those of the Communist captain with an indifferent hostility. Recognizing each other, they were silent. The airman passed on with a pappat of heavy boots. Storman looked after him and suddenly sent his immense laugh booming down the Embankment.

The tramp awoke, the pigeons rose in a cloud. His unhumorously humorous eyes a-twinkle Storman turned again to the River. The tramp swore, subsided, pillowed a short-cropped chin in his elbow, and slept again. The pigeons, flittering, strutting, resumed their pecking.

Suddenly two hands covered Storman's eyes.

Unalarmed, his thoughts elsewhere, he stood for a moment half unaware of his blindness. Then he raised his hands and clasped two slim wrists.

"It is little Norah Casement," he said.

Subchapter iii

The Air Force private was the son of a Unitarian minister. He had been born near Bulford, in Salisbury Plain, and from early days had learned the way to Stonehenge across the windy moors. Stonehenge had first awakened his nameless curiosity—a damnable, ceaseless, hopeless curiosity which had wrung him like a pain throughout his thirty years of life.

His name was John Garland. And this name pleased him. A name of iron garmented in velvet. Like a purple note of music . . . John Garland. . . . Walking the Embankment towards Victoria, he fell to thinking of his name idly, pleasantly.

7

"Sometime, maybe, I shall be like it. Old and mellow and full of the illusion of disillusion. In that undreamt-of peace that men call age."

He grinned. He was very hot. There were no military policemen about. He loosened the collar of his tunic. Twenty paces in front of him a car slowed down.

It was a Daimler. It drew up by the kerb. The chauffeur descended. Blasted old blood-tub. A fat woman, in furs, descended. Ere she comes. Nah for a song and dance.

"What's wrong, Ernest?"

"Near rear wheel ripped, Muddim. Ave to jack it off."

The fat woman, swaying her stomach, beckoned Garland. "Help with this wheel, my man, will you?"

"Go to hell," said Garland, equably.

He passed on. The chauffeur licked his lips. The fat woman stared after him, crimson. And Garland thought:

"Why didn't you? Angry because she went by your uniform and assessed you as aitchless and obliging?

"Then get out of uniform. Get a job in the City under some bulbous-nosed go-getter who thinks Wells should be shot and that Anatole France is a hair pomade. Lead a pleasant, respectable existence. Marry. House in Purley. Get the *Daily Express* every morning. Turn the cat out nightly. Assure the next-door-neighbour over the wall that the days are drawing in. Grow chins and line your soul with suet. . . . Great God, I'd rather be an airman suckled to salute the ineffably brainless."

As ever when he allowed his thoughts to run riot, he felt pleased and invigorated. He lit a cigarette. A stout figure, with musing eyes, he halted and waited for a bus. It was nearly five o'clock.

He boarded a green pirate and rode west. Thirty years of age that day, he was conscious that his outlook on life was more appropriate to seventeen. Or seventy. He believed nothing and everything. He did not believe in himself. He watched the passing pageant of life with ironic humour, yet constantly found himself plunging into that pageant, grabbing a banner, insisting in joining in the song. And always, sooner or later, because he was conscious of singing out of tune, because he saw the ludicrousness of the banner and his fellow-marchers, he deserted. He returned to the pavement to stand agaze, speculating on the processionists, their lives, their indecencies, their lusts, whether they approved of Mr. Churchill and artificial silk stockings and believed in God.

Love, life, planets, stars, death, fate, the worm that dieth not, and words like widdershins and swastika intrigued him. He was interested in them as a scientist—with the wish for knowledge and with no ulterior hope of gain from that knowledge. Sometimes, as a result, a loneliness and a horror of himself and his incessant, ruinous curiosity would come upon him. He would long with a cynical passion for personal love, quarrelsomeness, children, slippers before the fire and a belief in the disinterestedness of Reuter's correspondents.

Goddilmighty, to escape and rest from oneself!

Reddened in the colours of the sunset, the green bus drove into the west like a chariot of God. Wide and brown and thronged branched the streets. They contracted and elongated in the sunset light. Over all hung the fainting Spring. A newsboy cried in the gutter of the discovery of a woman's head in an ashbin and the search for the murderer. In the windows of butchers' shops the dead bodies of animals, emptied of their intestines, hung pink and bloody and legless. Girls, short-skirted, eager-eyed, passed in and out of multiple stores. They had discarded the large breasts and broad buttocks of their mothers. Alert, quick, confident, and owlish, they made purchases in the Spring sales, paying an increase of 25 per cent on the usual prices. In bookshops, casually turning the leaves of chance volumes, their eyes grew gawked and contemptuous at some phrase or fantasy beyond their understanding. Throwing aside the book, they would walk out, counting their change and humming pieces of song about blue birds which were all day long. Cheered, emancipated, they walked the streets, or stood in little groups, or applied to their lips the reddening and men-alluring chemicals inherited from the courtesans of Sumeria and Thebes. The sunset brooded redly upon them, then closed and died in the face of the rushing bus whereon rode Garland.

He was late. Getting off the bus, he hurried, his hobnailed boots slipping on the heat-moist paving-stones. He swung his stick, turned into a doorway, and climbed three flights of stairs. Down the well of the staircase came the sound of a piano and a man singing in a strong voice, with jagged edges. A girl's contralto joined in. Garland halted upon the third landing and listened, for he loved the song. Emitting blurred sounds in place of the words he had forgotten, he opened his mouth to a vague, pleasurable humming.

> "I must go down to the seas again,
> To the lonely sea and the sky,
> And all I ask is a tall ship,
> And a star to steer her by,
> And the wind's song, and the tiddly um,
> And the whatname flying,
> And a grey mist on the sea's face,
> And the seagulls crying."

And Garland thought: "This is a lyric of the wanderlust— the wandering being over and the lust a memory. It is Romance. It tells nothing of the obscene stinks of a sailing ship, the bugs which habit the bunks, the sea that seen through mist looks like bad soup afloat with mildew, the meat that rises up and walks the decks and makes mewing noises. It is Romance. It has no connection with life. It is glorious."

And standing bulkily upon the landing, he grinned and rang the bell. Instantly sound of piano and song ceased. There ensued a hesitant, soundless blur of no-silence. Then the door swung open.

"Why, John, you're late."

And, from the same shadows that had an hour before projected upon her the Aztec face, Thea Mayven reached out to kiss John Garland upon the lips.

Subchapter iv

They kissed with a clean, unlengthy deliberation, touching hands the while. Drawing back his head, Garland felt, faint and sweetly bitter upon his lips, the moisture of Thea's.

"Sorry I'm late. How are you?"

"All right. Oh, happy returns."

"Thanks."

He laid aside his cap and stick. They spoke to each other in raised, laughing voices. Their natural manners changed. In the dimness of the little hall they glanced at each other with wonder and uncertainty.

In love, they quarrelled continually. Sometimes, when the ironist was uppermost in Garland, Thea would grow angry and silent and forget the fun of life while he dissected God and marriage and the ectoplasmic theories of Sir Arthur Conan Doyle. Garland's attitude—his multitude of attitudes—to life, moved and disturbed her profoundly. In his jesting she sensed falseness, just as in his bitterness a tongue-in-cheek insincerity. Knowing him better than did anyone else, she distrusted him, feared him not at all, and loved him passionately. Sometimes she wondered if his romantic poet's love for her was merely one of his attitudes, and, so wondering, would stab him with pinpricks of malice and a tentative coarseness. Remote in her mind, a thing she hardly dared uncover, was the knowledge that the asexual tenderness of his love was a treason to love. The desire which had given her birth and a woman's body cried for lust in love.

A remote cousin of Garland's was a friend of Thea's, and at the home of this cousin, in Chertsey, they had first met, three years before. Garland, in shabby civilians, was on a week's leave from his camp; Thea weekended with her friend. It was the blue-hazed weather of a mellow September.

So they met, and always was Thea to remember that queer pang of tenderness and wonder that sprung within her when first she looked in Garland's eyes. Remembering it, and believing the first her truer vision, she could disregard much of her later impressions.

As for Garland, the romantic was uppermost that weekend while he rowed Thea upon the River, and the ironist only a pale shadow a-rock with ghostly mirth.

So they fell in love—love which Garland, according to his mood or fantasy, either adored and glorified with a passionate tenderness, or else dissected into its constituents of animal conceit projected upon animal desire. Looking at Thea, he would feel a soft drowsiness grow about his eyes, feel a strange looseness of limb, hear the blood sing in his ears. Or a sudden tiredness, a longing for the benediction of her hands, to lay his head in her lap, to kneel by her, unthinking, in the shadows of

11

a sunset-flooded room, would come upon him. And the pain of his longing for her he would taste slowly, lingeringly, with ironical laughter.

"Come into the sitting-room. It's cold after the sun's down. Norah hasn't arrived yet—she's bringing a boy to tea. Did you hear us singing 'Sea Fever'?"

Speaking, Thea opened the sitting-room door. A beam of light sprayed into the little hall. Walking it, Garland entered into a smell of toasting muffins.

"Hello, old bean."

"Many happy returns, Mr. Garland."

"By jove, yes. Best of them, old bean."

It was a room twelve feet by fourteen. It held for furnishment a sideboard of imitation walnut, a gate-leg table, a deal bookcase, three armchairs and four armless chairs. The window-curtains were yellow. The three armchair cushions were yellow. The shade of the electric lamp was orange. This was artistic. There were five pictures on the walls. Two were lithographs of infants who appeared to have developed dropsy, two depicted battle-scenes where elegant men in tight trousers and calm smiles rescued side-whiskered comrades from under the obligingly poised hooves of charging horses. The fifth reproduced in an uncertain fadedness of colour the Heir of All the Ages.

The yellow window-curtains flapped in the evening breeze from the River.

A girl was toasting muffins. She had wished Mr. Garland many happy returns. Twenty-eight years of age, her name was Ellen Ledgworth. She was a milliner. Her hair was fair and fluffy and bobbed, her teeth complete and false. Her figure, broad at the hips so that she walked like a sedate cow, was at the moment squatted in an armchair and a black dress. Placid, she looked up at Garland hospitably, kindly. She did not believe in the Old Testament because it was silly. Strikes were caused by agitators . . . Though you mightn't believe in the Old Testament, there was certainly Something. Socialists, labourers with patches in the seats of their trousers, and people who quoted poetry without a placid cough were funny.

Opposite her sat her lover, Edward Snooks. With retreating chin and forehead, he had been a second-lieutenant in the

Tanks during the War. On leave in England, he had been snapshotted by press photographers as a typical Army officer. Both eyes an indeterminate grey, he had a slight impressive cast in one of them, and an unhealed, powdered sore on his chin. He hated his name, but Thea Mayven loved it. She would lie abed thinking of it, and gurgling with delight over it. Snooks! Oh, lord!

Looking across at him, as she followed Garland into the sitting-room and their greetings, her eyes twinkled at thought of his name. Snooks smiled back at her, fascinatingly, in answer. He appreciated her slimness. Shouldn't wonder if she was a warm little devil. He pulled forward the third armchair for Garland to sit upon.

"Sit down, old bean. Well, how's the Air Force?"

"God knows."

Thea had gone to the window and looked out. Her small head was enflapped by the uneasy curtains. She gurgled.

"And d'you think it makes Him bitter?"

Garland laughed and sniffed with a hungry appreciation the smell of the toasting muffins. He hated the Air Force. Like ninety per cent of those in the ranks, he had enlisted under the compulsion of hunger and unemployment. His stomach had conscripted him more surely than any Man Power Act could have done. He had never forgiven the Service the fact of its feeding him.

"Sick as a dog, I should think. Let's do some toasting, Ellen. You'll ruin your complexion."

And, spearing an untoasted muffin upon a fork, Garland held it out to the red glow of the coals.

Relieved, Ellen panted back into her chair and watched the muffin. Lighting a cigarette, Snooks asked questions about the Air Force. He was genuinely interested in it, especially in the pilots, who were officers, wearing collars and ties and having batmen to brush their shoes, rebuking unshaven parades in cultured tones. He still associated himself with the Services and talked to Garland with the kindly understanding of an officer appreciating a private's grievances. This condescension delighted the cruel ironist in Garland. He would retreat into his mind with a chance phrase of Snook's and extatize upon it, like a dog with a bone.

13

Meantime Thea, leaning out of the window, watched for the appearance of Norah and her boy, breathed the night air through small, oval nostrils, and, looking up at the sky, prophesied good weather for the morrow.

"It must be glorious to live in a camp down in Surrey in the Spring."

"There's nothing wrong with the location of the camp, though the camp itself . . . It's set high on a hill. I must take you down sometime. Wave-troughs of grass and trees in tides to the horizon; you can hear the nightingales in the woods at early dawn. . . . Oh, it's a pleasant place enough."

"But not for the rankers—eh, John? The officers have a decent time, though, I'll bet. I remember at Boulogne in 1915—an Officers' Rest Camp there. We used to laze all day with cool drinks. Motor jaunts in the evening. Back for dinner at seven. Good old War! . . . And those same lads up in the front line, Gad, they were splendid."

And Edward Snook's eyes grew bright with emotion, for he had read Mr. Frankau's book about Peter Jackson and modelled his war sentiments upon those there recorded at such generous length.

Garland nodded and turned the muffin on his fork. "Yes. Splendid. I've seen them sleeping three in one dugout, with only a single batman to look after them. Remember one especially in the Spring retreat of Eighteen. He must have been a Marathon champion, for he passed me; and I can sprint myself. He was crying and naturally very upset, for he'd mislaid his batman and his sergeant-major and didn't know what to do, and the night was coming on. There were shells churning a quagmire of marsh spanned by a half-submerged pontoon of duckboard. I caught him up there and as I started to cross he screamed out an order to me to get off and let him go first. He grabbed my leg and tried to hold me. But I was lost to all sense of discipline. I left him there, still screaming."

(How he had screamed! As a spectator Garland looked back across the years at that twilight struggle amidst the mud and the falling shells. From the dim picture-galleries of his memory he brought forth and looked again at the streaked face and slobbering mouth of the man with whom he had struggled for the right of passage. He'd given a woofing gasp as Garland's bayonet was driven into his chest; he'd gurgled and fallen and scrabbled in the mud. . . . Amazingly remote and unimportant. . . . That shaking bridge in the hellish flare. . . .)

Snooks threw his cigarette-end in the fire. He had never been far up the line, having acted as a stores officer in the Tank Corps. So, from his own experience, he knew that Garland was lying. He shook his head. He disregarded the story.

"Oh, there were rotters here and there amongst us, but, say what you like, John, blood tells. It was the public-school boy who won the War."

The father of Edward Snooks had been a butcher in Bristol. But Edward, after graduating from an orderly-room clerk to a commission, had forgotten this. Unconscious of snobbery or falsehood, he believed himself of aristrocratic descent and education. He believed in the Conservative Party and in a God of Battles with a sword and white whiskers, like the brigadier in charge of the Military Police at Le Havre. A clerk in the City, he would, when riding past the Cenotaph on the top of a bus, raise his hat gravely, as though returning the greeting of fellow ex-officers and acknowledging the salutes of defunct but still respectful privates.

"Yes, say what you like . . .."

"Well, perhaps they did." Garland finished toasting the last of the muffins. "Only, I wish they'd done it without asking my help. Isn't that someone coming up the stairs?"

Thea went out into the hall. In a moment a latch-key slotted into the outer door. In the sitting-room they heard the voice of Norah Casement.

"Miggod, r'we late, Thea? 've we kept you all waiting?"

"It's all right. The muffins are just ready."

"Oh, Jim, this is my friend, Miss Mayven. Thea, this is Captain Storman. Come in and meet the others."

Subchapter v

Storman and Norah Casement had first met at a dance of the Civil Service Clerical Officers Association. Norah was a clerical officer. She did not believe in the Association because of the ferocities of Mr. W. J. Brown, and his habit of referring to clerical officers as though they were workers, like

15

kitchen-maids or shop-girls. Nevertheless, she paid her subscriptions for the sake of peace and dancing.

She loved dancing. Prancing in grave, animalistic fox-trots originally fashioned to stimulate virility in the cave-shelters of Atlantis during the Third Inter-glacial, she would feel young men, holding her, grow excited and unnerved, and would laugh up into their faces with Irishy and insouciance.

Storman attended Association dances for two purposes. He enjoyed dancing and he enjoyed making converts. A personal friend of a high Association official, he preached seditious disregard of Association rules and the necessity for revolutionary tactics to young women who had previously believed that Communists always wore topboots and drank human blood with their porridge, the while they read the *Daily Herald* propped up against the body of a slaughtered Capitalist. But Storman did not wear topboots. It was inconceivable that he was an upholder of anthropophagy. Troubled and mentally colic-stricken, young women would listen to him and then return to their homes in Brixton and Wimbledon, whence they would emerge, scared into action, at the next meeting to elect officials, and vote Conservatives into the executive.

On the third occasion Storman and Norah met and danced Storman had halted abruptly in the middle of a step. "You know nothing of dancing," he explained, casually. "Come out into the corridor and I'll teach you the elements."

Dazed, she had followed him. They reached the corridor. Waiters lounged with empty trays. Disregarding them, Storman stamped and padded and pirouetted. They stared. Norah blushed. The agony was but begun. Commanded to imitate his motions she found herself obeying. Grinning, the waiters exclaimed poor tart.

And Norah, angry and shamed, was strangely attracted. She danced with him often thereafter. He never made love to her. He never paid the least attention to her remarks. He seldom spoke on a subject that was even faintly intelligible. He kissed her once with a cold and passionate precision and then asked if she would like an ice. He took liberties, boredly. In a fight for her self-respect, she sought to win him to a continuance of that passion which his kiss had promised. For this reason she had invited him to tea at the flat which she shared with Thea Mayven and Ellen Ledgworth.

After tea, they left the flat and went down to the River in search of fresh air. It was a soft, amethystine night. Couples walked the Embankment arm in arm. The arclights glowed dully. White and broad and light-dotted, the dim waters gurgled seaward. Overhead were stars.

"Have you and John Garland met before?" asked Norah.

Storman, pipe-smoking and looking up at the stars, came out of a brown study. "Yes," he said.

"Miggod, I thought you had. Why didn't either of you mention it?"

"It was in time of war, our last meeting, and we were on opposite sides. He tried to brain me with the butt of a rifle."

"Biggod, and what did you do?"

"I was riding a motor-cycle," explained Storman, "so I slowed down."

And, abruptly tickled, his laugh boomed out. Then, he pointed to a star burning low above the evening roofs. It was the planet Mars. It was probable that there were canals on Mars. Made by intelligent beings, organized to fight for life on a dying planet. A civilization greater than any on earth.

Norah looked up uninterestedly at the far, red glow of the Marxian world. What the divvle was he talkin about? Men in the stars. She gave a short, bright laugh. Unconsciously, she attributed animation to only a few intimates on her own planet. To conceive it existing in the sky was foolishness.

Storman ceased his astronomical exposition, and stopped, and looked down into the Thames, even as he had done earlier in the day. Norah, bored, halted beside him, and in a little silence they looked across at the yellow festoonings of lights on the Surrey bank. Then Storman tapped out his pipe, methodically, and put it in his pocket.

"Are you tired?" he asked.

Norah, sick of stars, nodded, yawned with mouth finger-covered. "It's been a sleepy afternoon. And this place gives me the shivers. Let's go."

He paid no heed. He had apparently forgotten his own question. Dim, tall, alien, and uncomforting, he leaned on the Embankment wall, and turned his face towards her.

"Norah, I love you."

"Eh?"

She was stricken mute with a contemptuous surprise. A prostitute passed them. Behind, at a short distance, trailed a soldier. Storman looked after the two of them till they faded into the greyness. A fog was rising from the River.

Norah felt as though a weight had been lifted from her heart. Biggod, now she'd show him. In love. The same as all the others, in spite of his Communism and jabber. Who the divvle did he think he was?

"By the way, Norah, are you technically what is termed 'pure'?"

She found that he had come closer to her. A warmth emanated from him. At her gasp he put his hand upon her shoulder, lightly, firmly.

"Don't answer if you don't want to. It makes no difference. Women, I suppose, have the same curiosities as men."

Norah found her voice. She had twice given herself to a junior clerk of the Civil Service, and had once staved off pregnancy only by an intimate knowledge of certain appliances. But anger and disgust shook her voice.

"If you think I'm that kind of girl . . ."

Suddenly his arm encircled her shoulders. In the rising fog they now stood alone, enswathed. The stars had vanished. Like dying suns in the dim heavens the distant arclights gleamed. Storman's arm tightened.

"Do you love me?"

He asked it with a wistfulness which gripped her heart. The night was very still. A London lovers' night. Norah felt a subtle warmth spread through all her body, and, in a numbed disgust, knew it for what it was. But love . . . only a name. She put her hands against Storman and tried to push him away, her throat grown dry in memories of the awry, insipid taste of afterlust. Love?

Perhaps it might be. Something that was different. She glanced up, sideways, at Storman. But for that encircling arm, he had attempted nothing. Contempt and an angry impatience returned.

"I want to go home," she said.

Still wordless, he bent and brought her body close against his

18

own. Then his thin lips met hers. His kisses blurred to warmth.

Norah's arms gathered him closer. Lost in a sensuous extasy, she believed in love.

Below them, the River sang its seaward-making song.

Subchapter v (a)

The fire smouldered and glowed with little bluish flames. It flung the shadows of the fender and two armchairs gigantic upon the ceiling. And a ruddy, furtive underglow stole from it across the floor, imposing mystic significances upon the entortured whorlings of the linoleum. Garland, deep in one of the armchairs, pointed a hand at the fire.

"Notice those bluish flames and the soft porous pieces in the coal?"

"Yes. I love blue flames."

"They are caused by the carbonization of animal fat."

"Uh." Thea, remote in the other chair, a shadow, a mystery, from which projected towards the fire two long, slim legs, shuddered. "Why do you always think of the unpleasant side of things?"

"But I don't. Animal fat isn't unpleasant. You often cook your food in it."

"You're hopeless."

"I can't see much of you, but your legs are adorable."

"Nice legs, aren't they? First time you've noticed them?"

"No. I've noticed them often. They are slim, with just that smooth curve at the calf which seems to us shapely. Yet, you know, of all amazing and unpleasant evolutions, that of the human body is the most futile and unwarranted. Man is the ugliest of all the animals."

"Thanks."

"But it's nothing to the ugliness he'll ultimately achieve—a large skull and a group of feelers. Then he'll look back on us, the ancestral type, with revulsion and disgust."

"Let him look. Beast. Ugh, I'll never have children."

"But perhaps they'll merely laugh at our skulls, same as we do at Victorian sidewhiskers."

They both laughed. They were alone in the flat, for Ellen and Edward Snooks had gone to the Chelsea Palace. Sitting in

19

the unlighted room for the past half-hour, they had talked lazily, disconnectedly, appreciatively. In the darkness they were shielded from each other and yet, subtly, made intimate. And Garland thought:

"We are pleasantly soothed and excited, sitting here, because of our inheritance of two conflicting race-memories—or perhaps three. Darkness is a thing of terror; but locked doors and a fire spell security; lastly . . ."

"John, have you met Captain Storman before?"

"Storman?"

"Yes. Norah's man."

"Yes. We stared at each other on the Embankment this afternoon."

"Was that all? I thought you both looked . . . funny when you were introduced."

Garland poked the fire. The bluish flames vanished. In their place uprose and hovered thin yellow convex sheets of flame. Thea drew in her legs.

"Why did you do that? It was more comfy before."

There was a little pause, Garland leaning forward, his ruddy face fire-ochred. He sighed. "Life's the foe of comfort."

"Goodness." Thea had clasped her hands about her knees. She considered him. "Wonder what they'll think of you up in Scotland when I take you home this summer?" She mused. "For that matter . . . "

"Yes?"

"What does England think of me when it takes *me* home?"

Garland still stared into the fire. He began to speak softly.

> "Behold, thou art fair, my love, behold, thou art fair,
>   Thou hast doves' eyes within thy locks;
>   Thy hair is as a flock of goats that appear from Mount Gilead. . . .
>   Thy lips are like a thread of scarlet, and thy speech is comely . . ."

The yellow flames died away.

"John."

"Thea."

"That's wonderful. But—is it me, or just poetry?"

"Oh, my dear!" He turned towards her and caught one of her hands and held it. An inarticulate pity came upon him. Goddilmighty, the hyena-like laughter of beauty! Never for

20

Thea Mayven or any other woman was that song sung; I've clad you in my dream-mate's garments and you question their texture and cut. . . . My dear.

The fire sank to a glow, a presence, a thing apart. In the darkness he still held her hand. Suddenly he spoke in a clear, shrill voice.

"You're lost in that chair, you know."

Wondering, yet knowing, she sat and waited. A bitter-sweet panic choked in her throat. Garland's right hand moved up her arm and touched her as with a frost; it crept betwixt the chair-back and her shoulders till his arm encircled her. His left arm below her, she felt herself lifted . . ..

Suddenly she was conscious of the horrifying, unclean kisses of a stranger.

Subchapter v (concluded).

At half-past ten John Garland went by Underground to Charing Cross, left that station, and walked across Hungerford Bridge. Here and there, in the embrasures above the water, gigglingly amorous young men held prostitutes in their arms. Overhead, on the Surrey bank, flicked and flashed bluely an advertisement of whisky. A thin rain came down in greasy pellets and then passed seawards.

Two young women, loitering past Garland, invited him with chirping lip noises. He cursed them with an absent-minded foulness and finality, and walked on. Behind him, they protested shrilly and obscenely. Garland leant his arms on the bridge and looked into the water and then across at the lights of Northern London.

They looked beautiful. All the night had a certain beauty, wrought of the Spring and the River. Even the voices of the starved shadows drinking of sex in the bridge embrasures had, in distance, a cadence of beauty. And because the beauty of unbeautiful nights and days, the beauty of bleak and evanescent and unexpected things, had the power to stir him darkly and wonderingly, Garland thought:

"And damn fools speak of the Sea as the Mother of men. She is the City: she is ours, the Great Mother, with the sunken eyes and the painted face and the strong, vile hands. She is ours as never was sea or mountain or heath. Blind, drunken, whored, she is ours. The beauty of a passing smile upon her face stirs us with a passion and pity as does nothing in Nature . . . The Great Mother. Bedecked in her whisky advertisements, her lighted ships, her roaring factories, her creeping clouds of disease, her whimperings of song and her tollings of deathbells. . . . Murderous, pitiful, whimsical: with a song in her heart and a sneer on her harlot's lips."

For a little, exalted and ironic in a breath, he lingered on the bridge, then went along it and descended into a network of thin, greasy streets, darkly-lit, mouth-organed, fish-and-chip-smelling. Four young men swayed upon the pavement. They were singing, lifting up vacuous, grave faces towards the sky. They drew aside courteously, swayingly, to allow Garland to pass. And Garland thought:

"The desire for expression is of all desires the most universally human. Between the singing of these boozed louts, Shakespeare's Hamlet, and the Ring of the Nibelungs there is only a difference of degree."

And, under the high shadow of Waterloo Station he chuckled. "You bloody prig."

Entering a sudden luminous doorway in the dark greasiness of the street, he found himself at the foot of a staircase that crept up to a far shimmer of brilliant light. Nor was this any illusion. Like a serpent, undulating, the stair arose out of blackness, and, like a belly-tender serpent, climbed. Mounting a serration on the monster's back, Garland was borne aloft into Waterloo Station. He passed quickly through the crowds, stopped to show his pass-form to a military policeman with a Yorkshire accent and the small, stern eyes of a dyspeptic swine, and then descended through ringing corridors to the cab-ranks and stifle of the Waterloo Road. Crossing to the right, he climbed the steps of the Union Jack Club.

Two Artillerymen, a Scots Guard, a Marine, and an American sailor were sitting in the entrance-hall. The American sailor, his small box hat toppling over his face, snored nasally, confidently. The Marine was eating chocolates. The Scots Guard and the two Artillerymen were talking about women.

Garland, bulky, clad in his shoddy blue, swung his stick and began to climb the stairs. Within view of the entrance hall these stairs bore a carpet; their walls were decorated with spears, javelins, testimonials, blowtubes, and the heads of animals. Beyond view of the entrance hall, the floor again rang beneath Garland's feet. On the third landing he diverged into a maze of corridors lined with the doors of cubicles. He was in a hive, cleanly, dim, murmurous. And about him arose the smell of week-end baths and the fish-and-chips smuggled to their beds by the inmates. At room 599 he stopped, inserted a key in the lock, swung open the door, and entered.

The cubicle contained a bed, a chair, a washbasin, a chest of drawers, a looking-glass. Upon the bed lay the attaché case which Garland had laid there earlier in the afternoon. Beside it was a copy of "Crainquebille".

Garland closed the door behind him, sat down on the bed, lit a cigarette, and stared unseeingly at a notice on the wall. It read:

SMOKING IS FORBIDDEN IN THE CUBICLES.

Garland began to unwind his puttees. The whole floor on which his cubicle was situated was very still. Garland's cigarette drooped its ash tentatively towards his breeches. He became aware of the fact that he was sitting, his mind a fogged blank, staring into vacancy. Half-unwound, the roll of puttee hung in his hand. He looked down at it, then flung it from him. Its hairiness of touch had made him shiver.

He began to undress recklessly, with speed. His whole body burned with a disgust of his clothes. He kicked aside the heavy boots, ripped off the thick socks, presently stood naked. Broad-shouldered, white-skinned, the hair here and there on his body was fair and silky, soft matts which he touched tentatively. His hips were narrow, but his loins curved strongly. Interestedly he passed his hands over the bulging calves of his legs.

"I was made for a breeding animal."

He suddenly raised his head and looked at his reflection in the mirror above the chest of drawers. His eyes were shining, his heavy lips hung slack. He shivered again.

Cold.

From the attaché case he took out a suit of blue pyjamas.

Clad in it, he turned back the blankets from the bed, picked up "Crainquebille", stood hesitant. Then he walked to the window and pulled it up.

Far below was the deep, dim well of the courtyard. Garland looked down at it, then up at the stars. He addressed the night in curious, guilty whisper.

"By God, that was a narrow escape."

He stood listening in that silence above London. No reply came to him. He drew a deep breath, put the cigarette between his lips, then suddenly spat it out. It sailed outwards, like a rocket, spun and wavered in some eddy of air in the courtyard, then disappeared into the darkness. . . . By God, a narrow escape. For Thea. For yourself. . . . You damned, filthy fool.

It was that nerved passivity of hers which had stopped him. Quite suddenly. As suddenly as it had begun. He had taken his lips from her face and his hands from her body. There had come from her a tearless, choked sob. In another moment she would have been as he had ceased to be. . . .

"It was that which was the third race memory upon us in Thea's room. Sex. Something greater than ourselves. A memory like a poison gas. It makes a goblin of the sun."

He was smitten with a sudden, still wonder at the silence of the Spring night, and, in the midst of that wonder, was slowly aware that his self-horror and self-loathing were slipping from him. He reached to light another cigarette and looked up at the sky with a detached curiosity. A moment before, consciousness of his own physical lusts had moved him to an almost physical sickness. Now, carefully, meticulously, detachedly, he built up a wondering thought. . . .

All the beauty and delightfulness of Thea. That curve of her throat. The winey hair that smelt like and tasted like an old, grave wine. Those archings of her brows. The queer, delicate beauty of her hands. That shy, impertinent gurgle. That adventurer's mind of hers. Her twists of phrase and accent. Her memories and likes and patriotisms. . . . All Thea, all threads of lovableness to lead love and adoration to her.

And each and all of them but enticements for him to rape and fertilize a female beast in order that she might bring forth young.

Those things of the Spirit that were apart from Lust—Lust

was their essence and connotation. But for one foul biological accident, Man would never have been Man. Unlike all other animals, he ever longed, in an insensate biological vanity, in and out of season, to fertilize the female of his kind. Urged forward and unendurably pressed by this longing, his history has seen arise marriage, love, prostitution, morals, art, Right and Wrong, God, the Virgin Birth; and Marie Stopes. With but a subtle difference in his chemical composition—with but some glandular modification to induce that trait of normality in the procreative organs which was the characteristic of all other animals, Man would not yet have been Man. . . .

Garland was suddenly conscious that the stars glowed no longer. They leered. Sadistically. Sex everywhere. Up there as down in Chelsea. Sex, Nature, God, the foul Trinity back of Life. It was God who had stooped with him in that moment of black lust, stooped with hot breath and eternal, wearied, unwearying, mindless purpose. . . .

A dim Ape-shape that squatted against the stars.

"You Beast," said Garland.

CHAPTER THE SECOND

Wherein Divers Folk react to God and Man as beseems their Natures, and in a Fashion beyond the Author's Powers of Précis.

Subchapter i

EARLY on the Monday morning Mrs. Streseman Mullins, owner of the millinery establishment of Cocotte Sœurs, sent for Ellen Ledgworth. Mrs. Streseman Mullins was a tall woman, handsomely clothed and with a powdered face. Her breath was rank, for she suffered from pyorrhea and dreaded consulting a dentist. Owing to this, her husband had proved unfaithful and she had divorced him. Craving sex-companionship, she had promoted a designer to managership, and, inviting him to her house for dinners, had constantly sought to seduce him. But the designer was a Fascist and occupied with politics. Seeking the salvation of the Empire, he noted neither Mrs. Streseman Mullins's breath nor the cravings of her desire. For long hours he would lecture her on Signor Mussolini and the tactics of Bolshevism the while she writhed in the agonies of pyorrhea and longing. Then he would return to his wife and four children in his flat in Brixton.

Her breath odouring the room, Mrs. Streseman Mullins spoke to Ellen, ordering her to take a selection of hats to a Mrs. Gayford in Mayfair, to await a decision and selection, and to make notes on any alterations in design which might be desired. Ellen listened with cheerful eyes and placid face, and then went down to the shop, picked up the large box which had been prepared, and set out for Mayfair.

She went by bus, first purchasing a copy of a London weekly to read on the way. The weekly was a literary one. It contained short articles on the private life of a mistress of King Charles and the Riviera as a holiday resort, a weekly excerpt from

27

Pepys' Diary, a page on matters of grammar and syntax, book-reviews, a photograph of Mr. H. G. Wells, and a leader by the editor describing how he himself had risen to literary eminence. Ellen read the leader with unimpaired cheerfulness, skipped the book reviews, and had completed the selection of Pepys when she arrived at her destination. Having no further use for the weekly, she left it lying on the seat. A Communist navvy, seated next to her, picked it up and, looking with contempt upon the photograph of Mr. Wells, spat.

Ellen rang at Mrs. Gayford's door and was taken up to a bedroom. Mrs. Gayford was sitting up in bed dictating letters to her secretary, a girl of sixteen. She took no notice of Ellen's entry, but stopped now and then to tap her teeth with a gold-mounted pencil. The room was tastefully furnished in blue and white. Einsteinian decorations whorled upon the walls. On the mantelshelf was a bust with a sneering face. This Ellen thought was Pan. But it was Lenin. Mrs. Gayford was clad in a dressing-jacket and embroidered pyjamas. Beneath the throat of the latter her neck showed creased and yellow. Round eyes protruded slightly from her cultivated face. She was forty years of age, and had sought for twenty of these to create a sensation. She had lately publicly disowned her son, had had her house burgled four times in succession, had addressed meetings on Free Love, Woman's Right to the Illegitimate Child, and Christ an Impostor. A convert to Communism, the damage sustained to her toilet by a fascistic egg at a Peace meeting had shaken her convictions to their depths. Nevertheless, she dictated now, in a clear, sharp voice, as to an underling:

> The Editor,
> *The Red Republican.*
> Dear Comrade,
> How long will the British proletariat allow to pass without protest the latest outrage upon Communists in Latvia? Following on the suppression of the trade unions, it is now stated that the right to strike has become illegal in that dark land. Our Latvian comrades' hour of trial is ours: their menaced rights are ours. Let demonstrations be made at the Latvian Embassy and the murderers'

envoys shown that we workers in Britain know how to resent an outrage upon the liberties of the entire proletariat.

Long Live the Revolution!

Yours fraternally, ——

Ceasing to dictate, Mrs. Gayford turned her head and looked Ellen up and down with a cold criticism. Loving revolutions, she switched her mind reluctantly back from the fraternal huzza concluding the letter.

"What do you want?"

"I have brought your hats, madame," said Ellen, placidly.

"Cocotte Sœurs? Very good. I will examine them, choose, and return those I do not require." Mrs. Gayford spoke with deliberation, moving her lips gracefully in the fashion which she had long practised in front of a mirror. Slipshod in speech, she attempted to improve herself for public occasions by the study of books on Good English. From those books she learnt that though the English language had no infinitive verb yet to split that infinitive was a grammatical enormity, and to end a sentence with a preposition a sign of under-education. Guiding herself by these rules, porters, taxi-drivers, and literary folk with whom she came in casual contact regarded her either as a foreigner or a mental defective.

Ellen, turning to leave the room, was halted by a question.

"Do you belong to the Garment Workers' Union?"

"No, madame."

"Why do you not?"

"Because I don't choose to, madame."

Mrs. Gayford sat up more rigidly in bed, thereby revealing the well-developed bust which she had never been able to suppress since the bearing of her one and only child some twenty-three years before. The pores pitted her skin like miniature extinct craters. The secretary, by a deft manipulation of the muscles of her mouth, grinned unpleasantly at her employer and pleasantly at Ellen. For the secretary was sick of workers' unions and Communist societies and suchlike unsanitary organizations. She considered Mrs. Gayford required scrubbing, mentally and physically. Ellen, calm, broad-hipped, stood by the hatbox.

"Do you know to whom you are speaking?"

"Mrs. Gayford, I believe, madame."

"What is your name?"

"Ellen Ledgworth, madame."

"Very good. I shall report your insolence to your employers. And I think the Union will take care that you are not provided with another situation. You can go."

"Very well, madame. Good morning."

Ellen went downstairs. It was near the lunch-hour. She regretted she had nothing to read in the restaurant on which she was already intent.

As she reached the foot of the stairs, a footman, tall, imposing, and limping a little because of a soft corn between his toes, was attempting to restrain a young man from entering the hall. The young man, dressed in a well-cut lounge suit, argued with virulence. As Ellen appeared, he turned to her.

"Is my mother up there?"

"I don't know. Who's your mother?"

The young man looked at her with surprise. She was evidently not a servant. But also, she was plainly not of any well-bred or sheltered class. Assuming a cultured voice nervously, he said:

"I beg your pardon. Mrs. Gayford, I mean."

"She is in bed," said Ellen, placidly.

The young man flushed. "Bloody old fool," he remarked.

At this the footman, spite the agony of the soft corn, grinned. Ellen, forgetting the servants' entrance, made to pass out through the open door, then stood aside to allow another visitor to enter.

It was James Storman.

"Good morning, Miss Ledgworth. Didn't know you visited here."

Swaying her broad hips preparatory to leaving, Ellen smiled.

"I don't think I will again."

"Oh. Why not?"

"Mrs. Gayford has just told me she's going to ask my employers to dismiss me for insolence."

Footman and young man stood listening. Both reared in different sections of a large house, they were unacquainted with good manners. They stood and eyed Storman and Ellen with mouths slightly opened and fishlike eyes.

Storman smoothed his hair. Clad in plum colour, he looked well. He wore no hat. His eyes shone humorously.

"Bloody old fool." He came into the hall. The young man, regarding him dazedly, stood aside. The Footman stepped forward.

"Mrs. Gayford expects you, sir. You are to go right up."

"Right. I'll settle things for you, Miss Ledgworth. Don't worry."

He went swiftly up the stairs. Ellen passed through the doorway and descended to the street. The young man followed her, indecisively. Sinking into a settle, the footman removed a shoe, and, stroking the soft corn, moaned.

Out on the pavement the young man, coming near to Ellen, raised his hat.

"I beg your pardon, but do you know who that fellow is?"

Ellen nodded. "He is Captain Storman, a Communist agent."

"Good God!" The young man swore carefully, then apologized. "You see, I'm her son. She forbids me to enter the house and yet invites that rotter up to her bedroom."

"I don't think she's in much danger."

They smiled at each other, Ellen with a placid coarseness, the young man with a flush. He was Robert Gayford and was twenty-three years of age. He had gone to Harrow but not, subsequently, to any university. Disowned by his mother after a police-court case of petty larceny in which he had figured, he lived on the charity of an obese uncle who drank Younger's Ale, read Gibbon, provided his nephew with an allowance, and swore whenever he saw him. As a result, Robert Gayford stayed mostly at his club. Without an occupation, he had become a Roman Catholic and upon occasion sought to gain admittance to his mother's house in order to convert her from the atheistic life which she was leading. At other times he sought life and adventure. Thought of sex thrilled and terrified him. Consummation of desire he had never yet experienced, though, brooding upon it, his blood purred. "What," he pronounced "Hwaw", uneasily. In stressful moments his voice fell to a thin flatness. He wore under his coat a knitted woollen jacket of vivid colours and obscure design. Believing in God, he read the *Morning Post* and was thrilled by its leaders.

Ellen's last remark had given him his cue. With questioning

31

eyes he surveyed her figure. It was good. Perhaps he might make her acquaintance to good effect. Perhaps she lived alone. They would spend the day together. She would invite him home after dinner at a restaurant. There would be soft lights and warmth and tenderness and she would love him. He would seduce her.

His face becoming bright, he spoke to her again.

"Come and lunch with me. Hwaw?"

"Pleased," said Ellen.

A bus came. They boarded it. Throbbing, it sped along the street. Its driver went off duty at Charing Cross and he was hungry. The bus fled at unusual speed. Road-workers cursed it. It splattered through a stretch of tar. Overhead the sky had of a sudden cleared to a wild, strange blue shadowed by sunshine.

Robert Gayford and Ellen had mounted to the top of the bus. They sat side by side on the front seat and peered into the dust. Ellen's knee touched the young man. Absorbed in thoughts of her, the touch thrilled him with a sweat-pringling extasy. Ellen smiled at him placidly.

"We'll go to the Strand Corner House."

And, swaying upon her broad hips, she felt the gastric juices stir pleasantly within her stomach.

Subchapter ii

Meanwhile Storman sat on the edge of Mrs. Gayford's bed and talked to her. The secretary stood impatiently by the window. She wished to leave and type the letters already dictated. Further, she loathed Storman, for the latter treated her as he did most women unconnected with his political faith—with the insolence of a complete indifference.

With Mrs. Gayford he was otherwise. His primitive sense of humour tickled to a cruel under-laughter the while, he listened to her patiently, agreed with her tactfully, bullied her and lied to her flatteringly and basely. He patted her mind and stroked her brain. Had it suited his purpose, he would have burned her alive with an equal thoroughness.

His purpose was to procure money for the Anarcho-communist Party. Pursuing this aim during the last two years, he had cajoled trade union leaders, wheedled Socialistic authors, begged from Moscow, borrowed from the French Communist Party, and blackmailed business firms in Manchester. To the same end, he would have sold the bones in a London cemetery.

He thrilled Mrs. Gayford, who, blind enough in most things, yet sensed his inhuman, selfless cruelty of purpose. It made her draw her bedjacket about her and snuggle down into the sheets. He was as stimulating as electric treatment in a beauty parlour. Speaking, he looked her straight in the eyes.

"You have done the Cause a service, comrade. In our narrower interests we are apt to forget the broader issues. The Latvian persecutions will certainly be made the subject of demonstrations. Better still, if we can collect the money, we will send a donation from the workers of Britain to fight the White Terror of the Baltic."

Knowing that this style of speech pleased and impressed, he addressed her with the sterile blood-and-iron pomposity of a Moscow thesis. Mrs. Gayford sat up and nodded.

"Yes, we can raise a fund. I will set about it through the columns of *The Red Republican*, if you will give me some space this week."

Storman shook his head. "And the Latvian workers meantime—rotting in their prisons, dying by gibbet and firing-squads? . . . My God, when I think of it! But for our poverty, the poverty and the apathy of the workers here, Latvia might be freed even yet. Even yet might the red flag rise in her streets behind the workers' barricades . . .."

He had stood up, emotional, and turned away from the bed towards the window and the glowering face of the secretary. Behind him, Mrs. Gayford sat with wrinkled skin and shining eyes. Barricades delighted her. The thought of machine-guns and brave, clean sanitary workers pumping lead into attacking Whites moved her with an extasy that was religious.

"You mean—there could be an insurrection?"

Storman turned back towards her. "We were discussing those demonstrations at the Latvian Embassy, comrade. Could you arrange for a woman's contingent?"

Mrs. Gayford understood. At a motion of her head, the secretary left the room. With thankfulness. Mrs. Gayford addressed Storman in a whisper.

"The Latvian workers would revolt if . . .?"

"If they had the arms and ammunition. But there's no use thinking of that. By the time our fund has collected a few pounds—well, it will be useful for burying the corpses."

"But where could these arms be procured? Not in Latvia?"

"A Swedish firm would send a boatload across the Baltic. All the details have been gone into. . . . If we had a millionaire in our party he might provide those guns and his name live for ever in Latvian history as Byron's does in Greek." He gave a weary laugh. "Only, we've no millionaire."

Mrs. Gayford was pressing the secretary's bell. Upon her face had come a light that transfigured it.

"How much would the arms cost?"

Looking at her, Storman calculated swiftly. "Eight hundred pounds."

"Comrade, I will give you it—in trust for the Latvian nation. I am no millionaire, but—Miss Robson, my cheque-book. Be quick."

As she sat signing the cheque, Storman, brown and tall, looked at her. The light had not gone from her face. For a moment a contemptuous wonder held the mind of the ex-captain of artillery.

"Oh, there's another thing, comrade. A girl—a Miss Ledgworth—came here this morning. I believe she interviewed you, and there was some disagreement."

The light faded from Mrs. Gayford's face. She frowned.

"Ledgworth? No . . . Oh, the girl from Cocotte Sœurs?"

"I met her as I was entering. She told me you had threatened to have her discharged."

A faint, thin colour, leaving the wrinkles still white, came on the woman's face, and with it a certain hauteur. By a strange change, she was moved back into the point of view and demeanour of the class into which she had been born.

"She was insolent."

"A revolutionist has no dignity, comrade."

At Lenin's phrase, a mere sulkiness replaced the hauteur. Storman, folding the cheque and putting it in his pocket, felt glad of the fact that it had already left Mrs. Gayford's hands. Otherwise, the Latvian workers might have been constrained to storm the barricades with toothpicks. (Where the devil exactly was Latvia, and what was happening there?)

Mrs. Gayford tapped her teeth with the pencil.

"I did not mean insolence from a personal point of view. But this girl is a blackleg. She is not a member of her union."

"She will join to-morrow. I'll see to that."

"Then, of course, I'll let the matter stand."

"Thanks, comrade." The ex-captain of artillery prepared to leave. "For what you have done to-day I know that neither Latvia nor the Republic of the World will ever forget."

Nodding good-bye, Mrs. Gayford, comfortable amongst the pillows, was scarcely conscious that he had left. Instead of the room-walls surrounding her, she saw the Latvian workers' groups, bayonets a-glister, marching through the bitter snow of a storming nightfall; heard, far on the winds, the music of the Marseillaise and the crackle of machine-guns. And then she saw the People triumphant, saw in the great square of a Baltic town the statue of a woman in symbolic dress, reared to overlook the Sea and City. . . .

And the garments were the garments of Liberty, but the face, fashioned by a master-sculptor, was her own.

Subchapter ii (a) Anticipative

A week later the secretary of the Blackshire Miners Association, which had been carrying on an independent strike for the past six months, forwarded to the headquarters of the Anarchocommunist Party a receipt for £800 and a promise to support the Anarchocommunist affiliation application at the next Labour Party Congress.

Subchapter iii

Suddenly, at noon, the Spring sun breathed upon London with a warm, malarial breath, and it was Summer.

Through the long corridors of the streets, in a tide that was almost visible, advanced the heat; and through the heat the bus from Mayfair carried Robert Gayford and Ellen Ledgworth to the entrance of the Strand Corner House.

Streams of people eddied in and out. The streams were

hurried and apologetic. Men with chalky faces predominated. Hurriedly, fearing indigestion, they left or entered. Tables were crowded. Queues waited on each floor. The band played from Lohengrin. It was stiflingly warm.

Smiling, Ellen led the way to the third floor.

At length they found seats. Ellen ordered steak and onions and rhubarb and cream. Sickened, Gayford ordered the same. Sweat stood on his forehead. As though it also sweated, his brain was in a dull, warm daze. He leant uncertainly across the table.

"Look here, let's spend the day together."

Surveying him, Ellen discovered his face to be splotchy and unhealthy. He wanted exercise. She nodded, placidly.

"Don't mind if I do. It won't make much difference, as your mother's going to have me sacked."

She was undisturbed at the prospect. A good milliner, she would soon find another position as good as or better than that held by her at Cocotte Sœurs.

Food arrived. They ate. A tenor sang "Sweet and Low". They clapped. Stout men laid aside their spoons and beat their moist palms together. Girls chattered, bringing out mirrors and powderpuffs and dabbling warm faces. Food introduced into their stomachs exuded heat and comfort through the pores of their skins. Mollified and dyspeptic, they surveyed the surrounding tables and listened to the band with a feeling of pleasant security.

Suddenly, while the musicians rested, a voice rang out through the restaurant, down the wide well from floor to floor. It was the voice of a man singing.

> "Arise, ye outcast and ye hounded!
>   Arise, ye slaves of want and fear!
> For Reason's thunderous tramp has sounded
>   And the day is drawing near . . ."

A wild gibberish, sung in a sweet, cracked voice, it stilled the restaurant. Wondering faces were lifted. Beside the well on the third floor a man had risen and stood singing, his hands outstretched. His face wrung with a pallid sorrow, he stood and sang. Open-mouthed, a waiter stared, scratching himself intimately.

36

The floors hushed a moment, listening politely, with jaws poised. A faint clapping arose. The singer stopped, glared, made an obscene gesture common in the bazaars of Jerusalem, wheeled about, and was gone.

"What was it he sang?"

"Did you see his face?"

" . . . a stunt of the management."

This became the general opinion. The song was recognized and verified as the new *Morning Post* patriot chant, the Hungarian National Anthem and a lyric from the Hollywood talking-picture "Speakeasy Love".

"Damned funny, hwaw?" said Robert Gayford. "Did you know what he sang?"

"Oh, yes," said Ellen, placidly. Then was a little worried, remembering her companion's social status. She searched carefully among her accentuations and then decided against the "h". "It was a nymn."

Subchapter iv

At three o'clock on the afternoon of that day Storman's typist brought him a cup of tea. She was a small, dark girl with earnest eyes and horn-rimmed glasses. All day she typed to Storman's dictation and at night attended classes in ambulance work, so that she might be prepared for the Revolution. She and Storman each had an office at the rear of the printing and publishing works of *The Red Republican*. In these offices they planned the overthrow of Capitalism and organized for the dictatorship of the communes.

"A man wishes to see you, comrade."

Storman took the tea, tasted it, and resumed work on the pile of manuscript in front of him. "What's his name?"

"Cooper. From Egypt, he says."

"Cooper. Cooper? . . . I'm damned. Ask him to come in, comrade."

A moment after the typist's exit, the door opened and a man stood looking at Storman. Then, hand outstretched, he limped into the room.

"Koupa!"

"The same. And yourself, my Storman? Little Christ, it is

37

good to see you. . . . Eh, a card-index? What fate for a rebel! Tea? It is a swinish drink. Besides, I had five pints of the so-good beer for my lunch. Eh, Storman!"

He stood with his hand on the shoulder of the ex-captain of artillery, then shuffled to a chair and sat down.

They had not seen each other for five years.

Andreas van Koupa, a Dutchman who had once lived sufficiently long in England to take out naturalization papers, was a poet and a tramp. He liked tramping. He had once walked from Paris to Cairo without crossing other water than miniature streams. The world in undress amused him. Over the backyards of the bourgeoisie human nature was revealed to him. He spoke nine languages and had three wives—one in Leningrad, one in Cairo, and a third in Alexandria. Vain of his appearance, he had the pale, still face of a Da Vinci Christ and beady, birdlike eyes.

Before the War he had starved in most of the capitals of Europe, writing verses which no publisher would accept. In Paris, after the outbreak of hostilities, he had lived by writing obscene little sex stories which were privately printed and sold in brothels to English soldiers. In London, in 1916, he had been conscripted and sent to the Somme. Terror and distaste filled him. He attempted to commit suicide. One night he stormed a German trench, single-handed, bombing its occupants to submission. He was decorated. Still terror-stricken, he volunteered as a sniper. He bore a charmed life. Finally, in an advance, he was crippled by a British bullet and invalided out of the Army. At the conclusion of the Armistice, however, volunteering as an interpreter with the Army of the Rhine, he was accepted. Six months later he was tried for embezzlement of commissariat funds, found guilty, and sentenced to six months' imprisonment. At the conclusion of that time he tramped eastwards through a starving Germany and Russia to Moscow, where he was imprisoned on suspicion of being a spy of Mr. Churchill's. In prison he preached with a passionate earnestness the communist doctrines which imprisoned him. He was speedily released as a consequence and appointed to a post on the 'Tcheka in Petrograd.

In that city he spent two years, clad in leather, carrying a revolver, and searching out counter-revolutionary traitors.

Then, when the Kronstadt sailors mutinied, published their famous indictment of the Bolsheviks and called for free councils, Koupa, profoundly moved, left his wife and the 'Tcheka, and threw in his lot with the sailors. Night after night he addressed them, stirring hundreds to enthusiasm by his passionate sincerity; his golden voice. Snow fell. Moscow delivered ultimatum after ultimatum. Kronstadt, angry, justice-seeking, confident of the redress of its grievances, dispatched delegations to argue the matter. One grey dawn the boom of heavy guns filled the air. The Workers' Government poured high explosives into Kronstadt, then advanced their battalions of conscripts, stormed the town, and made of it a blood-sacrifice of death and fire to the unquiet manes of the Revolution. Koupa escaped to England on a Latvian cargo-boat.

After two months' tramping in England, he applied for a position with a company which specialized in conducted tours to the East. His excellent knowledge of languages procured him the position of assistant-conductor, and a fortnight later he was on his way to Egypt with a party of tourists. Landing, the smells and scents of the unforgotten East went to his head like wine. At Cairo he deserted the party and went to live in the Wagh el Berka with a Greek harlot from Lemnos. There, in an attic, close to the stars, he sat all day drinking Greek brandy and writing verses, the while the woman earned their bread. Of nights, restless, Koupa would walk the streets and stand by the river-bank, and listen to songs borne on the waters from the lost Mountains of the Moon. Sickened, and longing for sight and sound of the sea, he set out one night and walked to Alexandria. Arrived there, he sat in the morning light at Mustapha and watched Storman bathing in the Mediterranean.

When Storman came out of the water, they talked. They talked all that forenoon. They talked for days. Storman, a civil engineer, had just completed a two-years contract in the Sudan. He was recuperating prior to a return to England. From excess of expenditure of purpose and energy in the work he had just completed, he was wearied and convinced of the purposelessness of life. To Koupa he listened with a cool detachment, till the latter found his measure.

"You are a Positivist," said Koupa. "But the only active Positivists in the world to-day are the Communists."

And, lying on the warm sands, he was smitten with vision of the inhuman drive and purpose of Communism.

"The Communists?" said Storman. "The Russian half-wits?"

And Koupa, still visioning, looked in his face and sang him an epic saga—of a doctrinaire's dream that shod itself in blood and iron and climbed through wreckage and destruction to Purpose, pitiless, selfless, and sane. Listening, there had kindled in the narrow, disciplined mind of Storman a slow fire. Watching, Koupa had seen it and tended it, till a weariness came upon him and one morning he was gone and Mustapha knew him no more.

And now, looking at Storman from his bright eyes as he sat in the offices of the Anarchocommunist Party, it came upon Koupa that he had lit a torch of a quality and glow beyond his dreaming. God mine! he believes! Such a light as no man shall ever put out. . . . This little Storman will surely find me a job till we wring the Capitalist neck.

Chuckling, he talked of his life during the last five years. Desiring to improve his Arabic, he had crossed the Red Sea and entered the Wahhabi territory. In disguise, a pilgrim, he crossed the dreary camel-routes to Mecca, had prayed in the Kaaba, had discoursed sterile futilities of conduct with Shiite sheikhs. In the guise of a Coptic convert to Islam, a puritanical reformer, he had stirred up the Wahhabi rebellion against the Hedjaz and had taken part in the triumphal campaign which ended in the entry into Medina. Then he had deserted and gone northwards to Sinai, and so, across the desert, to Kantara and Suez. He had obtained work on an England-bound tramp and, four days before, had arrived at Liverpool. From there he had walked to London.

"Eh, Storman! London magic! I could have wept as I came within the so-dreary miles of the redbrick: wept with gladness, as one who had come home again. She is the mother of aliens, our London. So I tested her spirit again. I climbed up to the third floor of the Strand Restaurant, and, while the greasy little clerks fed, I sang them a verse of the Internationale. God mine, how they stared! Eh, but yet it is the old London! I heard one say to the other as I slipped out that it was a hymn I had sung!"

Koupa's thin ripple of laughter and Storman's bass boomed out together. Looking at him, Storman was without illusions. This Koupa was of the order that the organized State would utterly stamp upon and destroy—shiftless, shameless, a vagabond, unreliable; probably treacherous. But he worked his work; he dissolved and destroyed; he was a wrecker. And in the house of Communism there are many mansions.

Said Storman:

"Let's go and have some food together. I'm hungry."

They went to a small place near Leicester Square. People stared as they passed. Under his arm Koupa bore an immense, ribboned sombrero. About his shoulders was an opera cloak. He wore flannel trousers and muddied boots. Seeing the glances cast upon him, he chuckled delightedly.

The waitress served them doubtfully, looking at Koupa's clothes and untrimmed hair. Koupa poured the tea, ate a chocolate éclair, and fixed his bright bird's eyes on Storman.

"Eh, Storman, it is something to have climbed from the ape and the Wahhabi—to eat éclairs with a silver fork! God mine, do you not love them also? Or is it indigestion or love?"

Storman nodded. "Love."

"Ah. She is a comrade?"

Storman stared at him abstractedly: then laughed. "Love of éclairs, I meant. It prevents me eating them."

"Ah, I had hoped some woman it was who steals your thoughts at these times. To bear you children for the Revolution and wring your heart with pity that ever love was evolved."

Storman drank tea. "You go too fast. I fell in love three months ago."

"God mine! Is it so?—And a comrade?" Saying this, Koupa grinned internally. Eh, a comrade, for certainty! One who had bedded with Spartacus and Karl Marx and believed in throat-cutting for political reasons. Storman shook his head.

"She is an empty-headed little ape, Koupa. Brainless, and with a rather long upper lip. Like a cultured monkey. Some day I'll marry her, and then, I suppose, breed the Revolution's cannon fodder from her."

"Take care that you breed not that which ousts the Revolution from your heart." Koupa, speaking without thinking, was himself half-startled. He ate an éclair with

41

methodical abstraction, and was disturbed. God mine, the poor Storman, with his so brave, so honest stupidity! Aloud: "You know her—so?"

"Better than she will ever know herself."

"Then it is bad. For it is not love. God mine, no!"

"Then what?"

"Pfuu! Love! A tinkling thing of tendernesses and caresses and sweet dreamings—a thing of empty adorations and desires. You may see its results rise staled from any marriage-bed: down in the Strand to-night—God mine! the good old Strand!—you may purchase it at anything from a half-crown upwards. Love! . . . It is Lust that has gripped you, Storman. It will suck your blood, maybe for years."

Storman's enormous laugh startled nervous tea-drinkers. "And that—it is not poetry, as you think, but paradox. How long has it sucked your blood, Andreas?"

But the poet was grave. He was dreaming a poetic defence of harmless love against the blasphemous Swinburnian lusters. Indigestion growing upon him from the éclairs he had eaten, he looked around the tables with a sneer.

"Boghe! Is there anything on earth more to disgust than public feeding? In the civilization of our communes, my Storman, eating will be classed with the obscene, secret bodily functions."

But Storman was indifferent. He cared nothing for the table etiquette of the Communist state: he cared nothing for the art and literature that would arise in it. He cared only that in the state he wrought to build men would rise from their beds for work that had selflessness and purpose; would procreate children who would also serve that unending aim; would stand clearly forth in the sunlight and never again go faltering back to darkness and the deeps of night.

With whom the millenniards would share their beds and brothels, tears and tribulations, was no concern of his. He had little or no interest in human beings, recognizing, as he did, that man is an abstraction.

"It may be classed with arson and simony, for all I care." He surveyed the tables as might a buccaneer, and, even so, with little humour. "This is a well-equipped place. It would melt down well for the party funds."

For money poured in the party funds was as water poured into a sieve.

Koupa chuckled and rose carefully to his feet. "Let us go." He belted his cloak round him and put the sombrero under his arm. "And you will tell me how I may help the little party."

The waitress came quickly to their table after they had gone. She counted the teaspoons and the forks, swore under her breath, and presently sought out the manageress.

"Two forks have gone. From that corner table. It was the dirty man, I think."

"A good job they're imitation," said the manageress. "Even though they're hallmarked."

Subchapter v

"Miggod, where've you been?" said Norah Casement.

Ellen sank into an arm-chair and laid aside her bag. "Had such a nice walk," she observed, placidly, tiredly.

It was the sitting-room of the flat which the three girls rented jointly. The mantelshelf clock had just recorded the hour of eleven. All Rosemount Avenue was very silent under a crescent moon.

"Where's Thea?"

"Gone to bed. Biggod, I thought you were making a night of it somewhere." Seated, Norah yawned, elevating her book in the air. Ellen smiled placidly.

"Oh, no. But I've had a glorious day and a glorious walk. Such a nice boy. He wanted me to spend the afternoon and evening with him in London, but I wouldn't have that. So I took him out by Edgware and we walked for miles and miles in the country. A nice, shy boy. Hardly spoke all the time. We lost ourselves for an hour or two, then found a bus-route." She mused, reminiscently. "I think he was a bit tired when we got back."

"Deadbeat, if you walked at your usual rate."

"Oh, and I'd just put him in a taxi at Hammersmith when I met Billy Newman. He wants you to go to a dance with him on Wednesday."

"Does he? Well, I'll—" Norah's voice tailed off. A flush came on her cheeks. She avoided Ellen's eye, petulantly. Ellen purred placidly.

43

"And how about that nice Mr. Storman?"

A creaking noise sounded and the sitting-room door opened slightly. Round the edge of it projected the head of Birch, the household cat. Norah stood up and flung her book at it. It vanished.

"Oh, I don't know. I'm going to bed. Fed up." With sudden passion: "Boys are the very divvle."

CHAPTER THE THIRD

Wherein the Bracing Effects of Military Life are demonstrated, the Meditations of a Lady in a Bath recorded with Due Indelicacy, and some Sympathetic Insight shown into the Difficulties of compiling the First Novel of an Ironist.

Subchapter i

JOHN GARLAND awoke in a hut in Burford Camp. Sweet and clear through the dawn rang the notes of reveille. A blackbird was whistling in a tree outside the hut.

His pillow made of straw cased about by yellow cloth, Garland lay with his mouth slightly open. His lips felt foul and edged. He pushed aside the shoddy blankets. Thereat the reveille abruptly ceased, and the door of a distant hut banged in the morning air. The trumpeter had gone back to bed.

And, muddily, Garland thought:

"Oh, Christ; morning already. What a damned stink. The proletariats smell bad this morning."

He yawned profoundly, sat up in bed. It was a Macdonald, made of transverse lathes of iron. It creaked and swayed. Garland lit a cigarette. He sniffed the air again.

"Like a dung-heap."

He slept in a corner. Down the length of the hut were thirty-six other beds, eighteen on either side. Beneath their blankets the occupants lay in varying stages of crumplement. Tunics hung from hooks. Breeches, boots, and puttees lay upon the floor. The airmen slept profoundly with open mouths and evil breaths. One of them had been sick during the night. Outside the blackbird whistled.

"Gaily," thought Garland. "Birds always whistle gaily, we imagine. But that is mere anthropophuism. They are neither

45

glad nor sad. They open their windpipes to ease their stomachs, most probably."

He chuckled and tentatively extended a pyjamaed leg from the bed. None of the other airmen wore pyjamas. For it was bloody swank. Perspiring in their thick shirts, they would lie abed of an evening and watch Garland change. But because of his D.C.M. and his extraordinary command of foul language, they would say nothing.

No one stirred as Garland put on his trousers, socks, and shoes, took a towel from the locker above his head, and went out of doors. There, in the silence, among the long rows of huts and with the sunshine in his face, a happiness came upon him. For once he did not pause to think it out. He walked to the open-air ablution rooms whistling. Arrived there, he filled a zinc basin and washed himself. Then, stooping, he cleaned his teeth and drank a mouthful of water as it gurgled from the tap.

Abruptly, raising his dripping head, he began to sing. His voice was powerful, untrained, harsh.

> "Mademoiselle from Armentieres
>   (*Parlez-vous?*)
> Mademoiselle from Armentieres
>   (*Parlez-vous?*)
> Mademoiselle from Armentieres—
> Oh, every night for sixteen years
>   Inky Pinky
>   (*Parlez-vous?*)"

Still the huts near at hand slept. But remote in lines at the other side of the camp voices rose and fell. The orderly sergeant was on his rounds, tipping airmen out of bed. This he did by seizing the lower halves of the collapsible Macdonalds and jerking them forward. At such a moment the entire contraption would fall to pieces and so awaken the occupant.

As Garland entered the hut, a voice came from the bunk of the non-commissioned officer. This was the voice of Corporal Mackay. He shouted to Garland to stir the lazy bastards out there.

"Stir them yourself," said Garland, and poured oil on his hair.

"Do what I bloody well tell you, or I'll put you under arrest."

"Arrest your grandmother," replied Garland. For he had a D.C.M. and cared nothing for corporals. He began to fold the blankets on his bed and to set to rights the kit and equipment above his locker. Presently there came a steady snoring from the corporal's bunk.

At seven o'clock the trumpeter sounded cookhouse. Instantly the hut sprang to life. Men leapt out of bed and into their trousers. Socks, boots, and tunics were rapidly donned. Then, with plates and mugs in their hands, the airmen ran rapidly towards the shed which was the dining-room.

Arrived there, they paraded in a queue past an opening in the cookhouse wall. Two cooks served out the food. Each portion consisted of a sausage and some blackened potatoes. The tea was black and boiled. Carrying plates and mugs, the men seated themselves at long plank tables. By a quarter past seven there were over two hundred men in the dining-room.

Garland sat midway the length of a table. About him, hungry, simple, unwashed, the airmen ate. They talked as they ate, with full mouths and unscrubbed teeth. Their laughter was unwholesome and high, their appearances and demeanour truculent. From listening to lectures and reading Mr. Kipling's poems, they considered this attitude proper and resultant upon their vitality and courage. It was, however, largely due to indigestion and cowardice. Drilled and directed, punished like children and rewarded like children, they looked from shallow, muddied brains with pithecanthropic eyes. Even oaths were standardized and mainly concerned various obscene sex-functions. Eating, they related stories of their adventures on the previous night. Prowling in alleyways and back kitchens, they had each raped a woman.

"Where were you last night?" asked one of them of Garland.

Garland speared his sausage and looked at it. "Last night I stoned a dog that had a funny smell." He sniffed at the sausage. "Yes, it's the same."

The table roared its appreciation. By such means Garland had attained a flickering popularity. Sometimes, however, when the moody spell was upon him, his humour was a savage bludgeoning of cruelty. At such moments, each apprehensive that the lash might be laid across his own shoulders, the airmen would laugh with scared eyes, and Garland's popularity, fed on fear, would soar. Yet, fearful of N.C.O.s themselves, the other airmen secretly resented Garland's indifference and occasional insolence to a corporal or a sergeant. By God, if I'd stripes, I'd have shoved him in the digger for that. Further, as Garland had been heard to state that he did not believe in marriage, he was secretly regarded as immoral and shocking. For without exception the other members of the barrack-hut believed in marriage and children and virtuous wives. But the women with whom they consorted before marriage were bloody pros.

At five minutes to eight the four hundred airmen in the camp had gathered on the tarmac in front of one of the hangars. Presently the camp sergeant-major appeared. He was a little man, his breeches sagging at the seat and knees. From his face and voice he was known as Bonzo. During the war he had been a warrant officer in a military prison on Salisbury Plain. As a consequence, he had never been on active service and had no medal ribbons. This fact galled him. Medal ribbons grew to be a craze with him. He would carefully survey the tunics of ex-army privates and reprove them if their ribbons were soiled. He had cold, glazed eyes, like a bullock in a panic. His moustache was twisted to fine points. He lived in a dim cave of drill formulæ, and, transferred to the Air Force, had been puzzled and alarmed by the impact of new ideas and necessities. He would ask newly joined recruits if they had been trade unionists, and would then relate to them how such bastards had been licked into shape in Salisbury during the War.

With a limited vocabulary, he clung firmly to the word bastard. Airmen who did not shave properly were bastards. Strikers were lousy bastards. Socialists were bastards. Fearing his wife, he would upon occasion privately record her bastardly in his thoughts. His only daughter, whom he loved, was alone exempted from the general accusation of illegitimacy which he levelled against the animate world, and she had been born ten years before, at Salisbury, as the result of the clandestine embraces of her mother and a conscientious objector.

The parade lined up. The sergeant-major called it to attention. Then, bringing the drooping knees of his breeches in close proximity to each other, he lifted his hand to his face. At

48

that, a young man who had appeared on the scene also lifted his hand to his face, as though to draw attention to the rows of pimples with which it was garnished.

He was Pilot Officer Brougham, and orderly officer for the day. Gazetted to his commission six months before, he was the son of a Liverpool grocer. He had already crashed two aeroplanes. His face lacked a chin. For three thousand years men—Dædalus, Da Vinci, Lilienthal, Wilbur Wright—had dreamt and adventured and visioned greatly that he might ride the skies. Now, his stick under his arm, the projecting teeth of his upper jaw resting upon his nether lip, he walked along the ranks, inspecting chins and buttons and hobnailed boots.

And Garland, in the front rank, standing rigid, indifferent, with the D.C.M. ribbon on his tunic, thought:

"How the anti-militarists flatter militarism! It is no monster clad in steel and fire, ruthless, relentless, inhuman. It is only a shambling, cowardly ape, underbrained, with stinks and fuddled scratchings. Its impressiveness is that of the Zoo orang with a newspaper cocked on its head. Oh, its cage has opened upon occasion and it has torn and smashed and snuffled blood till some impact on the lewd brain has sent it whimpering and slinking. . . . Tanks and poison gas. Lord! How it does fear at such times the new clubs and battering-stones thrust in its hands, and, in sleep, in lulls, dreams with simian snortings of the cage and vermin-picking and a paper hat. . . . "

Meantime, as the names of the owners of unshaved chins and under-blacked boots were, at the orderly officer's instructions, noted down in the sergeant-major's notebook, there spread throughout the entire parade an increasing disbelief that Brougham had ever been fathered by the Liverpool grocer.

Subchapter ii

The bathroom in the flat in Chelsea was a miniature apartment. Its frosted window looked out upon a backyard where a dead cat had lain so long that the flesh and fur had partly mouldered from its bones. Enclosed on all sides, triangular, this backyard had no apparent entrance or exit. It belonged to no one. It was a place apart, unclean, rubbish-heaped. It lay and festered amidst the flat-blocks. It was Property, proud, unassailable, law-defended.

Thea Mayven had raised the bathroom window that afternoon and had wrinkled her nose above the backyard. She had the afternoon free, and was preparing a bath for herself. This could be done only by stoking the kitchen stove for an hour or so, and then trusting to the pipes to carry the hot-water to the taps. For once the trust had not been misplaced. Into the bath, steam-emanating, poured the water. Thea, undressing in her bedroom, listened, knowing by the depths-descent sound of the water how full the bath had become.

But for herself, the flat was always empty on Wednesday afternoons. So it was her bath day, and of the bathing she made a rite solemn, sensual, cloudily humorous. It was the only occasion, save in hurried glimpses at night or morning, when she ever saw her own body. And her body amazed, pleased, and amused her.

Undressed, proceeding from bedroom to bathroom, she never wore her dressing-gown and seldom went by the directest route. Naked, she would pose, walk like a bird, placing one foot in front of the other, delighted at the quaintness of herself. She would enter the kitchen and look round it as though she had not been there for a week; would walk into the sitting-room, occupy one of the chairs, light a cigarette, sit cross-legged. . . . Delightful to be naked, without the swish and feel of clothes. Naked came I into the world. Goodness, if someone came in just now—John, perhaps, on half-holiday from the camp. . . .

But even thought of Garland was not disquieting. She was not Thea Mayven. Thea Mayven was lying alone there in the bedroom—a camisole, green dress, stockings. Poor young Thea! Wouldn't she like to be me?

Idiot! this'll grow on you. You'll walk out of the flat some day and put Rosemount Avenue into fits. Go and scrub yourself. Eaughow! This is good. 've to go back for that damned towel.

Mucky mess this bathroom. Never mind. Some day you'll have a real one, enamelled and shining, with rubber mats and squeejees and a husband to soap your back. . . . John. Hard at work in camp, trying to earn that bathroom. Poor John!

Ouch—hot! Grrr. . . . Scalding. O God, our help in ages past. Grit your teeth, girl. Stick it. Lord!

Tha's be'r, 's I used to say when I first came to London. You're like a Red Indian. Are Red Indians red? Gently till you're flat. Inch by inch.

Her body covered with water, she lay flat in the bath. Above her rose the steam. She raised her arms and clasped them behind her head. Upon those arms was a faint, golden down.

Her rounded breasts showed flattened in the water, like spread lilies. She splashed with one foot. At that a wave arose at the far end of the bath, flowed up betwixt her breasts, and gurgled against her chin. This amused her. She splashed again, looking down at herself consideringly. Glad my skin's like that—snowy, with blood under it. A nice skin. Worth a lot. Any husband should be proud . . ..

Married. Lord!

Her face grew crimson, her eyes suddenly angry and shamed. She had remembered that Saturday evening when she and Garland had been left alone in the flat. Abruptly she began to hum, to soap herself, to thrust that memory back. The steam rose up towards the half-opened window. Birds in the garden, six feet long. Where's that sponge? Ouf! Have to hurry up if I'm meeting Norah for tea. Else I s'pose Ellen and her Snooks 'll be back. Our aristocratic Snooks. How do ex-officers treat girls in baths? Oh, badly. Wicked Snooks. Love, you have left me. Rotten soap. Oh, damn, I've forgotten to go down to Oxford Street for the boat tickets. Time John sent the money for his. . . . John.

Thought of him was unescapable. She stopped soaping and leant against the side of the bath, her chin in her hand. Very grave, poised so, like a nude Greek koré of the Athenian vase-makers, she pondered on the riddle of desire, and twiddled her toes, and for a little was still.

That Saturday evening. If you hadn't stopped him. Poor John, poor boy. Funny boy. Sulky. Likesome. Your funny, tender hands. If you hadn't been stopped what would have happened? All of it? Every little bit? Down to unbuttoning and repentance and an offer of marriage? Oh, damn it, don't fool. And you didn't really stop him. You know you didn't. He stopped himself. You wanted him to go on. And then—if he had . . . And then.

51

You fool, fool, fool. Filthy. Beastly vile. Both you and John. Damn him. What does he think I am?—Filthy little privates should keep to filthy little slaveys, and then talk about them in their barrack-rooms. Probably been talking about you. . . .

She swore, splashed, and, in a whirl of white legs, narrow-hipped body and strong arms, jumped out of the bath and seized the towel she had brought from her room. In a fury of energy she began to scrub herself with it. Her hair, thick, short-cut, wine-tipped, fell over her face and she flung it back with the gesture of a boy who has been running. She scowled at herself in the mirror for a moment. Then, still looking at that reflection, she watched her eyebrows draw apart, quiver a little. In the corners of her eyes little lights twinkled.

She smiled at herself, secretly. She began to towel herself with swift gentleness.

John's not like that. And don't be a fool. Be decent, not a damned animal. Never mind the queerness, the delight, the singing sounds when he touches you. . . . Oh, be quiet. Plenty of time for that when you're married. And not too much even then. Sparing of the whole business. Separate beds. Love nights. Soft like velvet.

Nights in a room in a house above the sea.

The farmhouse lights couthy and dim and paraffinny across the moors.

Such nights!

In the sound of the sea.

Nakedness.

And the sound of the sea!

A warm mist blurred her vision. Half-adream, she was yet conscious as never before of the life within her—of the blood quivering through each vein of the stroke-beats below her left breast, of the cloud-drifts of thought across the mind-tracks of her brain. Oh, my dears—life and love and Thea—there are miracles awaiting you yet!

Suddenly the skin of her breasts blushed red and a sharp, stinging tide of colour poured up her throat to her cheeks. Puzzled at this strange occurrence, she raised her eyes.

Through the keyhole of the bathroom door she saw the water-glint of a close-pressed eye.

Excitement hung over Waterloo Station like a malarial fog. Policemen, blue-garmented, contemptuous, stuttered and shooed the crowds. Large men, they were interested in strike-breaking, dog-racing, batoning, pensions, and solicitous women. They believed that drunks should have their arms twisted, that you should always be courteous, that promotion was bloody favouritism. Stamping large feet, they awaited reinforcements, and meantime attempted to hold the crowds at the Station in check.

Momentarily the throngs grew more dense. A woman fainted. Railway porters stood around, stroking their red ties and smiling. Near the far end of the taxi ranks booings and cat-calls burst out, rose tremolo, spread, and split apart into two parallel banks of hiss fringing a narrow lane to the Southampton platform.

Meaken, the noted Labour leader, was leaving for a tour in South Africa. Unemployed, organized by their leaders for the occasion, had marched to Waterloo to demonstrate. At a coffee-stall outside the Station they had halted, eating cakes, sausages, and drinking cocoa. A few straggling, detached combats had taken place with patriotic sailors from the Union Jack Club. Those had ended by the sailors being arrested and marched away by military policemen. Then the unemployed had flooded up into the Station and awaited Meaken's arrival.

Through the lane he came, walking with a look of indifference upon his face. It was a mottled, unhealthy face, with sincere, shifty eyes. The Labour leader was fifty-four years of age. For twenty years he had been secretary of his union. Ever since entering Parliament in 1920 he had preached conciliation and peace in industry. In the House of Commons Conservative members had entertained him to tea, sitting far back from him because of the rankness of his breath. Overcome by their accents, he saw the folly of hasty reforms. He went to a manicurist and had his nails seen to. Sweating, he spoke of the oneness of employer and unemployed. With the coming of the Labour Government he had been given a salaried position and his daughter had been presented at Court. Heavy, sincere, he dominated his union, addressing his colleagues simply as Enry or Bill. When any agitated for high wages, he raged against them in the press. Subeditors, correcting his large, unpunctuated manuscripts, cursed him. He was made a Privy Councillor and had played rounders with the Duke of York.

His daughter was going with him to South Africa. She walked beside the Labour leader, sickened by the filth and smell of the unemployed. Why didn't the police clear the Station of these under-washed never-works? Frequently she pressed a small handkerchief to her nose, for she had never overcome the distressing habit of sniffling acquired in early childhood, when handkerchiefs were scarce.

Half-way down the lane, one of the unemployed, a slight, limping man, leant forward and knocked a policeman's hat over his eyes. The demonstrators roared their approbation. The policeman was knocked down and trodden on, joyously.

At that the lane caved in. The Labour leader began to wield his umbrella. Sniffling, his daughter was kissed by a scavenger, an ex-tramwayman, and a newsboy. The police drew their batons.

"Back, you sodamned fools!" shouted the slight limping man to the demonstrators. "Behind you there is a wagon with bottles. *Aux armes!*"

And, suiting his words to action, he leapt upon the brewer's wagon and reappeared with an empty bottle grasped in each fist. Shouting, the unemployed armed themselves. At this moment Storman appeared on the roof of a taxi which had slowly worked its way into the Station.

Hearing over the telephone of the demonstration, he had hastened from the Anarchocommunist offices in Leicester Square. Why couldn't the damn Unemployment Committee have first informed him? The baiting of Meaken, unless properly organized, would have little propaganda value. An autocrat, contemptuous of democracy, he had little faith in the ability of the unemployed to evolve spontaneously a scientific blackguardism.

Arriving at the moment when the police drew their batons, Storman climbed out on the roof of his taxi. For a moment, tall, bare-headed, he dominated the riot.

"Comrades . . . ."

A young policeman, skirmishing on the edges of the demonstration, looked up and saw the chance of promotion. Bursting through the unemployed, he leapt up the side of the taxi, seized Storman by the ankle and brought him crashing to the ground.

At that moment the rest of the police charged.

Dropping their bottles, the unemployed fled. The Labour leader and his daughter gained the platform. The remnants of the riot eddied across the Station, like the backwash of a tide. Ellen Ledgworth, hurrying to the Underground from a message made on behalf of Cocotte Sœurs, was roughly jostled. A man snatched at her bag.

As she and it shrank away, a fist smote upon the nose of the thief. He ran. Ellen, panting, placid, with her broad hips trembling, confronted her rescuer. It was the slight, limping man of the demonstration. From under his arm he brought forth a wide-brimmed sombrero, put it on his head, and took it off again with a strong gravity.

"You are unhurt, madame?"

"Yes, thanks."

"My name is Andreas van Koupa. I am an artist and a poet, a foreigner in England. Madame, these are hard times."

Panting, Ellen took a shilling from her bag and handed it to him. He bowed, looked at the shilling consideringly, spun it in the air, and then limped after the remainder of the procession.

Meantime Storman, stunned and bleeding, had been batoned and marched to the nearest police station. Koupa, standing on the steps of Waterloo and watching Storman being dragged away, was seized by a sudden thought. He limped down from the steps, and made up the Waterloo Road towards Leicester Square.

Ellen went down to the underground booking-office, bought a ticket, and entered the lift. Near her a man stood learning Russian out of a grammar with interlinear translations. With wrinkled brow, he raised his face, and, fixing his eyes on an advertisement, declined the reflective verb *smietsya*, to smile.

The lift shot downwards, sickeningly, like a lost foothold in a dream. It clanged quiveringly to rest. Iron barriers, trelliswork of steel, grated apart. Men and women hurried out, running for their trains. The man with the Russian grammar exclaimed "*smietyess, smieyutsya,*" with relief, pocketed the grammar, and also ran.

Reaching Charing Cross, Ellen ascended the escalator and caught an inner circle train. The carriage was crowded. At the far end she saw her lover, Edward Snooks, standing up. His face was pale and dejected. He had just risen, offering his seat to a fat woman. For he was an ex-officer. Calling him dearie, thankin' you kindly and I will, the fat woman smiled at him. Hadn't she seen him before?—wasn't he one of the butcher's young men? Offended, Snooks swayed down the carriage and raised his hat to Ellen.

"What's wrong, Ted? You don't look well."

His eyes had the appearance of small, poached eggs. Looking at Ellen, he tugged at his moustache.

"I'm in trouble, old thing." He looked round the carriage. "Can't talk here. It's serious."

They got out at Sloane Square and walked towards Rosemount Avenue. On the way Snooks told of his troubles. He had borrowed, from time to time, a total of about £5 petty cash from his firm. Tomorrow he would be found out. What was he to do? What the hell was he to do? My God, and it was you I spent the money on. Cripes, what a hass I've been. My God, what a hass. . . .

Emotional, his face worked. Small, unwashed children stopped and looked at him. He had lost his accent. Ellen put her arm across his shoulders. She loved him, motheringly. Without his accent, he appealed to her as a child with a lost toy. Placidly worried, she swayed her hips.

"It's too bad, Ted. And I don't know what I can do to help you. I've no money, either. I didn't know you had been stealing."

She moved beside him up Rosemount Avenue like a sedate, compassionate cow. Earnest, she was infinitely tactless. Glancing sideways at her face, Snooks hated her. She was like a piece of emotional suet.

"Can't you think of something? Haven't you anything you could sell?"

Ellen shook her head. "My stuff's cheap. It would fetch only a few shillings. Oh, Edward, I wish you hadn't—"

"Damn you, shut up."

Placidly surprised, Ellen withdrew her arm. They came to the flat in silence, mounted the stairs, entered. Noise of their entrance was drowned by the sound of a heavy thump, as of a falling body, beyond the bathroom door. Startled, they stood listening.

"Thea having a bath," explained Ellen. Then: "I'll go and take my coat off, then we can have tea. Shan't be a minute."

"All right." Snooks, taking off his hat in the hall and hanging it on a peg, eyed the bathroom door.

A minute later, powdering her face, Ellen heard a sudden crash, the splash of water, a startled ejaculation. Dropping her puff, she opened the door of the bedroom she shared with Norah, and looked down the corridor.

Water dripped from the bathroom door, rivuleted from the keyhole, and streamed from the head and shoulders of Edward Snooks who, half-blinded, was just scrambling to his feet.

Subchapter iii (a)

"I saw an eye glaring through the keyhole," Thea explained later to Norah Casement, "so I threw my bedroom ewer at it. Snooks said he was looking because he thought I had perhaps fainted. So I lent him five pounds which he wanted very badly."

Subchapter iv

Wednesday afternoons were half-holidays at Burford Camp. While Thea bathed in Chelsea, John Garland sat at the desk in his office, typing out the ninth chapter of his novel.

He typed in front of a half-open window. Looking out, he had a view of the aerodrome, where a Rugby match was in progress. Excited airmen ran to and fro, hustling a ball. They were sportsmen. But across Garland's vision, when he raised his eyes, they were only dim, gesticulating phantasms.

Remote above the horizon an aeroplane, homeward-bound from a cross-country flight, droned against a sky blue and grey and summer-stilled.

But the outside world had ebbed from Garland auricularly as well as visually. His ninth chapter was exasperating him to a sullen fury. His characters, intended to collide and produce ironic mirth from their abrasion-rubbings and ingenious theorizings on the subject of collisions, were becoming unmanageable. Frequently they completely escaped him, disappearing into jungle undergrowths of his mind; sometimes they shammed dead; occasionally they broke loose and played the devil till the whole story-structure tottered rottenly. Worst of all, he could not get the seduction of his heroine, in the ninth chapter, to go convincingly. And this he knew was damning and damnable. For, as he intended his novel to sell and make money, he had known from the beginning that a mere ironical portraiture of contemporary life was worse than useless. An excellent acquaintance with current best-sellers had prompted the remedy. Purple patches. Sex. With a few ingenious prostitutions and seductions his novel would be made.

Unfortunately, even the first of these was proving uncommonly difficult to handle. He felt a reluctant distaste for having his heroine lose her virginity—even though she was only an ironic heroine. The damned woman kicked up such an infernal row about it—as though it was the first happening of the kind in the history of fiction. And her face, foreshortened, tear-stained, that odd, gasping sob of hers. . . . Pfuu!

A bumblebee entered the room, flew against a filerack, fell to the floor, rose again, hit the ceiling violently, and, landing on the table in front of Garland, hummed despondently. Leaning his chin in his hand, Garland thought:

"You're a damn poor novelist to shy from a little muck. This woman—Lord, why should she want all the fuss raised over the trumpery happening? This is an ironic novel, not a romantic one, my good female. Damn you, stop sniffling, else I'll choke you. . . . Pornography's a sweated industry.

"Lord, pull yourself together. Leave the woman alone and go on with the stuff that counts. You can come back to her later. The stuff that counts—Goddilmighty, you can write it and it cries to be written.

"What's wrong with the other moderns is the lack of purpose in their infernal books. They believe themselves up-to-date, Neo-Georgian, yet in novel-writing they're a generation behind the times. They're obsessed by the Galsworthy-Bennett tradition. They don't realize that the novel of portrait and manners is a dead dog which nowadays attracts only a casual interest by the different types of blowflies in attendance. . . . The world is sick of mere matings and baitings, bickerings and successes and failures in novels. It's grown up, has the world, and knows our characters for mere sawdust puppets. 'We'll accept the puppets—if they're projections of yourself,' it cries. 'Live through them. Make them tell us *your* thoughts, *your* vision of life, *your* hopes, *your* hates, *your* beliefs. Never mind them acting in character—damn their sawdust little characters—it's you we want, if you're worth the having. . . . '

"And why does this earnest world want your purple patches, then? Because it's so made, because it's human and inconsistent, and likes an occasional distraction—lewdness and lingerie. It likes to scratch and snigger and guffaw subduedly in the intervals of knitting its brows. . . .

"The diversity of mistresses possessed by Wells' and France's heroes! Yet Clissold and Jerome Coignard are the only folk in fiction who don't fade on rereading. . . . Rabbits complete with intestines. . . .

"Good old H.G.!"

He grinned and lit a cigarette. The Rugby match was drawing to a close. Overhead, a mile or so away, the aeroplane engine was missing fire intermittently, going spat-spat. Garland knit his brows. Infernal things, radial engines. Those trees against the horizon—lonely. "Far off the trees were as pale wands." Rossetti. This damn woman . . . .

Lord, what an unending tweeter, in fiction and fact, the insects on their mud-ball raised over the matter of procreation! What thin immortal pipings of appeal and fear and hate they raised over some male wrongfully fertilizing some female insect! Without the female's permission! (She never wanted that larva.) Wrongfully begetting fresh larvae to join the lawfully begotten in creeping from the slime to a fluttering of wings against a twilit sky, to a freezing extinction on a falling night or the brief, agonized enscorchment of the candle flame.

Garland leapt to his feet.

Out of the sky, beyond the Rugby players, smoke-and-spark-emitting, winged, a thing of flame sputtered and flashed downwards across Garland's vision. Involuntarily, waiting, he gripped the table.

Came a far, dull thwack, a subdued, moaning roar. Then a bright yellow flame concaved to being against the twilight horizon.

Running across the aerodrome, Garland was one of the first to reach the crash. By now the flames burned with a curious geyser-like effect. Abruptly came a series of small explosions, scattering a shower of débris.

"Here's the fire-engine."

Crowded, it roared across the aerodrome, the ambulance following. Garland's throat grew curiously dry. In the midst of the geyser something was moving.

The front of the fuselage, spouting flames from its petrol-tank, lay jaggedly askew, as though smitten a blow by a gigantic, half-clenched fist. Half-clenched, for a portion of the cockpit had been left intact. And, abutting from this portion, inside the geyser-ring, something was moving.

Then, in the flame-glow, Garland saw it for a blackened, rounded object, eyeless, faceless, moving slowly, lethargically, above a reddened carbonization. . . .

"Come back, you damn fool!" The officer of the watch, jumping from the fire-tender, caught Garland's arm. "You'd burn to a cinder. You there—bring up the crocodile!"

Towards the yellow lowe of the flames four men advanced with a contracting steelgrip in their hands. Behind the steelgrip trailed a rope. On a spring being pressed the prehensile jaws of the crocodile shot through the flames. The officer of the watch pointed.

"There, below the cockpit. . . . Damn you, hurry!"

The jaws of the crocodile leapt and closed. Garland and half a dozen others seized the rope. Along the length of the steelgrip the flames danced bluely.

"Pull!"

As the men on the rope began to move, something came soggily. Then the weight lightened. Still grasping the rope attached to the crocodile, the men ran backwards.

Something shapeless had been dragged out of the geyser. The driver of the fire-tender, a boy, a recruit, stared down at it, white-faced.

Then he began to scream.

Late in that evening, while the remains of Pilot Officer Brougham lay in the mortuary, a camp policeman, passing the headquarters offices, heard the sound of a typewriter. He went up to one of the windows and looked into a lighted room.

Seated at a table, his face glowing, Garland was triumphantly engaged in the seduction of his heroine.

CHAPTER THE FOURTH

Wherein, after a Side-glance upon the Doings of a Poet in an Unnecessarily Conventional Garret and an Account of how the Salvation of Man is planned upon the Best Approved Pattern, the Moonlight is utilized for a Rapid Series of Snapshots.

Subchapter i

ONE midnight, a month after the arrest and imprisonment of Storman for his share in the Waterloo Station riot, Andreas van Koupa, acting secretary of the Anarchocommunist Party, arrived home with a bottle of Bass under each arm. On the steps of the tenement block near Charing Cross, where he had rented a room, he paused, turned round cautiously, and gripped one of the bottles by the neck. He was not mistaken. He was being pursued. It was the Shadow.

Taking careful aim, the poet hurled one of the bottles full at the Thing. Up the deserted street echoed the sound of splintered glass: rich Bass flowed in the gutter. Holding the other bottle against his breast, Koupa surveyed the street, then nodded satisfiedly.

" 'Sgone."

Turning about, he entered the tenement block. His room was on the third story. Carefully, he proceeded to negotiate the stairs. Half-way up he stopped, placed the bottle of Bass on a step, put his leg over the rail and looked down the black well of the staircase.

"The harlot," he murmured. "The so-poor termagant tart. Dry."

Thought of her moved him profoundly. He almost wept. He withdrew his leg from the banisters, sat down on the stairs, thought deeply. Some minutes later he awoke. Beside him glimmered the bottle of Bass. He shook his head and spoke aloud.

"God mine, what jinni have escaped from that neck of yours!"

His head continued to shake to and fro, a fact which interested him. Gradually the movement again lulled him to sleep. The next time he roused it was with the sound of Big Ben striking three hours.

Koupa arose, left the bottle of Bass on the stairs, and climbed slowly up to his room. Entering, he lit the gas fire and then knelt for a moment in front of a picture tacked up in a corner. It was a Russian ikon which he had looted in Leningrad. Slavic, ox-eyed, the Holy Mother gripped the Holy Child under elephantine armpits. Koupa grinned up at her.

"You are undoubtedly a virgin," he said. "If you had borne the unfortunate infant you would not be holding him as though you feared he might be forgetting of himself."

The Virgin stared over his head. An atheist by faith, inclination, and training, he adored her. She, the Virgin, holding in her arms so gingerly that which she had mothered and the Unknown had fathered—holding in her arms that which she feared and would never comprehend—symbolized so much. Matter holding Mind. Or Humanity Faith. Or Death Life. In the dead stillness of the room Koupa, with gleaming eyes and sardonic lips, bowed to her.

"You are the eternal Piggishness," he said.

He sat down on the bed, unlaced his boots, removed one, and dropped it on the floor with a thud. The sound echoed throughout the whole tenement block. Preparing to drop the second boot, Koupa had a vision. He saw innumerable weary heads turning on grimy pillows in rooms below him—heads of folk awakened by the familiar sound and waiting for the second boot to drop ere they again slept. They waited uneasily, sleepily, irritatedly, yet with certainty. The second boot will drop in a minute, was reasoned in the undertow of each subconscious. It must do so in the nature of things. But one must hear it fall before sleep comes again. . . .

With the same grin on his face as that with which he had regarded the Virgin, Koupa removed the second boot and placed it carefully on the bed. Then he sat still and stared at the unshaded gas-jet. Before his eyes it blurred to a flame-ringed globe. Like the sun in space, the chromosphere with its tentacles of fire.

He realized that his mouth and throat were burning. That bottle of the little so-good Bass? Step by step he traced it back. He had left it on the stairs.

He arose, put out the gas, and then, in his socks, descended the summer-moistened flights of stairs. Now and then a step creaked beneath his weight. Coming to the bottle of Bass, he picked it up and was just about to uncork it when he remembered the woman of the basement.

"God mine, if she has returned she will be dry."

Descending the stairs with unsteadiness, because of the chill breath of night-wind that blew through the open street-door, he turned to the left, down a final stairway of greasy stone. The bottle of Bass he held clasped to his breast. At a door he stopped and knocked.

Nothing happened. His feet becoming cold on the moist stones, he waited, then knocked again. Presently there sounded on the other side of the door the scuff-scuff of footsteps. Came a woman's voice:

"Watcha want?"

"It is I, Andreas."

There was the noise of a cautious unlocking. The door opened. A black hole showed in the dimness of the passage. Koupa went forward into it.

Behind him the door closed. He stood still, listening to the relocking. Then someone brushed past him, and a match-head, ignited against the sole of a shoe, spluttered. Yellow-haloed, the pineslip illumined a ghostly hand. Then the glare of the gas-jet smote upon Koupa's eyes like a sword.

A girl in the uniform of the Salvation Army, but without the hat, stood below the gas-bracket. She regarded Koupa kindly, from out brown, patient eyes and over the peak of a Roman nose. Approaching, she put her face close to his.

"Cha want?"

Koupa held up the bottle of Bass. The girl smiled, comfortedly.

"Yaint arf a toff, Andy. Corn in Jacob. Blime! Woz jest mopin fer a drink."

Swaying a little, Koupa chuckled. "Nothing for to drink at the little meeting?"

The girl was searching a cupboard for glasses. She shook her head. Her hair, uncut, was Titian red.

"Driest crush this side of ell. A cup o biled tea after free hours rescue work on the streets. Prayers an blood an God's all they fink ev." Sitting down, she yawned weariedly. A prostitute, she had been converted by the Salvation Army, had been found work in a box-factory and had enrolled as a voluntary helper in salvation work at nights. She had, however, soon tired of the factory and reverted to her former profession, though with caution. From it she earned a comfortable income and on free nights still went to help the Army at its work. With a passionate zeal she searched the streets, exhorting the erring and guiding the strayed to safety. Gradually, because of her zeal and fervour, she had gained a high reputation and was much sought as a speaker at public confessionals and such-like exercises. Frequently, her throat parched with the over-boiled tea of the Army canteens, she would return home late at night from her rescue work, glancing longingly at the dead-eye glitter of windows in closed public-houses.

"Ere's ealth, Andy. Ow's the Revolution?"

The poet had slid down into one of the dusty chairs and now sat staring at the floor. At her words he raised his eyes, took the glass from her outstretched hand. He slowly stood up and stood to attention.

"The Revolution!"

He drank and then flung the glass over his shoulder. It smashed to pieces against the faded wallpaper. The girl swore.

"Daft bawstid. You'll waken arf the bleedin tenement. . . . You and yer Revolution!"

Koupa stood looking at her with dreaming eyes. He was of a sudden very steady, and shook no longer.

"The Poet and the Prostitute—the sot and the bawd! Some day, little sister, the eyes of the Revolution's dear Unborn will look back and see us not as we seem, but as the children we are, beating our hands on the walls of life in the frenzied quiverings of nightmare. . . . The kind, so-sad eyes of the dear Unborn, weeping tears of pity for we poor children of Change! We shall be a song and a story then, you and I."

"Ere, sit dahn. Gord, you aint sife. Worse'n that loopy old

bawstid, Crookshenks, at the meetin this evenin. Only it was ell an fire an brimstone an burnin an screamin that got *im*. *You're* nutty on the Unborn." She loosened her Army jacket, flung it aside, and looked at Koupa with contempt. "You an yer damned Unborn. Oo the ell are they to pity us? Easy for you ter go nuts on em—yer a man. They'll never exist but fer the women that'll be sick and ill an beastly bearin them. . . . "

Suddenly she was weeping—slow, greasy tears coursing down her face. Koupa stared at her, patted her shoulder, sat down with eyes and voice alike interested.

"What did Cruikshank say?"

She was drying her eyes, calmly, with an unclean handkerchief. "Cruikshenk? Wy, the usual stuff. Only—e's a devil. Blieves all e syes. Blast im."

"Do you believe it?" Incredibly gentle his voice, incredibly gentle the touch she felt upon her. In a moment the harridan had vanished. She was a quivering, fear-stricken child, clutching him close, his arm around her.

"Oh Gord, Andy, I dunno, I dunno. Scared stiff I wos. . . . Wot the ell's it all for, anywye? You an me an all the other wasters—our lives are muck an pyne an opelessness. An after we kick it we're ter be tortured an burned fer ever an ever because Gord mide us like this. An ow about Jesus syving us? . . . It's all a bloody cheat, Gord an Jesus an the rest. . . . "

But Koupa, shining-eyed, held her close and soothed her. Drunkenness had fallen from him. Vision, exquisite, torturing, was upon him.

"No cheat, child—only Jesus has been forgotten—forgotten by God himself, grown old and weary. By God! What theme for a poem—a sonnet!" He thrust the prostitute aside, stood up, began to search the room in a frenzy. "Paper, damn you, have you no paper?—I must have it—here!"

He found a sheet and a stump of lead-pencil, sat down, buried his face in his hands, sat erect, began to write. Terrified, wide-eyed, the girl stared at him. Once she moved and he turned and cursed her foully. His pencil flew in wavering lines. He groaned, beat his head, finished on a sudden spurt, stood up.

"Listen:

"LOST

"In wonderment God stood amidst the throng,
  Gathered on London's fringe this haggard night,
And heard afar the beating ways in song.
  The passionate speech of one whose face shone bright

"With extasy unquenched, had drawn a crowd
  Encircling, from the street-glare and the strife,
And God, unnoticed, bent, and old, and bowed,
  Heard clarion words: 'Lo, I am Love and Life.'

"Soft-voiced, God asked: 'Whose message bring you, Sir?'
  When, at the end, these two stood there alone.
'Whose message, friend? Why,' cried the minister,
  'The Christ's!' And God said: 'Who is Christ?'

                                "And blown
  About the streets that night the voice of One
  Cried terribly: 'My Son! My only Son!' "

Smear-faced, grotesque, standing in the light of the gas-jet, he read the sonnet. Then, looking across at the girl, his face crinkled angrily.

"God mine! This is the inspiration—this so footling spaff-doodle. . . . I cannot write—I cannot! (That tenth line—it is a so-damned five-legged mule.) Yet, if I write not, there comes and eats eternally at my heart the pain of thoughts crying for birth. And bring them to life I cannot. I am cursed. O God, God, God."

His insane agony horrified her. Then she saw small tears rolling down from the quick, bird's eyes. Understanding tears, compassion filled her. In a moment she was standing with her arms about him.

"Blime, Andy, wot is it? Don't cry. Lumme." Anxiously, pityingly, she held him, comprehending him not at all. With the maternal wisdom of the childless woman she soothed him, sitting again, his face against her breast. Kneeling so, he put his arms around her neck.

"Child, child. . . . Mother breasts to comfort me. I am tired, tired. Hold me a little close in your silence, mother child."

So, in a stillness of pity, they remained. Content, not moving, not thinking, she held him close. Time stood still in a mist of tenderness. Then his hands, holding her, tightened, then moved slowly down to her waist, then to the curves of her hips. He kissed her lips, snuggled close against her: his fingers upon her body trembled. . . . So it always ended. So men were. Always. The quiet pity was gone. Wearily her mouth surrendered to the clamminess of his kisses.

"Andy. Turn out the gas first."

Subchapter i (a)

In the quietness of the summer dawn Andreas van Koupa ascended the stairs to his room. From his window he looked out on a London which still slept. In a dusty mirror he caught a glimpse of his face. A thin trickle of blood from the cut where, kissing him, she had bitten him, had dried to a red serration on his chin. A sick disgust shook him.

"Bloody prostitute."

He sat down on the bed, yawned, felt a knobbly protuberance beneath him. It was the boot which he had carefully refrained from dropping some hours previously.

He picked it up and dropped it, thudding, to the floor.

Subchapter ii

At ten o'clock in the forenoon, with the summer sun raising a blue mist from the Thames, the Tenth Annual Congress of the Anarchocommunist Party opened in Shettlesea Town Hall. The delegates were welcomed by the mayor, a Marxian dustman who voted consistently for the Conservatives. This he did in order to help the Tory Party to power and continue its historic function of maddening all dustmen into revolt.

Close up to the platform four young journalists and three elderly ones reported the proceedings for their respective newspapers. Undereducated, intelligent, these men had developed side by side bluff geniality and the slyness of hunted animals. Unaccustomed to regular meals, they were cynical of all human aspirations towards social betterment, and believed the Anarchocommunist Party a semi-criminal organization, financed by Russia. One of them had once hung around the back streets of Leningrad for a month, gathering sensational copy. His stomach upset by some strange sausages on which he had fed, he had stopped at Riga on his return journey and wired the news that human flesh was on sale in the streets of Leningrad.

Kindly, contemptuous, the journalists listened patronizingly the while a spectacled professor of international repute read a survey of the prospects of the European wheat crops. Revolutionary phraseology, more cryptic and technical than that of chemistry, baffled the journalists, and, in a few hurried shorthand outlines, they noted down that a foreigner with a poor command of English had advocated the burning of the European wheat crops. Then a more fiery speaker followed the professor. He used the word murder, and then, three or four sentences later, the word justified. Genuinely shocked and horrified, the journalists recorded the speaker's conviction that murder was justified.

Concealed under the platform three plain-clothes policemen were also engaged in taking notes. In their cramped hiding-place they were almost suffocated. They knew of no means of exit apart from the raising of the two planks which had been unnailed to allow their ingress. The Communist speakers on the platform, aware that policemen were concealed beneath, sat row on row, on chairs, above the two planks. Frequently, stamping vigorous applause of a speech, they showered the policemen with dust and cobwebs. At length one of the plain-clothes men fainted, and his companions began to beat on the planks above them. They were disregarded. Warm-eyed, delegate after delegate arose and stood by the table and spoke of the Brotherhood of Man.

Motion after motion was tabled for discussion. The hall grew warm and there arose a smell of human bodies enperspired under the stress of emotional crises. Disagreeing, delegates cursed each other in many dialects. Scotsmen and Welshmen, using uncouth expressions, were listened to by fellow delegates with a shamed, amused contempt. English delegates would then arise and move enthusiastic condemnation of racial barriers in Kenya.

Representing a total of about 5,000 members, the Conference, in the name of the oppressed workers of Great Britain, passed a vote of thanks to the Soviets for their guidance and leadership in the march of the World Revolution, indicted the Spanish dictatorship with the suppression of free speech, and called on the English Government to resign.

A motion in favour of Birth Control then came up for debate. It was passionately combated by a tall woman delegate with kindly face and untidy hair. Discovering that she was a spinster, and presumably a virgin, the Conference rocked with laughter. Amidst laughter, catcalls, and amorous offers from male delegates, the tall woman subsided and the motion was passed unanimously, as was also one calling for the complete political, economical and social emancipation of women.

"Kumred van Cooper will now speak on the international political situation," said the chairman.

Koupa, bird-like, refreshed from the three hours' sleep which he had had after leaving the prostitute's room, stood up. Flinging out his arms in a well-practised gesture, his voice smote to silence the whole room.

> "The trumpets of the four winds of the world
> From the ends of the earth blow battle: the night heaves
> With breasts palpitating and wings refurled,
> With passion of couched limbs, as one who grieves
> Sleeping, and in her sleep she sees uncurled
> Dreams serpent-shaken, such as sickness weaves,
> Down the wild wind of vision caught and whirled,
> Dead leaves of sleep, thicker than autumn leaves,
> Shadows of storm-shaped things,
> Flights of dim tribes of kings . . ."

"Comrades, we have listened till we are a little so-sick, is it not, to our good friends with the so-brave statistics? They tell us of wage-struggles, of coming strikes and the rising price of bread, of electoral machinery and the massing of minorities. By these is the Revolution to come? For that and by that do we live and toil and dream? I tell you there is a greater thing in the world, a so-greater urge, a greater impulse. Listen, friends little. I have been in Russia, I have fought under the Hammer and Sickle and seen the Red Battalions storm impregnable Perekop. I have tramped through starving Europe, lived in a hut by Nile bank, heard the sunrise blow its horns from a

Beduin tent in the sands. I have had a great Visioning, friends
mine. . . . For, wherever I have gone, in gutters and slums, in
factories and fields, I have met that new thing in History, that
Promise of Dawn—the awakened soul of the Common People.
Austere and pure, unthinkably gracious, a thing so-shining, I
have seen it stir across the great battlelines of humanity. . . . I
have had a great Visioning. . . . "

He stopped. Tears were clouding his quick, bird's eyes. Leaping to their feet, the delegates cheered him and cheered again.
With English emotionalism, with lit eyes and uplifted hearts,
they looked up at the crippled figure on the platform. Had not
they also seen the Vision Amazing? Did not they also know of
the awakening soul of the Common People?—awakening somewhere, beyond the hills, in some place they had never had the
time or opportunity to visit. But this man had. His voice led
the spontaneous outbursts of singing:

> "Then raise the scarlet standard high!
>   Within its shade we'll live and die;
>   Though cowards flinch and traitors sneer
>   We'll keep the red flag flying here!"

God mine, what horrible doggerel! Sitting down, Koupa
seized a piece of paper and jotted down the words of a song to
supersede the "Red Flag." He did not continue his speech. The
delegates, well-satisfied, cheered the announcement that the
international political situation had been adequately dealt
with. At that moment James Storman, released from prison an
hour before, appeared on the platform.

Tall, spare, his brown face was thinner than usual, but he
was as well-groomed as ever. He had endured a month's
imprisonment for his attempt to restrain the rioters at Waterloo Station. And, by God, I have an account to settle with
Koupa over that business. Hm. A damn poor gathering. These
delegates have been badly elected. Wonder what fool has been
the secretariat for the last month?

He became aware of a thin and perfunctory hand-clapping.
Then, to his surprise, he saw Koupa sitting beside the chairman.
The poet acted quickly. Dropping his notes, he jumped up,
embraced Storman, and kissed him on both cheeks. Applause
broke out again. That little Dutchman. A card. A Real Comrade.

Storman sat down. Puffing, the chairman drank a pint of water. The question for the personnel of the delegation to visit Russia was now before the meeting.

"Before asking the Conference to nominate members, I ave to point out the slightly hunusual situation that as arisen. During the imprisonment of our Secretary, Kumred Storman, is work as been taken over, halmost entirely, by our very brilliant colleeg, Kumred van Cooper. In is interim position e as been brilliantly successful, and, halmost entirely through is efforts at Eadquarters, we ave added more than 200 new members to our lists. Further, e as refused to accept any part-salary for this work.

"The question as therefore been raised as to wether—seeing the Secretary must be one of the delegation—Kumred van Cooper or Mr. Storman his, for that purpose, to be regarded has Secretary?"

Storman's great laugh boomed out, startlingly, causing the chairman to jump. His eyes twinkling unhumorously, the man released from prison looked over the whispering rows of delegates. So that was the plot?

It was. Unpopular with the rank and file because of his opportunism and cold-blooded efficiency, Storman had hitherto swayed the Party by sheer force of personality and constant supervision of every activity. During his month's imprisonment, his power had been shaken by an uncalculated factor. This was Koupa's belief in the Awakening Soul of the Common People.

"Kumreds will now vote by show of ands."

Hands were upraised to successive questions. The tellers handed up slips with voting strengths to the chairman. The chairman drank a pint of water, stood up, and announced the results.

"Kumreds Pollock and Clanning hunanimously elected to the Delegation. With regard to the third member, the voting as gone: Van Cooper, 40 votes; Storman, 7 votes. Kumred van Cooper will therefore be the third member of the Delegation."

"No, no!"

Koupa, drawn from consideration of a new Revolutionary hymn, was on his feet. He had listened to the voting in terror-stricken silence. Once in Russia, he would undoubtedly be thrown into prison for his share in the Kronstadt Revolt.

Before he could speak, Storman had also stood up.

"Mr. Chairman, it would appear that both you and the Conference are unaware of the Party constitution. I am still Party secretary. As such, I shall be the third delegate to Russia. I am on a six-months' contract with the Party. It requires a special meeting of the Executive to dismiss me. And my successor must be approved by the Third International."

Shouts broke out. "We'll damn soon see to that!" "Executive! you're all up there—call a special meeting!" "Throw the traitor out!" Through the tumult Koupa, waving his arms, made himself heard, and the noise at once subsided.

"Comrades, I agree with Storman, and beg to decline the so-great honour you would do me. Russia—our Mecca—I have already visited. It is for the others to go there and seek the so-great inspiration and knowledge. And I know of the heart-hunger of my Comrade Storman, his devotion to the Revolution. Elect him to the delegation. While he is gone, I will, if the meeting so decides, carry on as acting-secretary."

Ceasing, he turned to Storman and held out his hand.

"Comrade!"

Storman surveyed him out of twinkling eyes.

Suddenly, unhumorously, his great laugh boomed out.

Subchapter ii (a)

That evening Storman spent in the offices of the Anarchocommunist Party, overhauling the confidential correspondence and examining the secretary's accounts. The conference, after voting Storman to the Russian delegation by a narrow majority and Koupa to the acting-secretaryship by an overwhelming one, had adjourned late in the afternoon to partake of high tea and afterwards attend a dance and social reunion. The while the records of his secretaryship were under scrutiny, the poet was engaged, half-a-mile away, in drinking beer, engaging in casual dances, and relating memories of the visit of Karl Marx to his parents' home in Holland.

Indexing and carding, fighting out balances in books, occupied Storman till ten o'clock. For weeks it seemed that nothing had been filed; ledgers were strangely and amazingly posted. Great heaps of unanswered letters lay on the typist's table amidst litter of cigarette-ends and scraps of verse scrawled on the backs of envelopes. But on the table at which Koupa had worked were scores of notes of appreciation and innumerable new membership applications.

Working steadily in the quietness, Storman at length came to the last batch of correspondence. As he picked it up, shook it and straightened it, a grimy card fluttered to the floor.

It was made out in Koupa's name, and was for the sum of fifty shillings.

He had pawned the office duplicator.

Subchapter iii

As from a giant searchlight, suddenly moved to a new position by the finger of God, the moonlight poured into a bed-sitting-room in Shepherd's Bush. Flooding across space, a distance of two hundred and fifty thousand miles, it came. Behind it, a giant reflector, blazed the great Lunar deserts and the ink-shadowed ring-mountains.

Above these, filling an eighth of their sky, mysterious and wonderful to Lunarian eyes, hung, ghostly and remote, canopied in its cloud-belts, the world that men call Earth.

And into the bed-sitting-room in Shepherd's Bush, across the unplumbed gulfs, the moonlight poured liquid. Each item of furniture offshot a velvety shadow. The table, round, three-legged, grasped the moon-spilt linoleum with grotesque claws. An alarum clock ticked hirplingly. Dried grass, in vases, oversprayed the mantelshelf. Upon the bed a shapelessness moved dimly.

So for a full minute after the entrance of the moonlight. Then the couchant shadow upon the bed split in two. One half, projected suddenly into the golden effulgence, budded forth a girl's head and breast. The alarum clock-face glimmered, dim seen.

"Oh, Miggod! *Billy*! Look at the time!"

Subchapter iii (a)

Checked, yet enticed, by a forest of grey gables, the moonlight flung a spear of radiance within a window in Mayfair. A bare three feet within the room, the spear-tip quivered to rest on a writing-table and an unfolded letter.

> The Secretary,
>> The Anarchocommunist Party.
>
> Sir,
>> I have to request that my name be deleted from the membership lists of your Party.
>>
>> I can no longer associate myself with either its beliefs or its so-called aspirations, and shall be obliged if the influence of my name is no longer used in propagating these.
>>> I am,
>>>> Yours etc.,
>>>>> GRISELDA GAYFORD.

Subchapter iii (b)

That afternoon, taking a boat from Westminster Pier, Thea Mayven and John Garland went down the River to Limehouse. Garland was in the civilian clothes he ordinarily stored at the Union Jack Club. They hung upon his stout figure with a baggy comeliness. He wore a blue shirt, a blue collar, blue socks, and a tie with a blue stripe. A bloody symphony. Under the turned-down brim of his velour hat the eyes in his ruddy, sulky face twinkled. He had with him a suitcase and a bundle which contained the MS. of his novel. For he had finished the first draft, and, typed, the front page awaited uncovering to reveal its legend:

FIRST NOVEL OF AN IRONIST

by

John Garland.

"Body and soul are twins: God only knows which is which:
The soul squats down in the flesh like a tinker drunk in a ditch."
—SWINBURNE.

This MS. he was to read to Thea during their three weeks' holiday. In Scotland. Beside a haystack.

Opposite him in the boat sat Thea. Her dress was green, embroidered with gold. Her hat was green, embroidered with gold. It had a wide brim, this hat, because Biggod, Thea, your nose has a bump in the middle and you need a hat with a brim. Her shoes were low-heeled, with papier mâché soles and whorling decorations. They were brogues, and she had bought them for long country tramps.

All her under-garments were new. They embraced her caressingly; she heard the pleasant underscuff of them whenever she moved. These garments included a thin vest, of a close, sweat-inducing fabric; stockings of artificial silk; cotton knickers which were hand embroidered by machinery; miniature, steel-sprung stays. For, after five hundred thousand years of the upright position, the pelvis of the human female is still incapable of supporting, without aids, the weight of the entrails and the womb, even of a virgin.

Looking at her, Garland thought:

"Ford Madox Hueffer's character is right. All attractive girls should be seduced and married. Then they trouble a man less and listen to his conversation." And he sighed, for he could not afford to seduce her.

Raising his head, he saw that they neared a wharf. Beside it was moored a ship. The boat of Garland and Thea drew alongside. Thea and Garland climbed aboard. In the middle of the ship yawned a large hole. Into this trunks, kitbags and motorcycles were being thrown by the sailors. Anxious men and women, boarding the ship from the gangway reaching to the wharf, attempted to catch last glimpses of their property before it vanished. The hooks of the donkey-engine derrick swayed threateningly amidst these people, and, cursing them, the deckhands would stop for a moment and wipe their faces and spit tobacco juice and declare their admiration for Mr. Havelock Wilson.

The ship was bound for Aberdeen. Men and women of the second class were sorted out into different sexes, and allotted bunks in separate divisions of the forecastle. These bunks lay in tiers of three. Garland found his high up, close to a porthole. Putting his suitcase and the bundle of his MS. into it, he went on deck.

Poor, romantic, unprosperous, many scores of Scots had come on board, bent on returning to Scotland for a fortnight's holiday. Years of residence in London had mitigated the accents of few of them. The men had sandy hair and shallow grey eyes and wore watch-chains with rows of medals. The women, broad-cheeked and with wide waists and the hips which told of much child-bearing, looked round the decks with innocent, kindly eyes, and, smiling, showed decayed teeth.

By the rails Garland found Thea, slim and green-clad and surveying the wharf from under her wide-brimmed hat. She pointed to the shore. "We're moving off."

The ship appeared to be slowly drifting out into the River. People on the wharf waved handkerchiefs. One woman cried. Excited, the passengers also waved. They laughed and spoke in soft gutturals. The ship began to move down the River.

All that evening they moved down the River, by docks of merchandise and trade, by hulls of rusty ships, against grey stretches of saline marsh. The sunset burned behind them. Gulls circled and cried. Still they held on. The River seemed never-ending. Then the ship began to rock in the rollers of the North Sea and the tea-bell rang.

Belly-stirred, the second-class passengers emptied themselves down the gangways to the plank-tables. Vociferating, they demanded seats. Two Irish stewards stood and separated them, men from women. And a stout, motherly stewardess, in charge of the women's table, looked about her with an austere, patient eye. She had the care of the women's morals in the second class. No harm would come to any daft young bitch while in her charge. Women passengers who had borne five children, and slept with their husbands for thirty-eight years on end, quailed under the look of this stewardess and, flushing, avoided the gaze of the menfolk, and ate hard.

After ten minutes at the table, Thea went on deck again and bargained with a steward for two deckchairs. It was inadvisable to leave any such bargaining to Garland. For he was dilatory and unsatisfactory in such things, being a funny boy.

In a little Garland, replete with tea and boiled eggs and salad, came and looked into the sea, then sat down in the chair next to Thea.

"Cigarette?"

"Please."

And, as she smoked and the English coast maintained its dim blur to the west, Garland stretched out his legs and looked at her and touched her hand.

"My dear," he said, "you are lovely. I haven't seen a girl on board to touch you."

Thea smiled, twinkling her eyes at him. And Garland, looking at her against the evening and the sea, thought:

"I might have told her that she was more fair than the sunset and changeful and cold and sweet as the sea; that she has mothered many tribes of men, that the ages have passed through her loins; that those eyes of hers have looked on incest and murder, warmly; that she is older than man or men and things nameless and horrifying and adorable is her body built from. . . . And all that would have been true; and she'd be angry if I said it; or troubled; look at me with darkened eyes. So I tell her there isn't a girl on board to touch her. And she is pleased. My dear, my dear!"

"Look down at the water," said Thea.

It was awash in the sunset like spilt blood; the English coast was a haze of blood; the sky was crimson—splashed. The ship moved through a silence of horror.

With shadows upon the sea, out of the veil of spindrift came the star-rise. Electric lights were switched on all over the ship. Grunting, she churned into the mysteries of the night. An old man leant over the side of the ship, vomiting.

The ship was overcrowded. Passengers who had not booked well ahead were given beds on stretches of canvas in the horse-boxes. The old man had secured such a bed but had been turned out of it by a later arrival, a young man who smelt of beer. The young man was burly and dark and angry; he had thrown the old man's shabby carpet-bag out of the horse box, had sworn at him.

"Old bastard," he had said.

Small, timid, feeble, more hopeless than hopelessness, the old man lay against the side of the ship, coughing. Every now and then he remembered the carpet-bag and outreached a shaky hand to it. He did not think; he had lived all his life in dim cellars of thought that grew darker day by day; he was old.

But up on the bow of the ship, in the keen of the wind,

wrapped with coldness and starfire, Garland sat dreaming by the side of Thea. They were almost alone up there, by then. Mysterious, wonderful, the grey heave of the sea, the dim horizon which towered and sank. Thea's face was a meeting-place of shadows; but for the warmth of her long legs outstretched against his own, Garland could have dreamt her also a dream.

But she was real; the only reality in Life; she, and the simple things—love, ambition, marriage, children, toil. He knew it now. He would forsake the Outer Wastes for ever. He also would be simple, guarded; think her thoughts, laugh with her, dislike with her. Work like hell, he would, now, so that they could build up a home together. A home, comfort, tenderness; the weeping horrors of Life locked out.

"Penny for them, darling."

He picked up her hand and kissed it, then held it close against his side, against his heart, held it fearfully. But he did not look at her. He was staring out to sea.

For towards them, like a rider triumphant upon the spindrift, was leaping a wild radiance, menacing, unearthly. Garland caught his breath in something that was half a sob.

"John? Cold?" She took his arm and looked up into his face. Before she could draw away he kissed her, suddenly, passionately, pitifully, as though hiding his face from a blow.

The moonlight poured over the ship in a cataract of silver.

CHAPTER THE FIFTH

*Wherein the Monotony of a Bucolic Idyll is relieved by
Various Interesting and Agreeable Purple Patches.*

Subchapter i

GARLAND and Thea landed at Aberdeen on a Thursday
morning. While they had been upon the sea the Government
had imprisoned five Communists, a high Church dignitary had
denounced communion as a superstitious practice, and a Royal
Princess had given birth to twins in the presence of a surgeon,
an anæsthetist, two physicians and three nurses.

They read of these things in a copy of the *Daily Mirror*
which Thea bought as they passed through the Fish Market.
At breakfast in the Station Hotel they read of them. Reading,
they first ate porridge, salted, with cream upon it. Then they
had eggs and bacon and tea and oatcakes. Then they ate
scones and brown girdle-cakes.

Eating a scone, Garland said:

"This bishop is right. Communion is a relic of cannibalism.
In eating the bread and drinking the wine we are devouring
the flesh and drinking the blood of the sacrificial victim. Symbolic cannibalism is the central rite of the Christian Mysteries."

But Thea was not listening. Scornful, republican, her face a
little flushed, she read aloud extracts from the account of the
Princess's delivery.

"All her family breed like rabbits," said Garland, and ate
another scone.

"Fancy all that amount of doctors! Though, of course, I
believe that all that kind of thing should be managed as scien-
tifically as possible."

And, earnest-eyed, she looked at Garland over a girdle-cake.

Garland said yes, and talked of science. Talking, he was
smitten with a sudden wondering amazement, and looked

away, and buttered another scone. She, Thea, the girl sitting opposite him—she had once been born. Once she must have been so small that her father had been able to lift her on the palm of one hand. And in her tiny brain had been no thought, no hope, no fear, no stir of conscious consciousness; her body had been a red little package of miniature and—heritage of the beast—largely archaic organs.

She had had no soul, no ego, no mind. Tiny, a feeble, weakling animal, she had lain. And days had passed, altering her; months had passed, building her; in a year her body had moulded to certain definite shapes; within the grey caverns of her brain crude, slow whorlings had involuted into a dawning consciousness. The outside world had retreated and approached and built itself on certain foundations before her eyes.

And slow years had passed. Her body had grown and changed and discarded. But her mind had retained, sifted away into different compartments of the subconscious, all the dross and dregs of vision and experience. The thought-whorls grew the more complex; below them, memories jostled the thicker. And, strangely antagonistic to the logic of these, ever more definite grew that consciousness that was now almost conscious of itself, that whispering knowledge of "I".

Most utter illogic. The Ego that then first stirred in her was an illusion—a thin wraith of a thing, a co-ordinated, energized memory of all the sights and sounds and touches of the outside world. It was a mere perfume, an effluvium—yet with purpose. Already, with a consummate daring, it was seeking to establish dominion over that outer world, over the outer world of its material body and instincts and stored remembrances. It claimed to direct, to lead, to suppress, to control. . . .

Her body grew. And then, in some year, came a time of physiological stress, of strange and disgusting changes to her body, of the first incursions of sex. And, with the coming of that time, a flower upspringing from the garbage-heap of Nature, her consciousness became conscious and she had said: "I am Thea Mayven."

Odyssey.

"John, waken up! We'll miss our train."

Thea was standing up and stretching, widely and luxuriously and slimly, by the table in the empty room. "Oh-h-h!
Glorious morning. Glorious day. Good as gold to be alive. I
want to go mad."

"So do I. It must be the scones."

Walking to their platform, they were conscious of reple-
tion and goodwill and happiness. Porters, carrying luggage
and talking of prices in the Fish Market, looked at them
sourly, surveying Thea's lightly-clad figure with interest and
the questioning greed implanted by Providence. For Thea's
skirt reached only to her knees, and those knees were round
and flexible and silken clad to an insolent sheen; her legs
were long and shaped to slim, flat ankles and small feet in
high-heeled shoes. So the porters at Aberdeen Station, filled
with the desire to propagate their kind, looked at Thea and
Garland cruelly, and suspected that she was a prostitute,
and felt stir within them the stern morality of their cove-
nanting forbears.

The train ran by the sea, northwards, for mile upon mile.
And of a sudden Garland and Thea saw that it was summer.
The corn was turning from greeny-yellow to gold. At wayside
stations they watched the waves come riding shoreward, heard
the wheel and whittoo of the peewits. They had a carriage to
themselves, and, looking out of the window, tears came in
Garland's eyes at sight of the corn, at sight of it climbing,
smooth and yellow and surgent, the sides of the upreaching
hills. And he knew that he looked upon the magic of the
ancient world as he watched that yellow cloakment suddenly
undulate in the passage of a morning breeze.

It was haytime. Through the opened windows of the train
they heard the clank of the mowers, saw bright blades flash in
the sun, the steamy breath arise from horses halted at the end
of a long ridge. In the fields wide lines of men, shirt-sleeved,
corduroyed, with drooping hat-brims and smoking pipes, blowing blue incense-whorls in the sunlight, flung the hay-swathes
apart with smooth-handled forks. And the smell of the hay
wrapped the train round like a garment, so that it went slowly,

sneezing, amidst the wide land of the haymaking, and, turning back to the sea, turned yet again, and was in the hayfields and the hills again.

"Summer," said Thea, and dropped warm hands on Garland's hands, and kissed his cheek, absently, eagerly, thoughtlessly, as a child might, then looked out again. "Look, there's Micklegarth and Morecalm; over there. And the Castle. There's Fluinn with its steeple; they take it in when it rains. Not long till we're at Leekan now."

It was three o'clock in the afternoon before they were through the pass in the mountains, and Leekan station came in sight. They got out. A place of corrugated roofs, red-painted, odoriferous, with drooping-headed horses in the railway yard. Through fir-trees, half a mile up a road, glinted the red granite of Leekan village. Then Thea cried, "Dad!" and danced up the platform, and put her arms about the neck of a man, and hugged him.

She brought him to Garland. Garland shook a broad, brown hand, calloused, and with serrated edges.

"Hoo are ye? Od, ye maun be tired wi the journey. An Theey's a gey responsibility, I'll warrant."

He said this in a slow, careful, doubtful voice, speaking carefully and slowly, knowing that all Englishmen were half-wits. Showing tobacco-stained teeth, he smiled cannily. He was of middle height, thick set, with enormous shoulders. A brown beard streaked with grey lay over the craggy whiteness of his collar and false front. He wore a suit of thick tweeds. His eyes were small and friendly and shrewd and oddly timid.

He was Thea's father.

He had brought a trap to take them home. Thea, light-headed, danced round it, embracing the head of Kate, the horse, a sonsy beast who snuffled at her and disregarded her, and, tail-switching, fell again into a dream in the sunlight. Roger Mayven fussed in the arranging of the luggage and a parcel of groceries he had brought from Leekan village. Speaking to his daughter, his tone was admonitory and full of a shamed pride and amazement, for he was still, spite the passage of the years, uncertain as to whether her conduct in refusing to become a bit servan lassie an milk kye an keep a man's house—na, na, she wad hae none o that, but maun

84

learn shorthan and siclike stuff and gae stravaigin awa to London—was decent and profitable, or not.

(And this bit cratur o an English mannie? Fit was it Theey said he was—an airman sodger? Od, no great catch for ony body!)

"Dinna cairry on like that, lassie. Fouk'll think ye're daft. Noo, Maister Garlan, sit up here in front wi me. Sit ye at the back, Theey, an min and no let the treacle rin oot o the jar in the bit basket. Noo, are ye a right? Wissh, Kate."

And Garland thought:

"That is interesting. Wissh is the eastern equivalent of the Western Lowland whiggam. From it the Whigs were named. I am listening to the encouraging hiss that gave birth to the Liberal Party."

They drove out of the station and turned to the right, away from the direction of Leekan village and towards the warm, purple bulking of the Grampians. Thea sat behind, among the parcels, for she was only a bit lassie. Thea enjoyed it. She was in the mood to enjoy anything. Going past remembered farms, she waved her hand to placid men in the fields. Her father was sair affronted.

Then out of the haze in front of them came another trap and spanked past them in the direction of Leekan. In it sat a man with side-whiskers, a large body, and a shy, supple smile. He waved to Roger Mayven, and they both cried "Aye, fine day," earnestly, reassuringly, at the same time. Then this man looked into the back of the Mayven trap and saw Thea, and waved to her also.

"Hullo, Theey, holidayin? Enjoy yersel!"

"I will, Dreaichie! How's the housekeeper?"

But Dreaichie was spanking on towards Leekan. Roger Mayven shook his head and looked over into the back of the trap.

"Ye shouldna hae said that, lassie."

"Why not? Doesn't he still sleep with his housekeeper?"

Garland, looking at Mr. Mayven, saw a tide of colour come up under his weather-roughened skin. The brown-faced, brown-bearded man, shocked, refused to meet Garland's eyes.

"Lassie, ye shouldna speak like that. I dinna believe ony o the stories about Dreaichie an his hoosekeeper. An he's a guid neighbour an a fine chiel."

For Roger Mayven was charitable towards the sins of the unashamedly sinful. Dreaichie and his housekeeper were just Dreaichie and his housekeeper. (A muckle limmer o a woman. And wi a tongue on her that wad clip cloots.) Why speak about it? Then, after such remark, he would moisten his roughened lips under his beard, and with kindly eyes and contemplative face, speculate on Dreaichie and his housekeeper.

But Thea, long escaped from her father and the fear of him, was unabashed.

"He's a good enough neighbour—at least to his housekeeper, else she wouldn't have three children. But what's happened? Has he fallen out with her?"

Behind his beard Mr. Mayven's face shrivelled. "Aye, so they say. There's a new bit lassie at Dreaichie's and they say the cratur o a hoosekeeper's fair daft with jealousy. . . . But there's things that a lassie like you has no right to speak aboot. Ye'll be wantin yer tea, Maister Garlan?"

"Horribly hungry, Mr. Mayven. Thea tells me that at Cairndhu there's real oatcakes and home-made, crumbly cheese, and curds and cream for tea."

"Oh, aye, but we'll be able to gie ye something better than that, I'm thinkin."

"Oh, my God," said Thea. "Don't tell me mother's been buying fancy cakes and getting ready an English tea?"

But Mr. Mayven said nothing, except Wissh, Kate, to the horse. They loped down a long, steep brae, the trap bumping against Kate's hindquarters. Above them massed firwoods. Up through those at a trot. Beyond, poised against the horizon and the mountains, with the gleam of the North Sea reappearing half a mile to the left, the biggings of Cairndhu.

In front of the biggings, out on the road at sound of the trap, in long skirts, hand-waving, appeared the figure of a woman. Thea, waving wildly in return, stood up in the trap. Garland looked up into a flushed, scared, bitter face.

Tears were in Thea's eyes, bitter tears, tears of an overmastering, heart-breaking pity. She and her parents were poles apart in all sympathies; she would never dream of turning to them for help in any emergency.

She was more alien to their lives and longing than a Kalmuck of the steppes. In youth they had loved her,

86

thwarted her, misunderstood her. She had hated them. (God, how she had hated them!)

Now, all unconscious of the reason, she was weeping because of that tragedy of existence which had led a woman to beget her.

Subchapter iii

At eight o'clock next morning Dreaichie was clearing a path round his hayfield in order to allow the mowing machine to begin. He used a long-handled, long-bladed scythe. Now and then he would stop to whet it, and the underskirl of the whetting rang soft and clear and sweet across the fields. Dreaichie's brown, red-ringed face dripped sweat. He worked in a drunken extasy. The cloverheads, essence-distilling, fell around him. Far off, a shimmer and a radiance in the sky beyond the brae, was the North Sea.

Dreaichie was forty-five years of age. Year after year, scythe-swinging, he had grown drunken of the smells of the earth and clover; it was, of all the earth-essences, the one he most loved. But there were others: the smell of sheep in winter buchts; the keen, metallic smell of new-ploughed earth; the biting smell of whin-burning; sweat-reeking horses' smell; smells without name, innumerable. He had made a cult of them. Simple, kindly, lascivious, he was descended from many generations of peasants who had tilled the earth, resisted their landlords, and begat many children upon the bodies of their womenkind.

"Hi, Dreaichie!"

The scytheman raised his whiskered, genial face. Gordoun, the local postman, a man with a squint and a belief in Scottish Home Rule, was leaning over a distant gate.

"Dreaichie, hae ye heard o that bit grave they've dug open at Pittendreich's? An awful auld place, wi a skeleton and stane swords in it."

"Eh man, fit's that?"

"A Stane Age grave. Dug oot hundreds o years afore there were ony English. Pittendreich and the Dominie's niece cam on't yestreen. I kent ye'd be interested." Squinting autonomously, Gordoun waved his hand and turned away down a steep path towards Cairndhu.

Pittendreich lay six miles away, high up in the mountains. Early in the afternoon, Dreaichie arrived there and dismounted from his bicycle. The sweat ran in greasy runnels from his brown whiskers. Both his feet were flat, and, as he pedalled from the middle of the sole, they ached. At the farmhouse gate, Pittendreich's wife, muckle and sonsy, directed him.

"I wouldna gang there mysel," she said. "There's only a heap o auld banes. The minister an Miss Domina an the Maudslay laddie were up at them yestreen."

Leaving his bicycle, Dreaichie climbed up a foothill of the Grampians. In the centre of a cultivated patch, a mound, grass-covered, had lain unmolested for centuries. Yesterday, however, engaged in cutting out new drains, one of Pittendreich's men had set to hacking a way through it. A few figures, sun-drenched, stood at gaze on the top of the mound. Amongst them was a girl, short-skirted, bareheaded, standing hand on hip. A narrow slip o a lassie.

Dreaichie walked across a pathway beaten in the late corn. High up above the East Coast valley was this land. The peewits moaned below in the misty mountain blueness. Pittendreich, crease upon crease of his flesh shining in the sunlight, was by the grave.

"Weel, Dreaichie, man. So ye've come to see it? There's a college professor here from Dundee the noo. He says the bit grave's twa thousan years auld, if it's a day; but I doot he's a leear, for the minister said it was sax thousan."

"Eh, man."

Dreaichie leant forward and looked down into the tumulus. The stone coping of the long barrow had been laid aside. At the bottom lay a dismembered, yellowy skeleton. Near the feet of the deceased the professor from Dundee prodded in the earth with a graip.

"Two thousand years ago," said a voice. "In the time of Christ."

It was the girl, short-skirted, hand on hip, her hair flaming in the sunlight. She was Thea Mayven. Beside her, pipe-smoking, stood Garland. Pittendreich and his folk glanced at them askance. English craturs. And, uncomfortable at hearing the name of Christ, they turned their eyes upon the professor from

Dundee. But Garland, taking his pipe from his mouth, shook his head.

"I doubt it. It's Epi-palaeolithic. Long barrow burial was a thing long past, even in Scotland, in the time of Christ."

The Dundee professor, black-moustached, quick-eyed, glanced up angrily. Thea smiled remotely and impishly. Garland mused aloud.

"Still, it's possible. They may have been backward folk in this district, keeping to the old ways of burial. This man may have wandered south, become a Roman legionary, have served in Palestine and assisted at the execution of the Jewish thaumaturgist. It may have been he who thrust the spear into Christ's side. Perhaps he returned after long years and told so many stories about the business that his neighbours buried him with all those pots of water in order that he might keep his throat moist to bore the afterworld."

"Perhaps he was a brewer's drayman," said Thea.

Their laughter rang out in the sunlight. Dreaichie, sweating, smiled sideways at them, doubtfully. Below, over the moors, the peewits cried unceasingly. Dreaichie bent down and picked up something by the side of the ancient dead. The Dundee professor looked up at him.

"What's that thing, d'you know? It's the only one I haven't been able to identify."

Considering, Dreaichie turned it over in his hands. It was a short dagger, of chert, stumpy, still-edged, dull-glowing in the light. "Och, man, I think this maun hae been a fairmer chiel in the lang syne, same's I am. I ken weel what it is. I've often seen the like in the Highlands when I was a laddie."

"Eh?" The professor from Dundee peered at it.

"What is't, then?"

"A gully knife."

"No, man, is that a fact?" Pittendreich and his labourers crowded around, interested. Laughing, they passed the ancient knife amongst themselves. Their faces, sun-reddened and high-veined, crinkled into knowing smiles. Then they recollected the presence of Thea. But she and Garland were staring into each other's eyes. One of the labourers, cupping the knife-handle in his palm, showed in shadowplay how the instrument had been used.

It passed back to Dreaichie's hands. Sweating, he turned it over consideringly.

The face of the professor from Dundee had grown red when he heard of the nature of the implement. For he was by nature shy of discussing all such things. He had been married ten years and his wife had borne him four children, but he had assisted at the conception of all of them in an absent-minded, delicate manner, his thoughts the while deliberately switched away to brooding upon the genesis of some stone implement or other. Also, he knew that if he took the gully knife back to Dundee, not one archæologist would recognize it under Dreaichie's nomenclature. For all of them were delicate-minded men, drinking tea and discussing lake- dwellings.

He moved about in the grave, the others watching him from above. Then Dreaichie noticed that when the professor from Dundee approached the foot of the grave, the soil there emitted strange under-cracklings.

"Man, there's something else below there."

"Eh?" The professor from Dundee peered and dug. In a little one of the graip's iron toes jarred against something febrile. Dreaichie climbed down into the tumulus and assisted. But first he slipped the gully knife into his pocket.

Remains of yet another inmate of the mound were uncovered. Shining with pleasure, the professor from Dundee motioned Dreaichie aside and prepared to photograph the bones in situ. Dreaichie craned over them moistly.

"What are they?"

"The bones of a woman. Can't you see? This man was doubtlessly her husband. She was probably sacrificed at his burial. Look at the base of the skull—there. That is the mark of the axe which must have killed her."

"Od, the nesty brutes," said Pittendreich.

" 'Man scores always, everywhere,' " quoted Thea, unstirred.

"Perhaps she poisoned him and then committed suicide," said Garland.

"She must have done it during a somersault, then."

Dreaichie climbed out of the pit, dusted his good tweed trousers, breathed deeply, looked indifferently away from the woman's bones to those of the man. . . .

A fairmer chiel, like himself, the man wi the gully knife. Often, maybe, he'd looked ower those hills on a summer afternoon. . . .

The genial brown eyes of Dreaichie blurred.

"Puir chiel," he said.

Subchapter iv

In the darkness Dreaichie rose from his bed, and, softly opening the door of his bedroom, went on bare and hairy toes along the landing to another room. Outside the latter he stood for a little, listening, then entered, cannily closing the door behind him.

In the bed Jean, the servant lassie, awoke and watched him. She had been in Dreaichie's service for a month. It was his third visit to her at night. She was seventeen years of age. Her father owed Dreaichie money, so she had been sent into his service. She was a neat, obliging girl, and had taught in Sunday school. She now fell to arranging the pillows so that they would serve for two instead of one.

But Dreaichie did not come to her immediately. Instead, after surveying her with shrewd, kindly eyes, he stood looking out of the window, holding his shirt cannily and respectably about him, for a cool night wind blew in.

The world seemed drowned in moonshine. Dreaichie shook an interested head. He broke into a husky whisper.

"Od, lassie, that was a wonderfu bit grave I saw up at Pittendreich this afternoon. . . . The skeleton o a chiel o aulden times, laid oot wi his pots and bit tools aroond him. A bit fairmerman, jist like mysel, he maun hae been. . . . Od, what can be on sae late at the Maudslay fairm?"

The servant lassie strained to see. Across the half-mile stretch of the valley they watched the flashing of a lantern in the farmyard of Chapel o' Seddel. Dreaichie's thoughts wandered away in an effort to apprehend some dimly sensed essence of romance.

"Jist think on't—that chiel in the grave—he's seen this same moon. . . . A fairmer-body just like mysel. He's the banes o a woman lying at his feet—killed to look aifter his speerit, the Dundee professor said. The English mannie wi Theey

91

Mayven was there, an he thocht that maybe the woman had poisoned the man, an then committed suicide."

"Whisht!"

They listened. The old farmhouse creaked unendingly, in the way of such houses. Nothing else.

"I thocht I heard the housekeeper," whispered Jean. Then: "You'll get your death o cauld standin there."

An hour later, his shrewd, kindly eyes heavy-lidded with sleep, Dreaichie went on tiptoe back to his own room. An hour after that a shrilling scream awoke the servant lassie from her sleep.

She awoke drowsily, taking it to be a yowl heard in nightmare. But it was repeated, raggedly, horribly. Jean sat up in bed, then cowered down into it.

The screaming rose and shook and wavered, then fell to a tremulous whimpering. Moonlight upon the planks, the servant lassie saw the door of her room swing open, saw the moonlight on the face and bared arms of Dreaichie's housekeeper. Then a dull something flashed in the moonlight and clanged on the floor beside the bed.

It was the gully knife from the Stone Age grave.

Subchapter v

An amethystine dawn came over the mountains, trailed its fainting colours across the Valley of Leekan, drowned them in the Eastern Sea. Behind followed the sunlight, strong and clear, dancing across the harvest-waiting fields. There was no wind. Sheep cried on the moors. The peewits whooped unceasingly. Soon the warmth grew such that a ground mist, blue in distance, arose, and the earth, as in some lost geologic age, steamed. Thea and Garland, leaving Cairndhu, went down across the shelving moor-ledges to the sea.

"What a day!" said Garland, and took off his hat to it.

"Clover and the sea!" said Thea, and no more than that. Her face was flushed, her eyes brightly drowsy. What a day!

Come to the cliff's edge, they stood and looked down upon the sea. The tide was going out. Lost rocks of granite were appearing above the receding waters. Seagulls dipped and cried. It was a little bay that lay below them, shaped like a jagged half-moon. It was gull-haunted, unutterably lonely. In that vivid dawn heat even the seaward-making waters seemed to roll sluggishly.

They climbed down the cliff by a path made by farm-servants stealing gulls' eggs, and so came to a narrow ledge of grey shingle, a beach of broken granitic fragments. Then they saw all the face of the cliffs spotted blackly with the mouths of caves. Thea pointed to one.

"The Covenanters hid there," she said. "The soldiers lit a fire at the mouth and smoked them out. As they came through the flames they were shot down. There's a tablet with their names."

They stood and read the tablet. Amongst the names was that of a Hamish Mayven.

"He was my ancestor," said Thea. "There have been May-vens in Cairndhu since the days of Duncan. So someone told father. Hamish and I used to get on well. When I quarrelled with father or mother I used to come down here and sulk, and talk with Hamish. He wasn't religious at all. He did it all for a lark, and because he was bored stiff. He used to sit opposite me there, and tell me so."

This was a new Thea. Garland ran his hand through his hair. Puzzlement came in his sulky, quizzical eyes. His stout figure stood silhouetted against the cavern mouth.

"Let's leave the sandwiches in here," said Thea. "They'll keep cool."

They went out again into the sun and sea light. Garland unwrapped the MS. of his novel. Squatting by Thea, he began to read it.

Thea lay on her stomach beside him. Thinly clad, she felt the sun-warmth penetrate her clothes and soak within her body. Listening to Garland and the gulls, she cupped her face in her hand and played with a little heap of sand. Sometimes Garland would pause in his reading and look at her; always he would find her eyes fixed on his face. In front of them, soft swishing, the tide went out.

Gulls and Garland and tide cried their story of Life in Thea's ears. Drowsy, she listened, sifting the sand, somnolent, adream. Once, somewhere, she had read that perhaps there was a universe within each grain of sand, even as the universe that we inhabit may be only a lost grain on some lost, unfertile shore. The idea pleased her. Trickling the worlds through her fingers, she caused planetary collisions, the extinguishment of suns, the wiping out of whole races. Black, red-and-storm streaked grew the Heavens, whereneath countless tribes looked up at the whistling approach of doom. . . .

When she awoke her head was cupped in Garland's arm and he was sprinkling water on her face. Far out in the bay the tide, ceasing to recede, poised and overflowed on a ridge of foam. Only the wail of the gulls was never-ceasing.

"You fainted, I think." Garland grinned at her. "Was it my novel or a touch of sunstroke?"

Thea shook herself, sat up. She still felt drowsy, as though her whole body had been punched by a flabby fist. Childlike, she rubbed her eyes with her knuckles.

" 'Fraid I fell asleep. Had you read much before you noticed?"

"Three chapters. . . . This is no time or place for interplane-tary communication."

Thea rubbed her head against his shoulder. "I must be still asleep."

"No." Garland hunched himself above the rock where he sat. "It came to me as I read. In matters of communication we are all as planets. Between us lie great gulfs of space. We wander in eternal loneliness. Dimly, from far off, we hear lost snatches of sound. Sometimes an enterprising planet, like myself, seeks to bridge the gulf with a message and a code. . . ." He yawned in the sunlight and blinked his eyes like a cat. "A damned strain-ing simile."

But Thea had sat up. "John, there must be something about this place—astronomical, you know. When you were reading I was sifting sand and thinking that perhaps each grain was a world, and wondering how many earthquakes I was causing. Funny."

"It's a special section of the earth set apart for dreams. You never know. Perhaps the earth was originally fertilized by seeds of life from outer space. Perhaps the meteor that brought them fell on this shore. Homer and Akhnaton and Queen Móo and Buddha and Mr. Baldwin and the megatheria were all here then—in essence. Young Thea Mayven was here,

94

indistinguishable from the aurochs and Lenin and the Princess and her twins. Anatole France and I and the Arbiter Elegantiarum were all here. 'The Revolt of the Angels' and 'The First Novel of an Ironist' were indistinguishable."

"There ought to be a monument," said Thea, and stood up, and sprinkled sand over Garland. "I feel hungry."

They sat in the coolness of the Covenanter's cave and ate sandwiches and oatcakes and grey cheese. Thea took Garland's case out of his pocket and lit a cigarette and attempted to blow smoke through her nose. Sneezing, she flung the cigarette away, and considered the sea. Suddenly she jumped to her feet.

"I know. Let's bathe."

"There's only one sea."

"Damn." Thea scowled at him with a sudden, unfeigned distaste.

"What?"

"The nuisance of you being a man. Or rather—oh, what does it matter? No one to see us. I'm not going to bother about you being here. . . . I'll wear something. Dry it afterwards in the sun. You do the same. Race you who'll be first in the water."

She was first. Naked, looking out from the mouth of the cave, Garland saw her, white and slim, like a boy of the Greek marbles, clad in something faint and negligible and wispy, run from the mouth of a cave further along the shore. She did not look in his direction, but leaping from point to point of the granite rocks, gained the water, dropped from a ledge, and began to swim out in the path of the sun. He stared at the flame of her hair, shivered, and laughed.

Following her, he plunged into water cold and grainily salt and vaguely sentient. Clad in white cotton shorts, he swam after the dipping dot of flame which was Thea's head. She was making for an out-cropping of rock, gull-haunted, in the centre of the bay. Looking over her shoulder, she began to go faster. It was a race.

Almost simultaneously they drew up out of the water. Laughing, panting, Thea flung back the short hair from her face. Her eyes were the eyes of adventure.

"Oh, good, good. . . . Don't look at me too closely, because I'm not respectable. Neither are you. . . . All right. Let's rest here."

They climbed up the rock. It was higher than appeared from sea-level. Thea gained the top first and gave a cry.

"John! Look at the grass!"

The top of the rock was shallowly concave. Innumerable rains, washing its sides, had silted particles of rock into a fine powder. In far-off years chance bird-droppings had brought the first seeds of life. Now the concave surface was grass-covered, green, a miniature island in the sea. When they sat down, the shore vanished from sight. Through the afternoon haze loomed dimly the purple mountains. Below, the sea whispered.

"It's an island," said Thea. "We're alone in the world."

Garland grunted and lay flat on his stomach. Then he rolled over and stared up into the blue-grey sky. Then he turned his head sideways and looked at Thea.

She sat cross-legged, backgrounded by sea-sky, her face not the face of Thea Mayven, but swept of personality, of expression, of emotion. She was utterly unconscious of his presence. The sea and the sun were hers.

In the croon of the gulls and sea-sound he watched her, content. Then a drowsiness began to come on him, and the silhouette of Thea grew gold, then blue, then a fainting brown.

"More comfy?"

He came out of a minute's sleep. His head rested in her lap. She was bending over him, her face grave. Half adream, he thought and spoke.

"Not for you." Then: "Your thighs are soft and sweet."

The lights twinkled in her eyes. She bent down and rubbed her cheek against his. "Listen to the gulls."

Unending. He put up his hands and held her face. Suddenly he was aware of the throbbing of her body. The lights had died from her eyes. He touched her breasts. Suddenly she sobbed and their lips met.

A pringling numbness leapt upon him. He thought "God," then ceased to think.

Subchapter v (a)

All a long hour had the tide hung poised. But now, suddenly, it began to enter the bay; in long lines of surf it poured across the shingle. Crooning inarticulately, the urge of the sea and the sky

96

behind it, it flooded, and the earth, understanding, shook and murmured at its coming. And a sound of tears and a sound of laughter rose and quivered and faltered to a voiceless extasy.

Never-ending was the wail of the gulls.

Subchapter vi

Late in the afternoon, limping homewards from his hayfield, Dreaichie stopped to watch with kindly, bloodshot eyes, two figures crossing the moor towards Cairndhu. They came from the direction of the sea. Mayven's bit lassie and the young English chiel.

"Hi!"

Raising his eyes, he saw Jean, waving. Aproned, hand upraised, she stood on the knoll outside the kitchen door. It was tea-time. There was no sign of the bitch of a housekeeper. She had left in the dead of night with her three weans. God blast her, the ful jaud.

Because of the wound inflicted by the gully knife, he moved stiffly across the fields. A headachy pain dizzied him. On recovering from the searing agony of the housekeeper's outrage, he had managed to light the candle and stanch the flow of blood by means of rough bandaging. Then, until morning, he'd lain almost daft with pain. At dawn he'd sent off Geordie, the plough-laddie, to Leekan for the doctor.

But when the doctor arrived he had been met outside the house by Dreaichie himself, pale, weakly moving, but refusing attendance.

He had been unable to bear thought of the scandalous story which would spread over the countryside if he submitted himself to the doctor's attentions. No one knew what had happened, except Jean, who had been awakened by the gully knife being thrown into her room. Puir lassie, she'd been gey frichted by that.

"I need a woman to look aifter me."

Shambling up the brae, that thought steadied Dreaichie, as it had done all the afternoon. Aye, he'd mairry Jeannie. Best thing for baith o them. She liked him weel. Wouldna mind though he'd never be able to be a husband to her. . . .

His footsteps soundless upon the grass, he crossed the knoll to the kitchen door. In the outbuilt dairy he heard a murmur of voices, a laugh, a clear sentence.

Geordie's voice speaking of castrated cattle.

Came the sound of a milk-pail being overturned, sniggers and whispered expostulation, then Jeannie, rumpled and flushed, emerged from the dairy. At sight of Dreaichie she stood aghast for a moment. Then, with a sly, contemptuous look, she disappeared round the corner of the house.

CHAPTER THE SIXTH

Wherein, whilst devoting Two Subchapters to the Interest of Philosophy and One to the Interests of Art, some Discreet, if Indirect, Propaganda is done on behalf of the Birth Control Movement.

Subchapter i

LATE in the afternoon Andreas van Koupa came into the Strand from a side-street. Extinguishing his partly smoked cigarette, he placed the unconsumed portion in his waistcoat, and yawned. Occupied with the accounts of the Anarchocommunist Party, he had awakened only half an hour before. Awakening, he found his mouth dry and sooty with over-smoking and his mind dry and sagging with mathematical effort.

The funds of the Anarchocommunist Party showed an unledgered deficit of £50. And Storman was due to return from Russia within a week.

Koupa had sought the pavements to think over the matter. Gaining the open air, however, he had lit a cigarette, and his thoughts on the missing £50 had gradually drizzled from his mind as he observed the various surprising phenomena of London. The sunlight falling on the gables of an old Georgian house, converted into a manure depository, had intensely amused him. He had stood still, moving his head from side to side and chuckling. Stepping forward again, a black cat had made to walk across his path, had hesitated, had only been induced to continue by the poet wheedling it with an inviting cheechee and then shooing it ferociously. Terrified, it had completed the crossing in a spurt of speed, thus showing a sign of luck. Koupa had then helped a blind man half-way across a street and abandoned him to look at a huge Shire horse in a lorry. Amazed at the size of the beast, he had walked round it several times. Descended from the small, dog-like archeophippus of the Miocene, the draft horse has progressed through a more amazing evolution than has man. But its brain has grown hardly at all. Why?

Intrigued, Koupa had stopped in front of the horse, inspecting its skull-formation. Then the carter had come out into the street with a sack of grain, and, observing the poet, had scowled. Noting Koupa's black eyes, broad-brimmed hat, and unclean fingernails, he had called out an obscene jest to another carter. Surprised and hurt, Koupa had walked on. And he thought:

"God mine, the cruelty of men one to another! And the essence of all the so-great cruelties—it is laughter. Without the curse of laughter it might well be that man would live just and sober and moral as the ant. But, observing the juxtaposition of things which to them seem inappropriate in juxtaposition, men find the muscles of their faces and throats relax in surprise. They laugh. The things seen as inappropriate in their relation then seem inappropriate and hateful in their essence. Then the sense of order which is in man creates in him the desire to stamp on and abolish that which has seemed laughable. From this have arisen all legal torments and watchings by priests and lawyers of the so-hideous tortures of rack and hoist."

He came into the Strand and put out his cigarette as he thought of these things. Now he observed that it was late afternoon, for the sun slanted. The Strand was moved, in the dusty and faded sunlight, as a river-mouth in the salmon-migration. An itinerant fruit-vendor stood by the kerb, wearing the Distinguished Conduct Medal and suffering from influenza. Struck by a thought, Koupa bought a banana from him and, eating it, walked along the Strand. Testing Koupa's twopence with his teeth, the vendor found one of them bend sinuously.

Engulfed in the throngs, Koupa finished his banana and put his hand in his pocket to bring out a handkerchief with which to wipe his lips. Pleased with the people who looked at him curiously, he had taken off his hat and now carried it under his arm, for he had a good forehead. Bringing out the handkerchief, he also brought from the pocket a small celluloid object. It slithered to the pavement. Bending, Koupa retrieved it.

It was a note-slab of Storman's and bore the addresses of various influential, but uncertain, friends of the Anarcho-communist Party.

Though carrying it in his pocket, Koupa had never before looked in it. Now, standing athwart the pavement and blocking the way, he flicked open its loose-hung leaves. Pinching his nether-lip, he leant against a tailor's street dummy, and consulted the entries.

For there was a deficit of £50.

An entry caught his eye. It read:

"Mrs. Gayford, 14 Poncefort Terrace, Mayfair. Rich. Morrisy revolutional. Statues and machine-guns."

"By the bones of Spartacus," said Koupa to an astounded Strand.

Subchapter ii

"It is Autumn," said Thea Mayven.

She spoke to herself. She had stopped under the plane-trees of the Chelsea Embankment. Leaning her arms on the place where Storman had leant his six months before, as he talked of Mars to Norah Casement, she looked upon the water and the yellow dimness of the opposing shore. She sighed. Upon her was a drowsy content. It was Autumn. Keats and quietness.

"Season of mists and mellow fruitfulness."

Autumn and London. How'll it be in Scotland? Oh, home-made cheese and oatcakes, stooks in a field of barley, peewits and the sound of a binder on a far-off rig.

Quietness. Some other word?

Fulfilment.

Looking over into the River, she leant and was silent. Good to feel good. Nice London. Good to be alive.

A numbing, painless drowsiness came suddenly upon her, a minute singing held her ears. Surprised, she looked down into the water, and, in the so doing, the delicious faintness passed.

"Funny," said Thea Mayven.

She turned then away from the River, towards Rosemount Avenue. It was a Saturday afternoon. John would not be up in London until to-morrow. Too busy with his novel.

Thinking his name, a secret smile came on her thin red lips.

John. Oh, hell, please leave me some peace. Just one little half-hour to myself. Keep out of my memory just this little while. Please, please. Oh, my dear, some day I'll curl up and fade away, and all they'll find of me will be a thought and a memory of John Garland. Throbbing on the pavement.

Every hour thought of him was upon her. Only by rigorous self-discipline could she go through the life of each day with an appearance of calmness and sanity. Even so, unawares, he would steal upon her. Before her typewriter she would of a sudden grow still. Her face, under the wide-set green-grey eyes, would pale and then flush till the blood of emotion covered cheek and neck and breasts and body in a startled amazement. For she would be conscious of the touch of Garland's hands, of his hungry, ironic, wistful lips, of the queer, adorable smell of his hair. . . . So, at meals, in the train, awakened suddenly from sleep, she would be haunted, and would swear because of it, with low laughter and a blasphemous tenderness.

Minute by minute, hour by hour, day by day—to see them flash and fade down the corridors of each week, till Garland come to her again.

Oh, good to live and be young and be loved! And damnable to be feeble and pitiful and incapable of telling oneself how much.

Awakened physically, she had been awakened mentally as well. Conscious of this, she had questioned Garland thereon, and he had stared and talked and explained, gesticulating and interested, till her hair against his chin made him halt and lose thread and grow crimson across his sulky face, and bend to kiss her and kiss her till she was conscious of Darkness itself beyond the abysses. . . . Alone, in soft, shameless impatience of the colourlessness of the labels she had been able to supply her sensations, she would repeat over to herself, word on slow word, descriptively, the happenings that were good. Indecently, calmly, she would specify them. And, in the midst thereof, she would suddenly colour in slow, mantling waves of blood, and her eyes would shine—the eyes of adventure.

Oh, fools that she and John had been to waste the last two years as waste them they had. They'd lived in shams and impatiences and mock angers simply because they had not lived. . . . Silly fools! Both of them. As if there could be anything wrong in being natural. . . .

Autumn. It had come so quickly this year. And, raising her eyes as she walked through Chelsea, she saw a flock of rooks going by into the west. How they'd be hronk-hronking over the white stubble fields in Scotland, with a storm blowing down from the hills!

She stopped at a florist's and brought irises – late irises, lifting blooms blue and grey-rayed above their green sheaths. Holding them in her hand, she walked out into the street. Had Garland seen her then he would have said that she looked like a sacrifice to Autumn.

The charwoman was cleaning the steps of No. 41 Rosemount Avenue. She moved aside her bucket to allow of the ingress of Thea. She was a short, stout woman with bulging breasts and scanty hair. She looked sourly at Thea's golden legs.

"Lovely afternoon," said Thea.

"Uh," said the charwoman.

Making tea inside the flat, Thea Mayven stopped to laugh. And she thought:

"Had John heard that he'd have had something funny and philosophical to say about it. . . . The Romantic and the Realist. . . . Pfuu. Poor thing. Perhaps she was once young and mad and had a lover."

She put down the cup from which she had been drinking, and yawned, stretching arms and legs, and finally all her body, in a taut extasy, so that the muscles cracked. Doing this, she was conscious, very vividly, of the beauty of her poise and of her body. No such consciousness had ever been hers before that happening in Leekan cove. She had accepted her body as she had accepted bacon for breakfast and shoes for footwear. That she possessed a temple of delight had never occurred to her till a worshipper had come to the altar of that temple.

Standing so, she thought of physical love and lust and the lies she had read of it. Its cruelty and its shame. Nothing had she ever seen recorded of its beauty, its tenderness—the queer, queer tenderness it evoked. Like the feeling that came to you holding soft pansies. . . .

Oh! Tired. A sleepy, lazy afternoon.

God!

Her body had just eased from stretching when it happened. Into her mouth came a strange gush of tainted saliva, acid and

103

bitter. At the same moment she was aware of a drumming in her ears and a contraction of her stomach.

A violent fit of sickness came on her and passed. She came out of the bathroom, and, standing in front of a mirror, looked at her face. It was repulsively pallid. As she looked, her eyes grew startled. A little froth spumed at the corners of her lips.

Suddenly she had remembered. For a full minute thereafter she stood still, staring. It was the pain of her bitten fingers which finally made her move.

She wrenched her diary out of her handbag and opened it with clumsy, shaking fingers. Doing so, she noted, with a vividness of utter detachment, how, under the tips of her nails, innumerable little white specks showed. Her mouth felt dry and crusted. She found the page she looked for, counted the dates forward, recounted them. . . .

Oh, God, God, it couldn't be *that*.

The second no go; Thursday the limit.

Then, with a concentration of interest, she noted how black the room was growing. Further, something else in it oppressed her.

It was filled with a low, horrible moan.

Subchapter iii

"A gentleman has called from the Anarchist Party, madam."

"Who?"

"A gentleman from the Anarchist Party, madam."

Mrs. Gayford, sitting writing letters in her library, looked up at the butler in amazement. Elected President of the White Arts Club, she had been unable to leave town, her time being fully occupied in organizing an exhibition for the Club's members. Her skin, being thick, dripped sweat in the warmth of the afternoon, and her hands, resembling carefully kept bunches of sausages, left brown stains upon the scented notepaper which she used. The butler regarded the crown of her head with eyes which resembled those of a dead fish. This, however, being his conventional aspect, had not stirred Mrs. Gayford's surprise.

It was the announcement of a visitor from the Anarcho-communist Party.

She had grown tired of Communism, had neither attended

meetings nor subscribed to funds for several months, had sent in a letter of resignation. To this, however, she had received no reply, and the fact had left her in a state of uneasy irritation. She had visioned a dramatic expulsion. Nevertheless, filled with enthusiasm for the White Artists, a new group which held that all drawing and colour were false art, she toiled daily and headachily in their interest. Far in the dim years, in the histories of the Arts, they would tell of the patroness of the White Artists, the woman who guarded the birth of Artistic Vision.

Convinced of these things, and regarding the butler the while, her expression changed from surprise and registered calm hauteur. The butler, imagining that she was about to have convulsions, modified his gaze till it was partially human. He was quickly undeceived.

"Show the man in, please."

She would deal with him quickly and contemptuously.

Andreas van Koupa limped into the room, stopped, looked at Mrs. Gayford, and then crossed the room, keeping his eyes upon her. These eyes, she observed, were insanely black. In a moment she found her hand in his. His fingers were cool and thin.

"Comrade, you have a beautiful home and beautiful eyes."

Saying this, the intentness left Koupa's gaze and was replaced by a simple admiration. Behind this change, in the reaches of his brain, he registered that he was adopting correct tactics. And a certain wonder held him. For, being startled at his words, the eyes set in the blotchy face had taken to themselves a certain warm beauty. Her fingers returned the pressure of his. She laughed uncertainly.

"The Party does not often send me flatterers. It more usually sends beggars."

And Koupa said:

"You so-abominable malnourished hog! To think that the fortunes of the Revolution should hang on the goodwill of the such-unbrained. . . . This ancient sow is out of mood with the Party; perhaps she thinks of leaving it, having taken to herself some new fad, some porous plaster with which to hold her unpleasant body in one and give the physical jerks to her bleached soul. . . . So, I must find what this is."

These words he did not speak aloud. Instead, glancing rapidly over the table at which Mrs. Gayford had been working, his eyes lit on a featureless drawing. It was upon cartridge paper, a tracery of white upon whiteness, mystic, unnameable. Interested in all Art developments, even in those which he considered as the tumours and cancers of Art, the poet had heard of the White Artists. Instantly comprehension came to him. It was in this bloodless botching of good paper which might have been used in lavatories or to wrap cartridges that this good Gayford found the Revolution-excluding interest. His gaze grew fixed. He stared.

"What is it?" asked Mrs. Gayford, sharply.

Koupa slowly turned towards her. He spoke with a certain stern intentness which quietened her as though he had laid on her shoulder his habitually chill fingers.

"Forgive me. You say the little Party so-seldom sends you flatterers. I flatter do not. But I love beauty. I come in this room, I see your eyes, I look upon the so-goodness of Nature's creation, then I see—that."

He pointed to the cartridge paper whereon faint outlines were observable. His eyes challenged hers.

"It is the work of the incomparable Briarton? I have not the right to look on it, perhaps? Comrade, I have no right to look in your eyes. I hold that all things of beauty are mine to share."

"You know Briarton's work?"

Mrs. Gayford, seated, looked up at the poet with mounting interest. For this drawing of Briarton's had perplexed and worried her. A reproduction of it was to appear in the third issue of the *White Artist Quarterly*, and Mrs. Gayford had been asked to write an appreciation of it in the same issue. For all articles in the Quarterly of the White Artists were appreciations. No writer ever found aught to criticize. All drawings, being colourless, were praised with thick smearings of colourful adjectives and thin daubings of uncompromising substantives. But, equipped though she was with an excellent dictionary of synonyms, Mrs. Gayford had found it impossible to write the article on Briarton's work. Owing to some inartistic coarseness of mind, she was unable to wield adjectives without a ratio of at least one to the dozen in substantives.

She had regarded Briarton's drawing from all angles of vision and under all possible lights in order to gain some insight into its meaning. Its title, "Nocturne", had merely deepened her perplexity. She had wavered between describing it as a "Night Attack on the Barricades" or "Moonlight on the Sahara". Koupa's words inspired her with sudden hope. Her slow face-muscles shook to a tremor of interest in his appearance. His eyes, still red from their sleep over the deficits of the Anarchocommunist Party, seemed to her to have vision and power within them. Koupa shook himself, as if coming out of a reverential reverie.

"Know Briarton's work? Even as you yourself do. We, the non-artists, sometimes we, is it not, have the vision? Briarton is but the instrument of beauty; you, or even I, we have a greater gift—appreciation, the understanding, is it not?" Saying this, Koupa rapidly and silently debated the meaning of the drawing. What was the so-infernal thing? Did it have a title? How would it help him to impress this so-rich cow?

Mrs. Gayford sighed, sweatily. "Ah, yes, that is very true. We can appreciate, but to describe in words—I have the pleasant but difficult task to review Briarton for the *White Artist Quarterly*, and it is—difficult."

Koupa chuckled inwardly. His line of action was suddenly clear to him. Pulling up a chair unbidden, he sat down.

"You also, then, are hampered by the inadequacy of words in describing the super-achievements of Art? Then let us collaborate. It comes to me—a palinode or distych. I shall write, we shall both compose. . . . Here is paper. Your pardon?"

"That bell-push beside you. Will you ring? For tea."

Ten minutes later, when the butler brought in tea, he found his mistress, her fingers staining the sheet of paper she held, sitting reading aloud the description of Briarton's "Nocturne". Koupa, seated now on the table, leant on an elbow and looked at his collaborator with shining eyes.

NOCTURNE

Crash on the heaving slopes of weeping Night
The lilies droop.
Let dawn be damned; night's here in shivering
Low
Blow

Wind of the wakeful woods.
A farthing? I see girls droop with powdered hair,
And writhen lips, and old men cry in dreams.
Hush!
A beggar selling brooches in the mist!

Subchapter iv

Not for another seven months or so, anyhow. Let's see. In
March. Perhaps. Couldn't be sure. How the hell to know *when*
it'll happen? No way of telling. Might have been any time
within the last two months . . . even the first time, out in
the bay at home. (God! Of all times I hope it was then it
happened. . . .)

Oh, God, God, God, but it's awful. John. My dear, my dear,
I'm scared. . . . What the hell will it matter to you, anyway?
You will be all right—can go on writing and sneering and using
me as you like. Oh, beasts we've been, beastly fools.

Be quiet. Pull yourself together. Fool. Can't go on like this—
hours of it. Dark. Must be late. Good job Ellen's away for the
week-end. And Norah can't be in yet. Pfuu! Pillow's sopping
wet. You fool. Don't think, don't think. Not any more tonight.
Read or something. John'll be here tomorrow.

Have to give up the office soon. Get a house somewhere.
Cost a lot of money. John must have some before he let all this
happen. Beast. Be able to live together. Have to furnish a
house, get all kinds of things, baby clothes . . . What a damn,
damn fool, after reading Marie Stopes and knowing all about
it. Sickening. And it'll hurt more later.

Uhh. Stiff. Have to change that pillowslip. Powder. Damn
dark. Oh, *blast* the thing. Not worth a light here. Dizzy. Headache—of course, you fool. . . .

She opened the bedroom door upon a gulfing tide of greyness
from the corridor. Her feet hurt inside her high-heeled shoes,
for she had neglected to remove those, and they creaked in the
corridor. Suddenly, spite their sound, she was conscious of a
deeper silence than that which had held the flat a moment
before.

She stood still. It was true.

Someone else in the flat?

At the thought she instantly saw a movement in the greyness

in front of her. With a cry she opened the nearest door, slipped inside, closed it behind her, switched on the light.

"Oh—"

She had entered Norah's bedroom. And from the bed, on her sudden entrance, Norah, red-eyed, had suddenly arisen. They stared at each other.

"Thea ... Scared me stiff. What is it? What's wrong?"

"I don't know. Thought I saw someone out there in the corridor."

"Lock the door, then. Quick."

They locked it and stood listening. Not a sound. For a full minute they remained rigid. Then Thea gave a short laugh, swore, lit a match from a box beside Norah's bed, and went out into the corridor. Then she searched the entire flat, flinging open doors with facetious queries and banging them behind her. Not a soul. She came back to Norah's room.

"Must have been a ghost, for he's vanished. What's wrong, Norry?"

Norah's face was ghastly and her underlip quivering. Thea stared at her, then put her arm round her.

"What's *wrong*?"

"Oh, everything.... Didn't know you were in. Where've you been?"

"Bedroom. Snoozing, I suppose. I just woke up a minute or two ago."

"I wish I could go to sleep and never wake up ... Thea, I've made a divvle of a mess of things. Oh, miggod, don't stand there. Come and sit down. You know I've told you about Billy?"

"Often. The bank clerk, isn't he? You used to meet him before Mr. Storman——"

Norah laughed, thinly. "And since."

"Yes?"

The other looked away. Her fingers were clenching and unclenching in the coverlet. Thea, sitting on the bed and leaning her elbow on the pillow, was suddenly conscious of a clamminess on her skin.

The pillow was damp.

"Thea, you can keep a secret? Swear you won't tell it to anyone else. . . . I must tell someone, or I'll go mad, I know I will.

I've been going with Billy while Storman's been away in Russia. And I'm going to have a baby."

"*What?*"

"Oh, it's horrible. It's true. I bought a ring and went to a doctor and was examined. And when I told Billy about it tonight he stared and laughed and then sidled away. . . . Oh, what a divvle of a mess!"

Suddenly Thea knew that she herself would burst into tears in a minute, or else laugh and laugh and laugh because of the funniness of that word divvle—laugh till she was hysterical and then mad. She heard herself ask a question.

"The baby—when will it be born?"

"Sometime in March, the doctor said."

Subchapter v

It was a night of stars. Mellowed by the half-bottle of Benedictine which he had drunk, to the stupefaction of Mrs. Gayford and her butler, Andreas van Koupa walked the Chelsea Embankment under the plane-trees. His cigar, red-tipped in the soft midnight, comforted his throat. Within his stomach the good Benedictine held drugged the malevolent gastric juices which an indiscreet dinner might have induced. Folded in his shabby pocketbook, next to his skin and held from slipping down by his waistband, was a cheque for £50.

He began to count the stars and stopped when he had reached fifty. Aldebaran held his attention a long, twinkling moment. He leant his arms on the wall, where Storman and Thea Mayven had leant theirs, watching Aldebaran and thinking of the saying of Anatole France that if one believed the stars inhabited it turned the sky into a horrifying shambles. Untrue. On such a night as this comfort and cheer signalled from life's innumerable outposts.

His thoughts diverged into speculation upon the inhabitability of the solar planets. Stroking his unshaven chin, he called to mind all that he had ever read of Mars, Venus and the Earth's moon. It was, indeed, impossible to believe them uninhabited. The canal theory of Mars had been built on the most exact data. Venus, with its dense atmosphere, would support vegetation, and therefore animal life. . . .

A dense and horrifying jungle of monstrous, insane plants upwreathed itself in his vision below a pair of hastening moons. Great seas roared with the rumble of hurrying tides on nightmare beaches; through the insane foliage green, macabre ghouls leapt and snarled and tore . . ..

"God mine, it is the Benedictine," said Koupa.

Whether these things were or no, everywhere life swung in rhythm of purpose. Beyond the jungles and the ghouls, secretly or openly, the Life-Force in every planet wrought and selected and toiled with its instrument reason and its goal immortality. Triumphant over itself, matter in motion conquered matter in stagnation, matter whorling in steady rhythm became matter in purpose and conquered matter in mere instinctive motion, matter in purpose intricated its whorlings till it was matter in reason.

The scientific Pentateuch. Reason, God, everywhere—in life, in death, in birth.

Looking up at the stars he thought upon birth with a sudden great wonder. Rightly had the Christians held it the holy mystery. The mothers of life—from the rat and the weasel to the girl with blossoming breasts—were partners fair and holy in the purpose of God; men but onlookers.

And a great tenderness and desolation came upon Koupa at this thought. Proudly must women walk, bearing to seed and fruit the miracles of their bodies. No man might share with them that pride, no man partake of the sacred mystery.

Goddess-cults—how understandable, logical, they had been. The coarse and fleshly cults most of all. Every woman with child was a goddess, an Ashtaroth, fit for reverence and obscene worship.

Mellowly, under the stars, he sat himself down on a bench. Overhead the plane-trees rustled. Sleep drew his eyelids down upon his cheeks, released them so that he might peer up through the leaves above him, then closed them again upon a thought that was a vivid prayer.

"God mine, a night of stars!"

Subchapter vi

John Garland stepped out into the colourful autumnal warmth

111

of London. Clad in the shoddy blue of the aircraftman, a blot against the sunlight, he emerged from Victoria Station into the arms of Thea Mayven. She stood awaiting him by the bus-stop. She was tall, clad in white and blue. Her face had the misty freshness of a flower. He noted with a strange little quiver the lobeless tips of her ears.

She put her arms around his neck, standing on the crowded pavement, and kissed his sulky face. And Garland thought:

"Great God, this woman and miracle is mine. Mine."

So thinking, he asked how she was, and looked at her with questioning, ironic eyes. For the ironist within him had been more watchful than ever since the happenings in Leekan Cove, defending the new Garland who quivered as a lutestring at the thought and sight of Thea.

"All right. Do you love me?"

" 'Thy lips are like a thread of scarlet'—I believe you've been eating cherries."

"I have." Thea sighed. "I'm too fond of them. But I'll be hungry again soon. Let's go to Putney Heath."

They boarded a bus, climbed to the top and found themselves riding alone through the heat-warmed smells of London. Thea leant her arm against the rail. The brimful of shadow cast by her hat lay upon her face in a semi-circle tipping her nose. Below that semi-circle her face was soft and relaxed; above, her face was rigid. Now and then she closed her eyes, and then opened them again quickly as if to surprise herself in the midst of thoughts and in the midst of a journey which was part of a dream.

But Garland noted none of those things. Upon his knee he had opened a copy of "Les Dieux ont soif", and gazed at it with an ironic sadness. Long the journey before he could write such stuff as this—the stuff that life is made of. Ironic life, at least. Thinking of the "First Novel of an Ironist" he felt a quiver of disgust.

Then he noted that his knee was touching Thea's. It had touched her naked knee before this. Think. The naked knee of Thea Mayven. A white knee, a dimpled knee. . . . Who would think it? Who believe that I had done this?

Riding up through London with the sun in his face a drowsiness came on him. He closed the book the better to think of the white knees of Thea. Once, absently, she laid her hand on his. Below them they felt the bus strain as it crossed the River and breasted the Hill.

"It'll be warm soon," said Thea, raising her head.

Grunting, the bus climbed the Putney reaches, past the Pines, where Swinburne was refused brandy. Garland, hobnailed boots pressed against an advertisement, abandoned for something bleak and disturbing the thoughts of Thea's knees.

But he would not tell her yet.

The bus stopped. They got off and walked across autumn grass, grown sere. A man was selling newspapers and ice-cream. Garland bought the *News of the World* in order that he might read of the murders. For no doubt there had been murders. Overhead were swallows. Garland lit a pipe and unfolded the *News of the World*. Thea walked humming.

Tell him. But not yet. Later.

Besides, the vivid horror of the business had vanished here in the sunlight. A baby. A son. Someone funny and quaint and sulky. . . . Be born with hobnailed boots or else clutching a copy of Anatole France. . . . John'll be with me; we'll be together when it happens. Wonder if I'll scream and scream? Like hell, no doubt. John's novel'll be published by then. He'll be writing others. He'll be able to get out of the filthy Air Force. Oh, we'll begin to live, we two . . . and—a baby.

Smiling they walked, and the world was young. And because it was young, its hurtfulness pained them with a sick intensity in the midst of their gladness. Shadows would come and pass upon their faces as they tried to remember the morning about them. Looking at Thea, Garland would lock his lips. Not yet. Not yet. And his throat would contract queerly.

They stopped at a stall where coloured water drinks were sold. Garland purchased two bottles and they sat down on the grass and drank from heavy, unbreakable tumblers. Then Thea bought cigarettes and they walked on, into cool jungles of heath and bracken and dwarfen trees. Below them London lay shining bluely.

"The City of the Sun," said Garland.

But Thea was still humming her song and did not hear. She had begun to feel tired. Her head ached a little because of the dancing heat-waves.

"Thank God for cool grass."

She sat down on it in the shadow of a bush, took off her hat and looked up at Garland. Their eyes met. Into Garland's came the warmth of desire. Pleasurably he looked down at her, noting the faint drops of perspiration on her brow. And a strange tremor, piercing in its sweetness, shot through him. For from where he stood he could look down and see the white hollow between her breasts.

He had kissed her there. Many times. He sat down, smiling at her, dreaming. But Thea lay flat on the grass, her eyes upon the faint wisps of clouds. He touched her throat with a gentle finger.

"Oh, let me alone, John."

Almost hysterical. Surprised, Garland withdrew the finger, opened "Les Dieux ont soif", lit a cigarette and began to read. But first he glanced at the swallows and at Thea, very still. An atmosphere to read in. In a little he had forgotten swallows, Thea, and all the world, forgotten technique and hints and style, the while he read of the priest and the atheist going to the guillotine. Oh, by God, by God, the Master!

Then a strange, black something struggled out of the story. He lost trace of its telling. He must tell her. He dropped the book, turned to Thea, found her lying as when he had last looked.

"Thea, I've got news—infernal news. I've been trying to keep it back, but you might as well know now. I've been posted overseas—to Egypt, I think. The boat sails three weeks from tomorrow."

CHAPTER THE SEVENTH

Wherein Full and Faithful Accounts, without Asterisks, are given of a Bridal Night and a By-Election, and, though We weep, the Skies are not Wet.

Subchapter i

JOHN GARLAND and Theodora Mayven were married at the Chelsea Registry Office on a Monday forenoon when a squally wind blew in the streets and the plane-trees along the Embankment wept dustily. For it was now Autumn, and to Thea, with child, and with grey-green eyes grown larger, the long, wet day passed in a drowsy mist of dreams.

They sat in a restaurant and ate a large and expensive lunch and looked at each other with a new curiosity. And the fact that Thea wore a wedding-ring was a strange and delightful jest. Then they went to a theatre matinée, to a play about a secret gang and foreign princesses and the machinations of the Communists. Holding Thea's hand, Garland gave himself up to the play, was thrilled, was indignant, cheered with the rest of the audience. For Thea was finally his and her hand was amazingly soft and warm.

Oh, God, and that look in her eyes . . . Love her, be good to her.

And, with a wistful humour, he thought upon her funniness of gesture and utterance, and that habit she had of saying, as one word: "Notatall!" Turning her head and looking at him the while he thought this, she smiled at him secretly, consideringly.

"Husband."

"My wife."

And the last word seemed somehow pitiful. But he would not think on that. Not to-day. This is ours, ours, mine and

Thea's. We shall not see its like again. And the little secret place between her breasts—I shall kiss it to-night.

They came out into the soft fall of the rain and stood, Thea's hand on Garland's arm, at Charing Cross, and watched all London go by. Indifferently by. And, at that sensed indifference, they held each other with a half-desperate tenderness. But of the unheeding menace they did not speak. Instead, they laughed, pointing out a man with a peculiar nose and the funniness of Nelson in the downpour, and a girl who passed, squelching, soggily, in Russian boots.

And, holding each other, they laughed.

And they went to a café for tea—to a dim, green room where smoke-clouds curled up scentedly. A dim, quiet place. The waitress smiled at them and at Thea's new ring, and Garland ate four scones and three large and squelchy cakes which he harpooned and then dissected on the edge of his fork. Thea had bought an evening paper. She propped it up against the water-jug and read it composedly. But ever and anon, catching Garland's eye over the top of a page, she would make a little grimace at him.

Married. Unbelievable. Married.

At eight o'clock they came out of a kinema where they had watched Miss Lilian Gish being made love to by an English baronet called Sir Devonshire. The rain had cleared away. The lit streets shone cold and alien. Thea held Garland's sleeve.

"John, d'you know you're my husband?"

"Suspected it."

"Be good to me, won't you?" And, saying this trite thing mockingly, she looked up at him so that he could have wept. For he saw himself as one in a drama of two, a drama acted everywhere in all ages, a drama weaving its plot to the end of marriage and consummation upon a marriage bed. (How right of the romantics to leave it there!) Endlessly.

And that drama was eternally tragic behind its last curtain. The curtain came down, the author spattered asterisks, the band played, and the lights went out. Then tragedy. The woman gave—herself. She became a loved, inferior, degraded thing. . . . Rightly did the Catholics prize virginity. Believing in the after-existence of the soul they yet, being cautious, heeded to keeping inviolate the impermanent body.

116

Thea. Soon she would not be Thea. She would merely be his wife. Not as a glorious gift would she give herself to him. He had a licence from the State to use her body. She had not even a name of her own, now. She had sold herself.

For what? God, for what? Oh, be good to her, as she's asked, you poor blackguard, for all this is of the rottenness called Life.

"I'm tired and sleepy," said Thea. They were within the room of their hotel. Street noises rumbled without. The fire-light flickered upon the hearth. "And I'm going to bed. So run away. Walk up and down in the smoking-room and throw away cigarettes and be nervous."

"Not I. I shall look out at the stars while you undress."

He went to a window and pulled the curtain a little aside. Then he looked up. There was not a star in the sky.

Something slipped into his hand, something warm and tremulous, like the heart of a captured bird.

Thea's hand. Stark, she stood beside him in the unlighted room.

"Well, am I a bad bargain?"

He put his arms around her, standing so. Her skin was soft, like velvet. Against the body that he held he laid his head, kissing her.

"I shall kiss you all over," he said.

And when he had done that, he sat for long on the edge of the bed, looking down at her. Sleepily she smiled up at him from the pillow. Then her eyelids slowly closed and she was asleep. Like a child she held fast to his hand.

Very gently he loosened her fingers.

Subchapter ii

Ten days after his return from Russia Storman flung himself into an active part in the St. Judas by-election.

The seat had been held for ten years by an Independent, a strong, simple man of the Cobbett stamp, who invariably voted in the Conservative lobbies. Unfortunately, owing to a cutting retort from an Under-Secretary at question time in the Commons, the member for St. Judas had next Sunday made an indiscreet speech in his constituency. The following day he had received a letter from the St. Judas Conservative

Association, apprising him of the fact that it would henceforth be compelled to cease payment of the annual subsidy made to him as an Independent. The member, an old man of expensive tastes and unimpaired virility, was overcome. For payment of his mistress, the matron of the St. Judas Rescue Home, he was entirely dependent on the annual subsidy. He went to his club and spent the evening there, mixing his drinks and brooding. Suddenly, at half-past nine, he was heard crying out in a threatening voice in the deserted smoking-room. On two of the waiters rushing in, they found him lying on the floor, attempting to strangle a portrait of Disraeli which he had dragged from the wall. He was secured and removed to a lunatic asylum.

The by-election which ensued was, as usual, regarded as a test one. All parties worked feverishly. The Conservative candidate, Leon Ropstein, canvassed from door to door in the working-class quarters and was photographed holding babies, stirring puddings, and assisting a pavement artist to lay out his materials. Nightly he addressed large meetings where free cigarettes were to be had at the entrance. Sincere, a zealot, he spoke of the glories of the Empire and the heritage of Anglo-Saxondom, and also of the necessity for strengthening the Aliens' Act, expelling all Reds and untrustworthy foreigners, and refusing to purchase Soviet petrol. From his father, a German Jew who had hawked old china in Frankfort, he had acquired a clear, penetrating voice which instantly won the attention his evident sincerity afterwards kept.

The Liberal candidate was Professor K. McGuire, who held the Greek chair at Rollchester. Stroking his stained beard, he would hold his audiences enraptured by pictures of the future, when the secrets of the atom had been discovered and electricity was available in the humblest home. He told how Mr. Lloyd George had saved Western civilization by taking control during the War and a leading part in the Treaty of Versailles. Planks in his platform were: Peace in Industry, Wider Education, Retrenchment, Economy, Reform, and Revision of the Versailles Treaty. He was supported by Grey Liberals, Lloyd George Liberals, a Labour novelist, the local Congregationalists, and the President of the Free Union of Seamen, which had a membership of eighteen.

The Labour candidate, General Sir John Browne-Lovitt, C.B., C.M.G., D.S.O., seriously alarmed his opponents. Gifted with a handsome face and cultured voice, it was feared that he would capture the women's vote *en bloc*. An ex-Conservative, he told, from platforms and hustings, from his car, from kerb and soapbox and wayside pulpit, how, when returned to Parliament, it was his intention to support a vigorous and uncompromising Socialist policy. Surrounded by a large audience whenever he spoke, he was for several days at the beginning of the campaign greatly enheartened—till a sameness about this audience caught his attention. It was always the same audience.

Thrilled by his words and promises, and the pictures of the Socialist Commonwealth which he painted, the Socialists of the St. Judas Division attended every meeting in scores, so that with difficulty the unconverted obtained seats in the various halls, or, at open-air meetings, succeeded in approaching sufficiently near to catch the drift of the speaker's argument.

On the third day of the campaign the Labour agent received a notification from the secretary of the Local Anarcho-communist Group to the effect that the St. Judas Communists would aid in returning General Sir John Browne-Lovitt to Westminster. The Labour agent instantly wrote back declining such aid, for, a grocer when he was not an agent, he believed that the Communists would confiscate all groceries without compensation. Also, they practised free love, which would complicate grocery bills. Sir John, at his agent's instigation, publicly declined Communist help. He did not wish Communists to vote for him. They should go out into the open and form a party of their own.

Hardly had he finished this speech when his meeting was broken up by a party of young men who played banjos and carried a Union Jack. Two of them wore black shirts. Next day the *Daily Beacon* denounced the Conservatives and their hooligan Fascist allies. Instantly Mr. Ropstein issued a printed circular disassociating himself from acts of violence, but stating that these were a natural result of the unpatriotic sentiments and anti-British policy of the Socialist candidate.

These leaflets, which had been in print a week before the campaign commenced, were scattered broadcast over St.

Judas. That evening the meetings of both Conservative and Labour candidates were packed, though Professor McGuire declaimed on atoms to an almost empty hall. Speedily General Browne-Lovitt, rising to speak, became aware that his audience was of a different order from that which had hitherto gathered. It was composed of the outside public. His usual Socialist supporters, rising to the need of clerical work in connection with the campaign, had stayed at home, addressing envelopes. Heartened, for, though naturally timid, he was relieved at the thought of conveying the Socialist creed to the unconverted, General Browne-Lovitt began to speak. At the end of ten minutes booing and persistent heckling caused him to stop. Then he was spectator of a welcome sight. From all over the hall strong young men uprose, seized the hecklers by the scruff of the neck, and flung them out into the street.

"B'Ged, I never thought they had it in them," said the Labour candidate. "Good lads, they'll keep things in order."

But at that moment, as he sat amazed at the virility displayed by those nurtured on the theories of Lord Passfield and Mrs. Sidney Webb, his agent leant across and whispered to him. "These young men are Communists. They've ruined the meeting."

The meeting went on. Turning from attacking the Empire Crusade, the General spoke of the weak and cowardly subterfuges by which the Communists sought to destroy the Labour Movement. Not at Reform, not even at Socialism in Our Time, did these Communists aim, but at bloody Revolution. Saying these things, the General, observing the demeanour of the young men who had evicted the hecklers, became sure that his agent was wrong. For the young men displayed no indignation. Two of them slept. They did not wear beards nor carry cameos of Karl Marx.

For, like many recent converts to the Labour cause, the General's ideas of Communists were gathered from news-sheets which in other circumstances he denounced as reactionary.

In the body of the hall Storman, in command of the detachment detailed by the Anarchocommunist Party to keep order at General Browne-Lovitt's meetings, listened to the speech in cold silence. A flicker of his old amusement came on him as the General caught his eye and nodded, friendlywise. For he and the General were old acquaintances. They had both received the surrender of Jerusalem. Storman's battery had dropped the screen of projectiles behind which the shattered British battalions retired after the second attempt on Gaza; for this, on General Browne-Lovitt's recommendation, he had received the Military Cross. Storman had accompanied the General on a night reconnaissance amidst the heaps of bloody rags and carbonized flesh which represented those unenterprising enough to profit by the projectile screen. The General, tripping amidst spewn entrails, had sworn and been sick. . . .

But Storman's amusement waned quickly. Instead, he was shaken with a sudden spasm of disgust. What hope was there for any party which returned these militaristic windbags to Parliament? What hope, for that matter, was there in all the weary business?

Yet it was the policy of the Anarchocommunist Party to help in the returning of Browne-Lovitt to Westminster—a policy for which Storman himself had always hitherto stood. It was policy to help in securing a Labour Government. With such government the Communists could carry on a widespread propaganda of anti-state agitation impossible under the overseership of a Tory Home Secretary.

So Storman had always hitherto held, but his visit to Russia had stirred in him anew his old passion for accurate blue-printing of a project. Further, that visit had aroused within him a destructive sense of humour. Now he sat sardonic over the planlessness of his own plans.

Meanwhile, two miles away, in the Memorial Hall of St. Judas, Andreas van Koupa, in charge of another Anarchocommunist detachment, had succeeded in reducing Mr. Ropstein's meeting to chaos. Shocked and amazed, the Conservatives on the platform listened to a derisive chant arise at regular intervals from amidst the audience and drown the candidate's speech. Anti-aliens, the Conservatives' most extreme policies were generally expounded by naturalized aliens. Other parties, brought up under the idea of pro-Britishism and Conservatism as synonymous, accepted such attacks and attackers without demur or questioning, the while they weakly defended their own alien candidates. By an infamous disregard of etiquette, Koupa had succeeded in

121

breaking up Mr. Ropstein's meeting. Regularly, at his signal, his supporters' voices would rise:

> "We don't want an Alien,
> We don't want a Jew,
> We don't want a Sheeny,
> And we don't want you!"

The meeting ultimately broke up amidst catcalls, whistling, and disorder. Next morning all the Conservative papers had leaders on the vicious anti-Semitism of the Labour Party in St. Judas, and leaderettes on the ruining of Russia by the gang of Jews which controlled the Soviet. But the *Daily Beacon* appeared with a Leader on the Equality of Races and a leaderette on Vote for St. Judas's Only English Candidate.

Polling day arrived. It passed in sleet. Next evening, at dusk, the results were announced. They read:

K. McGuire . . . 10,080
L. Ropstein . . . 6,540
J. Browne-Lovitt . . 6,450

Subchapter iii

Garland had a fortnight's leave before he sailed from Southampton. In that fortnight he and Thea had to find rooms where she might live and eat and sleep and bear her child.

Of the horror of Thea's position they did not talk. Garland had no money. He had never saved a penny-piece in his life. When he had told Thea this on Putney Heath, after their mutual revelations, she had stared at him like one gone mad— stared with drooping jaw and rounded, incredulous eyes. Then she had burst into high, thin laughter. What was to happen to her when he had gone to Egypt, when her condition made it impossible for her to work, thereafter lay like a red shadow across the brain of Garland. She would receive from the Air Force a pittance of marriage allowance insufficient to pay even for the rent of their rooms—those rooms that were still unfound. Even with all of his own pay that he would be able to send her, she would still be incapable of living anywhere but in the slums or on offal.

Once a helpful thought gave Garland rest for one night.

Thea could go back to her home in Scotland when the time came for the baby to be born.

Next morning he proposed this to her. They had newly got out of bed. Thea had bathed and was combing her hair. She said: "I would rather die. Perhaps I shall? What does it matter?" Then laughed.

It was the unacted, dead indifference of her tones that silenced Garland. Whether she might live or die when *that* happened she hardly seemed to care.

But sometimes, even in those first days, Garland would step out of the wearying, heart-breaking, foot-aching procession, and stand aside, as of yore. Smoking, seated comfortably, he would muse in the fashion which had become habitual to him. Strange that the bearing of life should be either a shameful or a pridesome thing. So thinking, he would again envisage humanity in terms of an insect-burrow. One insect—himself—fertilized a female insect—Thea—without apprising the other insects beforehand that he intended to fertilize. Fertilized, the female insect, overcome at the non-notification of the other insects, was shamed, and the male insect hated the whole burrow. . . .

But God, man, God, it's Thea—*Thea!* You swine.

And he would go in search of her and would kiss her suddenly, adoringly. He found a strange, wholehearted pleasure in devising new methods of kissing her.

Meantime, they searched for rooms. Flats were at impossible prices. So they searched for a bedroom and a sitting-room, furnished, with use of gas-cooker and bathroom.

At the flat Norah and Ellen were under the impression that Thea was honeymooning in Devon. Twice the newly married couple had to hide from Ellen, and once from Norah and Storman. Swearing lightly, but with her lips quivering, Thea would drag Garland into shelter.

So they searched London for rooms. North and south and east, on the trail of advertised rooms to let, they searched. Landladies would receive them in apartments decorated with the photographs of sons and cousins who had served in the War. But hearing that Garland was in the Air Force, they would shake their heads. They were respectable, and could not take in a soldier's wife, because the other tenants would not like it. Then Garland and Thea would board a bus for another place, where the rent would be twenty-five shillings a week and the walls stained with damp-mould, and they would be asked what Church they belonged to. Or, talking with some woman with rooms to let, a woman with breasts bloated by child-bearing and impressed to the extent of contemplated reductions by Thea's charm and Garland's frankness, they would become aware of a hiatus in the conversation. The woman, seated, would be regarding Thea sideways with wrinkled eyes and contemptuous mouth. "We're respectable people here," she would say, and rise up, and show them out. Unobservable though they might imagine Thea's condition, by that link of common motherhood it could not be hidden.

And their money was running short. One morning, in the middle of the second week, when Garland awoke he found Thea's place beside him empty and cold. Arising and dressing, a ghastly certainty held him. She had gone to the River. He saw her white, still face rising and falling on the ebb of the waters. . . .

He went downstairs and out into a forenoon of sunlight. On the steps he met Thea, her face paler than usual, but her eyes bright.

"Lord. Where've you been?"

"Replenishing the exchequer. Look."

She showed him a package of notes, and, at the dead, still sickness of his face, laughed with that never-far-absent touch of hysteria in her voice.

"Oh, I haven't come to that, yet. I took my slave bangles and wrist-watch to a jeweller's and sold them. Come and have breakfast, dear. My dear."

So they breakfasted, and, having eaten eggs and bacon and toast, loved each other. The black thoughts went from Garland's mind. He talked to Thea of the short time he would spend abroad, for he had only three more years to serve in the Air Force. Also, before he returned he'd have completed his novel, sent it to England, and had it published. Sure to find a publisher of some sort. One far gone in senile decay, for preference. Perhaps bring in fifty pounds. Or more. Good stuff in it.

He grew silent, remembering the novel, neglected during the past fortnight. A craving to rout it out and re-read it assailed him, for the MS. was at the hotel. But there were still the rooms to find.

Late that afternoon, they came to the last address on their list. It was a house in a road in Shepherd's Bush. It was a short road. A fried fish shop was No. I. On either side of the road were small, wizened plane-trees. There was little traffic. Children played and rolled podgily on the sidewalks. Dogs, released for the afternoon, sniffed and barked amidst their droppings in the dust. The houses, built in 1890, were small, semi-detached, with bower windows and narrow passages betwixt each block of two. One window held a placard advertising the Salvation Army, showing a stout man fighting a dyspeptic snake; another stated that light refreshments were to be obtained inside. Nearly all of those houses were occupied by a peculiar class of small tradesmen. They had been the failures or the rebels of their respective workshops or offices; yet cautious in rebellion or failure. For each, retiring from the jostle of mass production, had saved sufficient wherewith to establish a small business in a back room. These fugitive businesses they advertised with hand-painted placards or unshined brass plates. A vague smell compounded of many trades hung in the street. It was called Geranium Road.

"No. 24's the one we're looking for," said Thea, with weariness.

They rang and a woman came to the door. She was small, with mouse-coloured hair and a neck which showed traces of ringworm. Behind her spectacles showed a squint left eye and a doubtful smile. Talking to Thea, who always opened conversation at such moments, she eyed the fish shop and Garland's waistcoat. She bade them enter.

Entering, Garland almost broke his neck. The staircase came abruptly and at once down to the front door. To the right of the staircase was another door which the woman opened.

"This is one of the rooms, but I'm sure I don't know if I can let it. Not now. It's so long since I gave that address that you got from the agent. I'll have to speak to Daddy first."

"Who?" said Garland.

She smiled at him doubtfully. "My husband. I call him Daddy."

"Is he in?"

"No. He'll be back at seven o'clock."

Thea turned away. "We can come back at that time, then."

Out of her normal eye the woman considered her kindlywise, doubtfully. "Perhaps you'd like a cup of tea?"

"Love it," said Thea, "but don't trouble."

Smiling doubtfully, the woman went out and left them. They sat down. The room was furnished in red. It had two armchairs. Sinking back in one, Thea closed her eyes.

"I'm so tired. I wish we could get this place. It looks—livable. . . . But I suppose it's too dear."

Garland looked round the room. It seemed to him to resemble the antechamber of hell in its redness. A bookcase caught his attention. He got up and walked over to it. It contained a copy of Whitaker's Almanack for 1924, works by someone called A.L.O.E., two of G. A. Henty, and other such, of a past generation, bound in blue and with gilded edgings. Jammed betwixt "A Basket of Flowers" and "Under Two Flags" was a copy of "The Red Lily".

"Thea. There's a France here."

"Is there?" She remained with her eyes closed. "I hate him."

The door opened and the woman came in with a tray. Behind her followed a small boy of about eight years of age. He had a large head and sandy hair. His mouth dropped. With round blue eyes he looked at Thea. The latter held out her arms.

"And what's the little boy's name, then?"

"Now speak to the lady, Simon. Tell her your name."

Standing in front of the lady, Simon said nothing. Instead, his hand wandered to Garland's felt hat, left lying on a chair. He picked it up and put it on his head. He gurgled with his drooping mouth. "Funny," he said.

Thea, enchanted, laughed. The woman smiled doubtfully. Handing cups of tea, she stood sipping one and eating a biscuit. The boy, attracted to Thea, climbed on her knee, planting a dusty shoe on her lap. His mother, one eye on Garland at the bookcase, the other on her son, reproved the latter doubtfully.

"Now, Simon, you mustn't be cheeky."

But Simon took no notice. Still grasping Garland's hat, he proceeded to punch out the dent in it, till it stood up, big and circular, domelike. Repeating "Funny," the boy, seated on

Thea's lap, put his foot in it.

And Garland thought:

"By God, if ever I've children like that I'll birch the hides off their backs."

The woman and Thea talked of the autumn sales, window-curtains, and the cleaning of brass. Garland the woman referred to as "your Daddy".

"Now, Simon, you'll have to give the gentleman back his hat. There, there, now, the gentleman will be back again and will give you his hat to play with." The hat was restored. Simon wailed. Thea and Garland were conducted to the front door. A doubtful smile ushered them out. "Yes, if you'll come back about half-past seven."

They walked down Geranium Road. It was six o'clock. "Seems passable," said Garland.

"Mrs. Stickelly? She's a dear and it's a splendid room. Did you hear her say that if her husband allows she'll let the bedroom and sitting-room for fourteen shillings a week, with use of the scullery?"

"No, I was looking in the bookcase. That's the best we've been offered. Will we—tell her?"

Thea shivered. "No. I couldn't. And she won't take anyone who's going to have a baby. No one will. I know. Later, when she discovers it, perhaps she won't throw me out. . . . Oh, I'm tired."

At half-past seven they returned to the red-furnished room. Smiling doubtfully, one eye on the staircase and the other on the street as she admitted them, Mrs. Stickelly went for her husband and presently returned with him. He was tall, nearly six feet high, burly, and with a face curiously reminiscent of a bloodhound's. His complexion was mottled, for he suffered from constipation. He had a reserved, surlily secretive expression, as if he walked in constant dread that the numerous laxatives which he took might suddenly effect some internal and disastrous revolution.

"Now, Mr. Garland, what's your job?"

"I'm in the Air Force. I'm going to Egypt in three days' time."

"Oh, yes. And your good lady? Tired with the heat, missus?"

Thea smiled at him. "I am a bit, Mr. Stickelly."

"Oh. Yes."

Thea and Garland sat on the edges of their chairs. Mrs. Stickelly smiled doubtfully. Mr. Stickelly, seated, cogitated with an air of uncertainty. To Garland the silence grew strangling. He could feel his face begin to redden. Who was this fat swine to sit in judgement upon them? Why didn't he speak?

"I was looking at your books this afternoon, Mr. Stickelly."

"Oh. Yes. Do you read a lot, Mr. Garland?"

"Bookworm, I'm afraid. My wife reads a fair amount as well."

"Oh. Yes. Well, she'll have full use of my books when she comes here. Any book you want, missus."

But Thea did not reply. They looked at her curiously. She had fainted.

Subchapter iv

"Let's go out to the country," said Norah Casement to James Storman on the Sunday morning thirteen days after the marriage of Thea and Garland.

Storman was astonishingly free that afternoon. He had no meetings to attend, no proofs to correct, no rich patrons of Anarchocommunism to visit. Neither had these duties been taken over by anyone else—least of all by Koupa, whose help would once so readily have been offered. During the past week Koupa had disappeared.

But Storman was not thinking of Koupa. His eyes had lost their old unhumorously humorous glow, but, looking at Norah, he knew a stir of pleasure. Methodically he examined it, probing its causes. He desired her body. That she had anything else to offer was unlikely. Nor did he desire anything else.

For the love that is neither lust nor friendship nor kindliness he had never heard of. Within himself it had no seed. Self-contained, self-planned, self-knowing, he desired that certain of his appetites should be satisfied. Norah would do this.

"We'll walk to Baker Street and take an electric train to Harrow," he said.

Catching the looks he cast on her, Norah smiled and once blushed deeply and redly and vividly. And a prayer that was a blasphemy arose in her heart, the while Storman talked of Russia and autumn and unemployment.

They got out at Harrow-on-the-Hill and Storman led the way up the Hill. A tall church stood there amidst trees and clumps of aged school buildings. Now and then they met boys from the School. These walked with a cultivated waddle. Upon their heads they wore flattish straw hats. Short jackets reached to their waists. Beneath these their posteriors bulged respectfully. Extremely scrubbed, they showed a pallid aloofness. At sight of them Storman's old-time bull-laugh boomed out. But it died away almost at once. The blatant and the obvious had ceased to tickle him so easily. Russia. Forgetful of Norah, he strode up the hill. Ashamed of his lack of good manners, Norah followed.

They reached the top and passed through a churchyard where great pieces of masonry lay upon the dead, making certain of no premature resurrection. But roses bloomed through all the churchyard. Norah pointed to a group of them and stopped to smell them, pressing her small nose against a bloom. Standing so, she was slim and desirable, with narrow hips, breastless, with straight, thin legs. Hatless, Storman smoothed his hair with characteristic gesture. With his stick he pointed to the roses.

"They grow so well because they're manured with the dead," he said.

"You've a horrible mind."

Speaking to him, she seldom called him either James or Mr. Storman. Somehow, he was never either to her. But his attraction deepened. Walking with him, even while she plotted against him a great fear would come upon her. He was mad, mad, and she wanted someone sane and sly and reasonable and cruel.

She left him to peer at the inscription on a tomb surmounted with dog-roses. Storman stood still, looking at her with cold, clear eyes.

They came out on a terrace high above green Middlesex. Below were hedges and the whitenesses of roads and the long brown scaurs evolved of the Metropolitan Railway. It was a day of dead and level sunshine and down the hill gnats pinged and boomed.

"It's lovely," said Norah, leaning upon a railing and looking at the autumnal world. Storman pointed with his stick to the far horizon.

"Windsor is over there."

Unavailingly they searched the sky-line for Windsor. It was regally withdrawn. Presently their attention was attracted by a dog-fight on the terrace behind them. Two terriers, filled with Sunday energy, each abrim with the lust to assert its superiority and fitness to survive, fought. Wurring, they had affixed teeth in each other's necks and, rolling in the dust, tore out great lumps of hair and hide. A thin screaming arose from them. Their owners, respectively a middle-aged woman with red cheeks and a lanky youth with a pimply face, belaboured them unavailingly. Storman leant his back against the railing, lit a cigarette, and watched.

The terrace was filling with men and women returning from worshipping God. Shocked and eager, they crowded around the dog-fight, occasionally prodding the combatants with umbrellas. Becoming bored, Storman forced his way through the circle, bent over the two dogs and drew a small packet from his pocket. With his hand extended he emptied the contents of the packet over the heads and eyes of the two terriers. Thereat they tore themselves apart with ear-splitting yelps, and, capering and barking insanely, fled down the hill.

"What's in the packet?" asked Norah, wide-eyed, the while the occupants of the terrace regarded Storman with indifference and pointed out to one another where Windsor should be.

"Pepper." Storman followed the flight of the dogs with speculative eyes. "I keep it to throw in the faces of Fascists who interrupt public meetings."

"But that's not fair, is it? Fascists?"

"The bourgeoisie produces a certain romantic scum. Under proper conditions and temperature this scum froths and ferments. It is then Fascism."

"Oh."

"That is really all that it is." He mused over unseen Windsor. "The Fascists will never concern you. Unless they lynch me after we're married. Then you can sue them."

"We're not married yet."

"No." He looked at her absentmindedly. "Thank God."

They walked down the steep hillside to the lower churchyard. There graves were smaller and meaner than those around the church. Some were fenced about with iron railings, some

130

had new gravestones whereon the stonemason's name and address, in discreet capitals, apprised the living of the unostentatious comfort that the dead might cheaply attain. Storman pointed to the inscriptions.

"Competition. They lived their lives under it. Even in death they cannot escape."

"When I am dead," said Norah, "I'd like to be burned and my ashes taken out to sea and scattered on the water."

"When I am dead," said Storman, "they may put my head on Tower Bridge and dissect the rest of me. I shall be elsewhere."

"Where'll you be?"

"Organizing the Communists in hell, I've no doubt," said Storman.

Norah yawned and sat down on the grave of a greengrocer. She was tired. Storman looked at his watch. It was an Ingersoll.

"Let's go up to the Hill village for lunch."

There, in the "Swan" they sat long, till it was afternoon, eating watercress and trout and drinking cider. Made so by the cider, Norah's red lips grew redder. She talked of London, of the Civil Service, of Ireland. Storman leant his arms upon the table and looked at her gravely and absently. Outside the sun marched across the sky.

"It's cooler now," said Norah, in a pause. "We're wasting the day. Where can we go?"

"Down the Hill."

"So soon?"

"By a different way."

Outside the inn, they were conscious that it had not grown cooler. It was as if they stood at the mouth of a furnace-door flung ajar. After walking for a few minutes Norah's thin dress began to cling to her hips. She panted a little. Her face grew white. Swinging his stick, bareheaded and sated, Storman whistled the "Red Flag".

"I'll faint if I can't get some place to rest."

"You've eaten too much food," said Storman. Then: "I know a place."

He led her down the hill by a side-path through a narrow lane bordered by trees and red flowers. She never learned what those red flowers were. In remembrance ever after they danced in a hot-smelling wind, under a blue haze of heat. They passed through a wicket-gate, to a field set with scattered clumps of trees and the brown flanks of grazing horses sweat-gleaming in the sword-fall of sunshine.

"This is the place," said Storman and lay down in a shaded place beneath a tree. Norah stood looking at him and the grass doubtfully till he reached up a hand and pulled her down beside him. Thereat, of a sudden blotted out, horses and field vanished. They were alone in a dim, green world. In the grass a grasshopper chirped and chirped. Norah sighed.

"Miggod, this's better."

Storman lay upon his back and closed his eyes. Norah touched his cheek.

"Don't sleep. Tell me a story."

He rolled over and took her in his arms. "We will act one, instead," he said.

She trembled against him, seeing the look in his eyes. Nor, with the stirring of the commonest of desires, had these eyes grown the more human. They were a colourless flame. They seemed to look through her, through her eyes, through her brain, through her body, till they saw within her that nestling shape that shamed her. His lips met hers, and, pressure on pressure, kissed her, deeply and strongly, so that a wild surprise and fear came upon her. She struggled.

"No, please, Jim!"

He took his lips away. Thereat she wound her arms around his neck, impelled to the action by a force beyond herself. She felt his hands upon her body. In a delicious ecstasy she felt her bones and flesh melt and dissolve in a whirling dance of atoms. Faster and faster they whirled. . . . Lying together, they trembled as the strings of a violin played upon by a master hand. Storman's bull laugh smothered itself in her hair. . . .

Till late in the afternoon she watched him, where he had fallen asleep by her side. Sometimes she would draw the hair back from his forehead, broodingly, and then sit with her hand still on his hair, listening to far voices beyond the trees, to the trampling of the hoofs of the grazing horses. Content, sun-flushed, weary, she looked down on him.

She had found her salvation.

All the morning stout men had been engaged in carrying sacks of inferior potatoes and salted meat aboard the troopship *Culmer Castle.* In the Mediterranean this meat would mildly putrefy, giving off a sweetish odour sickening to the orderlies of the mess-decks. The troop-decks were in tiers of three, reaching far down into the bowels of the ship. An ex-German cattle-boat, she had been renamed in 1917 and refitted for her present purpose. But drinking-water taps were still labelled *wasser,* and in the lower decks a smell of cowdung, faint and musk, an aged, weary smell, lay quiescent till the Mediterranean suns that would sweeten the meat would stir it also to expansion and pervasion.

Above the central gangway was nailed a great poster. It read:

> IF YOU WANT A JOB
> that includes
> GOOD PAY
> GOOD FOOD
> GOOD HOUSING,
> A MONTH'S HOLIDAY A YEAR
> and
> WORLD TRAVEL
> You should
> JOIN THE ROYAL AIR FORCE!

Pointing at it, the stevedores laughed and said they didn't bloody well think.

Now and then a greasy rain descended on Southampton Docks. Customs officials sweated in close, small offices. To chance airmen they spoke with a brusque cautiousness which concealed a certain pique. For they were not entitled to salutes.

In the warehouse opposite the *Culmer Castle* berth Air Force embarkation officers walked to and fro, marshalling the draft and its two thousand kitbags. Bagging at the knees and the seat of his breeches, the sergeant-major called Bonzo lined up the airmen. Sweating, he knew them for bastards. On an officer approaching he would shout out "Atten" and pause, then add "shun". Hearing this last syllable the airmen would bring the heels of their hobnailed boots close together and sway. Bonzo would then salute the officer, and the officer salute Bonzo. Then the officer would say "Sergeant-major. Waw."

In these pastimes several hours passed and the day waned. Late afternoon drew on. A hurried medical inspection of the airmen began. Filing past the medical officer they removed their shirts and nether garments and stood with upraised arms. Four men were discovered to have syphilis. They were placed under arrest. Nearby, in the transport sheds, Air Force clerks worked with the collars of their tunics hooked up close to their necks. In this manner they retained a smart and airman-like appearance. Above their collars their faces shone red and moist and unset, and upon the many documents passing through their hands red-brown stains began to appear.

All afternoon a group of women and children stood and waited outside this warehouse. They were the wives and children of the airmen of the draft. They had thin Cockney voices and bright eyes. They wore cheap garments and the shoes of the children required mending. Now and then some woman would speculate aloud as to what was happening behind the locked doors of the warehouse. Then the other women would laugh or say that the speaker was a one. Underfed, nomadic, mostly shopgirls or domestic servants whom airmen had first seduced and then married, these women looked at the warehouse and the *Culmer Castle* with bright, interested, dead eyes.

Presently, unseen at its source, they observed a vast insect-crawl of pale blue upon the gangways of the ship. The draft was being embarked. At the same time a fog rose out of the docks, advanced in a solid wall, and obliterated the ship. At its coming one of the women went to the locked door of the warehouse and beat upon it. In cover of the fog, she found herself beginning to weep, and a low moaning that once or twice before she had heard escape from her lips frightened her. Her beating shook the door.

"Jiwant?" asked a voice from inside the warehouse.

"Let me in. Please, let me in."

The door opened. A sergeant wearing the red armband of the police looked out. Showing lead-stopped teeth, he grinned. A tidy bit of stuff.

"Now then, missus, what's wrong?"

134

"My husband—he's gone aboard the ship. I haven't said good-bye. Nor any of the women out here."

The sergeant removed his hat and scratched a close-cropped head. "Must be some mix-up," he explained. "Wait a bit." He shut the door in the woman's face and strolled away into the warehouse. Under a light at a convenient distance he stopped, pulled out an early edition of the *Evening News*, and read the winners of the 3.30.

The woman waited. Suddenly the door in front of her opened. She gave a cry.

"Oh, John, I thought you were going without—Oh, God!"

Garland, bebelted, sweating, grimy, took her in his arms. He panted as one who had been running, and kicked the door to behind him.

"I volunteered for baggage fatigue and managed to get back," he explained. "The gangways'll be up in a minute. Say good-bye, darling."

Blindly in his arms, Thea wept with the frenzy of a scared child. "Don't go. Stay with me. I'm afraid."

In the heart of Garland arose an insane hate—hate of the place, Life, Thea, himself. He shook her, kissed her.

"Don't cry. Thea, don't cry."

A thin scream arose and volumed piercingly outside the warehouse. It was the siren of the *Culmer Castle*. Garland's hands gripped Thea's.

"Dear, I'll come back long before three years. I swear I will. I'll come back before your time comes."

And, at the lie so told to her, Thea of a sudden grew quiet, wiped the sweat-laden face of Garland with her handkerchief, kissed that face, saw it disappear, and stood in a screaming sirocco of sound as the *Culmer Castle* flung off its gangway.

And a dead certainty came upon her. She would never see him again. Garland, her lover, boy and poet and care-free mocker, was gone for ever.

Subchapter vi

She hugged a pillow in bed that night and in the morning poked it, sleepily, to make it get out and turn off the alarum clock.

CHAPTER THE EIGHTH

Wherein Success, always a Pleasing Phenomenon, comes to Andreas van Koupa, Garland meditates upon the Grand Pyramid, and Storman is apprised of himself as an Agent of Mr. Shaw's Life Force.

Subchapter i

THE *White Argus* made its third appearance in November. Besides numerous drawings and colourless paintings, it contained three poems by Mynheer Andreas van Koupa. In one of these he questioned the existence of God and rebuked atheists; in another he spoke of the shadows under a girl's breasts; in the third he described the sensations of a man writhing in stomach-ache.

The poem describing Briarton's "Nocturne" appeared over the signature of Mrs. Gayford. It was hailed by the White Artists as a work of genius. Amazed and enthusiastic, shabby young men went to drink tea with the author and wonder how she had written such a thing; the fact made them vaguely uneasy. It was like finding the cook, an enthusiastic believer in the Holy Presence at Communion, indulging in cannibalism in the back-kitchen on the strength of that belief. Sweating, but less freely now, for the colder weather drew on, Mrs. Gayford held triumphant salons. But into the gatherings gradually crept the serpent of dissension.

By the majority of the White Artists the contributions of Koupa were considered to have defaced their journal. These contributions were denounced to Mrs. Gayford as reactionary and Victorian. Most violent in denunciation of them was Briarton himself.

This was at a tea-party. At that moment Koupa was shown in. He brought a poem and read it aloud in an unfriendly silence. It was called DUST.

"I have drunk deeply of the ancient wine,
    Wandered a summer in the Sumer land,
Heard in the dusk the bells of Cretan kine
    And maiden's song across the Cnossan strand:
Seen, in the sunset lowe against his God,
    The sculptor-scribe who carved the Runic plan
Of suns and shames and serpents intertrod
    On terraces of Toltec Yucatan.

"I hear new voices down the English morn,
    Alien laughter by the Lakeland meres,
The hymnal chorus rise to Gods unborn . . .

"Far in the seed-time of the sleeping years
I see the Christ, an outcast, stand forlorn,
A dream, a tale, a wonderment of tears.

"This so-little thing," said Koupa, "I wrote this morning."

He had written it many years before, but had newly revised it with a view to its publication in the *White Argus*. Mrs. Gayford refilled his cup with tea.

"It is exquisite," she said, and then became aware of Briarton's angry eyes.

"Is this—work—of Mr. Cooper's to appear in the *White Argus*?" he asked.

Something in his tone caused Mrs. Gayford to look at him closely. The other voices became stilled. Young men ceased to fill hungry mouths with cake and discuss Pirandello. It was felt to be a moment of crisis.

Mrs. Gayford considered Briarton, considered Koupa, and then made her decision. "It is," she said.

Briarton stood up. "Then no more works of mine, nor, I think, of my friends, will appear between the covers of the *White Argus*."

Koupa drank tea and to Briarton raised insolent eyebrows.

"Surely I have not yet seen any—works—of yours there, m'sieu?"

Briarton thereon walked out of the room. He was speedily followed by the young men. Next day Mrs. Gayford was informed that she had been discharged from the editorship of the *White Argus*; later in the day she received an urgent appeal to settle with the printer the cost of the *White Argus*'s third issue.

But, left alone with Andreas van Koupa, Mrs. Gayford had

listened to the planning of a new magazine. This also would be under her editorship. It would deal with modern poetry and would be called *The Lyre*. Real poetry, not the shams and symbolisms of Sitwellism and the like putrescent cancers, would be revived in its pages. It would purify the English language and inspire the English-speaking nations. Uplifted, Mrs. Gayford sat with shining eyes and skin, seeing herself in the histories of the future immortalized as the Reviver of Poesy.

"And, madam so dear, when we have lit the torch, when I have proven myself on that so-little field where I am armed to conquer, then shall I come to you and ask you to give me the right to conquest in a yet sweeter field."

Mrs. Gayford started. The idea was genuinely new to her. A startled blush mottled her skin. Looking at Koupa, she saw his shabbiness, the raggedness of his finger-nails, his frayed shirt. But these could be remedied. . . .

The wife of the great poet. A second Mary Shelley. . . .

Mrs. Gayford held out sudden, girlish hands.

"Are you not proved already?" she whispered.

God mine, the so-mottled old sow wanted a little of the love-making!

Subchapter ii

John Garland sat on the top of the Grand Pyramid of Gizeh.

It was Sunday afternoon. From the Air Force camp at Heliopolis he had taken a tramcar down into Cairo, had changed at the Esbekieh Gardens, had there inquired for routes and other tramcars to take him to the Pyramids. Four dragomen, wearing bowler hats and the tunics of colonels, had insisted on assisting him. In the heat and smell they had all piled in behind him on the tramcar for the Pyramids. The conductor had blown a small wooden horn. Streets, brown, dusty, uninteresting, had slid past. The conductor had come round for fares. The four dragomen had referred him to Garland.

"Go to hell," said Garland.

Protesting, the four dragomen had been flung off the car and Garland had proceeded on to Gizeh. Arrived there he had inspected the caves in the hillside below the Pyramids, had walked across the scuttering sand ledges till he stood in front of

139

the Sphinx. Looking up in the battered face, he laughed at sight of the wonder of the ages. For it had the face of an unfortunate pugilist.

It looked like Mr. Beckett.

"The dim savage who planned its carving can smile among the shades. Providing he ever dreamt of such a thing as pity or humour. It is a great thing to be funny—even unintention-ally—rather than impressive after five thousand years."

And, chuckling, he went back across the sands to the Pyra-mids.

Now he sat on the top of Cheops and ate peanuts. He had purchased a bag of them before he ascended. At that warm hour he was the only visitor who had as yet attained the sum-mit, though below him little specks drifted here and there amidst the great coned masses—tourist parties, these from Gizeh and Cairo. Beside him, on the top of the Pyramid, two natives squatted and scratched the soles of their feet. One of them had bottles of lemonade and obscene photographs for sale.

Garland cracked a peanut and looked out over the desert. The Moquattam hills lowered grotesquely through the sun-haze.

"They were like that five thousand years ago, when the queer, repulsive half-humans upbuilded these hideous masses of rock and brickwork. They hardly change, though the type of dark-minded savage beneath them changes eternally. The thousands who have come since the days of Herodotus to look upon the Pyramids and sneer at them! . . . Am I sneering? God forbid! They are not worth a sneer—those, the most boring monuments to futility that have ever been erected.

"But they have value. Their colossal conceit, had we but a single psychologist-historian with a spark of genius, could throw more light upon the evolution of mentality than all the rock-paintings and books of the dead and suchlike petrified snoopety whimperings in the dark. They mark that supreme apishness of the savage become a barbarian—an apishness far beyond the concept of any ape.

"For, at a certain stage in the evolution of man, when he was half-beast, half-savage, with his tail-stump still visible and hair in a mat across his shoulders and buttocks, it would seem

140

that he had little self-consciousness. He had lost, being then a mongrel, that animal swagger which induced him to antic at the watering-places and thump his chest over a disputed piece of carrion. He had no conceit.

"But the savage-barbarian evolved an apishness, a conceit, beyond thinking in the world before his time. Dimly conscious of power, those elevated headmen and witch-doctors of ancient Egypt—surely the most unattractive and owlish of all experimenters in civilization—grew out of their minds Conceit like a giant tumour. They invented immortality—an eternity of time wherein to fertilize the wombs of eternal squaws, to prostrate eternally their already-decaying bodies in front of other deified Conceits, to eternally eat and drink and perform all the obscene functions of the body. So, for that aftermath, for that everlasting time of stinking fecundity, they invented ways of preserving their bodies, and their slaves and sub-slaves, themselves victims of an insane Conceit in that they believed their masters divine and themselves capable of apprehending divinity, built those senseless monuments to the exaggerated struttings of the belly-filled ape."

Increasing, rather than waning in strength, was the afternoon sun. Upon the summit of the Pyramid it became scorching. Perspiration became sticky, but dryly so, like glue, around the inner rim of Garland's topee. He purchased a bottle of lemonade, and, inverting it, drank. Lowering the bottle, he wished he had brought his notebook in which to set down neat thoughts and aphorisms for insertion in the revised draft of his novel.

For his novel was now completed, and, as soon as he was definitely posted from Heliopolis to some Air Force office where a typewriter was available, he would set about typing the final version. Long ago his heroine had been successfully seduced, various other characters had died ironically, failed ironically, succeeded ironically, postured before the curtain for a grand ironic tableau. Thought of his novel pleasured Garland. Unfolding it in his mind, he proceeded to re-read the pages. The two natives behind him spoke thinly, pipingly. They pointed down the Pyramid. With grins, they touched Garland's arm and gesticulated.

"Well?"

He looked. A large American woman was ascending Cheops. Propelled behind by two Arabs, she clutched uncertainly up the gigantic steps. Her panting sounded like the beat of a dynamo. Half-way up she stuck fast. In response to cries, one of the natives leapt nimbly down from shelf to shelf to assist in the haulage.

Garland did not laugh at first. Then suddenly the irony of the business entered into his soul. He chuckled.

He himself, seated and philosophizing on the dung-heap of Cheops's conceit, was but adding to what that heap symbolized—the dung-heap up which another insect came painfully crawling to add its own special quota.

Subchapter iii

"God mine, at last. At last. *Post secula.* Dream not, little friend. It comes. At last.

"And the mottled sow purchases a magazine for the so-long forgotten little poems of mine. And they will succeed—now, at the last, when to me they are wind and water. They will succeed—now, when I need not fight and toil and strive for their success, when I need not pester the publishers and pay away the good guilders to the little sneak-dog agents. They will succeed.

"God mine, it is time, for I am weary. Grey in the hair that Laida used to comb those long-gone times in Haarlem. Where is the little Laida now with her so-sweet breasts? And from these so-damned rebel meetings I've gathered rheumatism—the windy sentiments of half-baked Prometheans ablow on me. . . . Growing old. Time to go home with the swallows, my little. Time to go home.

"Akh me, time to go home. And I will put by the dreams of Spartacus and Christ. Things are so. All strivings—they are but the spatterings of the insect in the wayside pool—the insect that hopes to alter the tides. I will keep me secure in the places to which I climb, fenced round with the politics and prejudices of the little bourgeois swine. I shall burn the torch of art behind their shelter, not see it blown to dust and ashes on proletecult barricades. God mine, Art cries for security, for shelter. Have I not earned the so-little share of those now?

"Share? The snivelling little puppety-dogs! Share? They will give me all, they who have sneered at and starved me and refused me. They will bow to me and photograph me and pay me for writings of fool-doodle in their little stink-muck reviews. They will make me the great, the eccentric poet, and, God mine, shall I spare them?

"Starving children and darkened brains, I have finished with you. Ergates, you are the great Beast, the devouring sick Beast that eternally cries for aid and sustenance from I and the other fool Prometheans. You fatten on our blood and sweat and ever weaken, ever cry aloud for new victims that your freedom be bought on guillotine and firing-squad. I have finished with you. Rot in your kennels. I have finished.

"Yet I could weep. Eh, but they would stare at you, here in this placid St. James, they who have lived their coddled, easy lives since their mothers' wombs ejected them, they who reserve their tears for the bridal chamber and the outsnufflings of their kin! And I go to join in their warmth and coddling. But I shall not be of them. All my life long shall I go with dreams and remembrances of horror and sweetness that they shall never touch. . . .

"Oh, God mine! the flags on the barricades and the dear, wild song of the blood revolt; the tramping legions in the snowing streets; the crawling prisons of foulness and the hymns of despair and the marching feet of the midnight jailers leading out the bloody wounded to the firing-squad. . . . Akh! And all the days and nights that thou hast seen—dawn upon the Red Desert, the stillness of the long flights of birds. Dawn, austere, unthinkable in purity above the Cairene hovels. Dawn in the so-dark forests of great Deutschland. . . . Dawns when in rags, in hunger, thou awokest to the sting of life and hope and cried thy little scream of wonder to the paling stars. . . . God mine, and the nights of love, the blue, soft nights: I shall not know them again. Tree boughs dappled with the so-shining stars, moonlight on the endless trails, darkness alive with the hands and lips and limbs of shaken love of women—I shall not know you again. . . . I go into the shelter, the safety, God mine, for I am old. I have paid. I go home. I shall marry the so-fat sow and live on clean foods and smooth beds and never again hear the midnight cry upon the mountains. I shall herd in a scented

sty with those who have never drunk of the blood of Life. . . .
But I have drunk! In the scented sty I shall not forget—God
mine, I shall not forget!"

In the London streets they stared amazed at a man who
walked into the evening, weeping, with blinded, unshielded
eyes.

Subchapter iv

"Oh. Jim."

"Hello, Norah. Alone?"

"Yes. I've tea ready in the sitting-room. There's a comfy
fire. It's horribly cold. Still raining?"

"Winter's knocking at the door," said Storman, removing his
gloves. "Listen."

A gust of late October wind wailed up from the River
amongst the houses in Rosemount Avenue. Against the win-
dow-panes sounded the sveet-sveet of thin, secretive rain.
Norah shivered.

"Come into the sitting-room."

It was warm in there, with a heaped coal-fire and dancing
shadows and still glow. Outside the windows, with the curtains
still undrawn, the evening tapped urgently. Storman went over
and looked out.

"Soon be night. I came down the street up there. A crowded
street. The folk were hurrying. Norah, I saw a sight that made
me sick."

"What?"

"An old man standing in the gutter. A draggled, aimless old
man. He had no laces in his boots. He wasn't selling anything.
I don't think he was even standing. He was just drifting in a
dead kind of way. His coat was a green mould rag. His face was
clouded with a dim trouble in the rain. It was a face like my
father's. My God, Norah, I thought it was my father."

Norah said nothing. She stood by the fire, looking at
Storman's back with startled eyes. He turned round suddenly,
and she saw upon his face a helpless terror.

"My God, Norah! I never realized it before—the abyss of
poverty. It might have been my father—that old man with the
eyes of a sick bird. I've done nothing for him or his like.

144

Communism's done nothing. All the world goes by. . . . I've schooled myself to be cruel and unwavering—for what? There's a greater cruelty—the Cruelty of the Streets, senseless, unemotional as that of an octopus. There is something worse than the beast in man—an evil older than Life itself."

The windows rattled in a sudden new gust and now came another sound—the flop-flop of blown wet leaves. Storman swung the curtain across the window. His great laugh boomed out.

"I've been frightening you. Where's the switch?"

Norah switched on the light. Storman sat down in an armchair by the fire and stroked his face with fingers that quivered. Then he took them away and looked slowly at the fire, at the tea-table, at Norah. He sighed.

"Comfortable here, Norah. If I weren't a modern Communist I'd marry you and you would have my slippers waiting for me nightly, and be an old-fashioned, illiterate wife, as are the wives of Revolutionists, and have mild flirtations with the gas-meterman and the butcher. . . . Three lumps, please."

"Here you are."

"Thanks. Damn."

His shaking hand had half-emptied his cup upon the carpet. He stood up, and poured himself fresh tea, not looking at Norah. His face was grey beneath the tan.

The sudden encounter with the old man had shaken him in a fashion unbelievable. He had suddenly and horrifyingly been humanized by a realization of the cold-blooded inhumanity of man.

"I'm sorry. This'll pass. Sit down, Norah. You look warm. Ah, me. Good for lying in a husband's arms these chill nights that are coming."

Norah drank tea. Her face had flushed. She always coloured at such references of Storman's. Since that day in the field below Harrow Hill she had not thought of Storman without the blood darkening her cheeks. Grown shameless herself in matters of sex during her years in London, she yet, by some curious inversion, associated Storman, even in his most frank remarks, with innocence. She ate brown bread and butter and rhubarb jam.

"Sometimes marriage doesn't mean a husband, anyway. I went to see Thea yesterday."

"Thea?"

"Yes. Remember that girl—red hair, grey eyes—at the flat when you came that Sunday? Ages ago. She married the airman, John Garland."

"Oh. And what happened?"

"Garland's been sent abroad—to Egypt or Palestine. Thea's living in two furnished rooms in Shepherd's Bush. She's horribly lonely. It's a shame. Just because she's so fond of Garland, she never has any other man for a friend. And I'm the only girl she knows. Now she spends days by herself. Moping. It's horrible."

Once Storman would not have thought her capable of such emotion, or, believing it, would have disregarded it. But the cracks in the walls of his world were shivering wider and wider apart.

"When are you going to see her next?"

"Wednesday evening, I think."

"I'll come with you."

"All right." Surprised.

"Unless you think her neighbours'll talk. Or her husband disapprove. But, being married, she should be freed from the convention which demands alike of you, Norah, as a Civil Servant, and of Mary, as the mother of a god, virginity."

"And neither of us . . . ."

"I am not responsible for both, Norah." He set down his cup and caught her hands and laughed into her eyes. The lights flickered to and fro under his even brows. She watched these lights, fascinated. "Am I? And you're glad I'm responsible for one—aren't you?"

She let her chin sink on her breast. Her eyes, on a level with his, did not return his gaze, but looked sideways into the fire. For the warmth and the sweetness of her and the picture she made, for the wantonness of her, her shy lustfulness and matter-of-factness, for these things and the comfort and homeliness of the room, yet another sigh was stifled in Storman.

The swallows were going home.

"Aren't you?" He repeated his question, idly, pleasured by stroking the soft skin of her arm, at the tingle of delight that went through him touching the skin sheath of her forearm. She turned her eyes on his slowly—bright, wavering eyes full of firelight reflections.

146

"Are you?"

"The man is always pleased, I think. He likes to believe himself a conqueror, though it's really the other way about. . . . Why, what's wrong?"

The brightness of her eyes had been the tears in them. Now they fell on Storman's face. He took her in his arms. As he did so she slipped her arms—fiercely, despairingly—about his neck, as on that day in the Harrow field.

"Oh, Jim, please be glad, please help me. I—we're going to have a baby!"

He held her without moving. She could not see his face because her own was hidden. A lump of coal fell out on the hearth. Storman thought: Coal, it will be scarce this winter. Nationalization . . .

She had said . . .

He had a sudden vision of the old man of the gutter. A dizziness, overwhelming, unphysical, closed his eyes.

She had said . . .

Subchapter v

Storman and Norah were married on the 18th of November—at a church to please Norah and at a Registry Office to please Storman. It was a dry, cold, wintry day and Norah's nose needed frequent repowdering. The best man was Edward Snooks, the bridesmaid Ellen. They had lunch at the Strand Corner House and came out to see a passing of the Prince of Wales, in state, and wearing a large, woolly hat. For the first time that day Storman's great bull-laugh rang out.

Earlier the same day there had been much confusion and hurrying to and fro in the house of Mrs. Gayford. Mrs. Gayford herself had risen an hour before it was necessary. She was bathed and perfumed and, standing the while like a stout sacrifice to the Sidonian Ashtaroth, buttoned into her underclothes. She trembled, and her eyes grew for an hour soft and youthful.

The wedding ceremony was at St. Judas's, the wedding to be performed by the Canon himself. Mrs. Gayford's friends assembled early; the Canon came early. The church was suffused with a bright, cold light. It grew to eleven o'clock.

"Here she comes."

147

Came the bride on the arm of a brother-in-law—he who had made the allowance to the disowned Robert. He had laid aside Gibbon for the day and, tall, stooping, asthmatic, moved angrily up the aisle with Mrs. Gayford's arm on his sleeve. He realized that he would have been much better employed reading the footnotes on Zozimus than in marrying this whore of Jack's to that unwashed Dutchman. And, with a Gibbonian irony, he looked round the church, at the stained-glass windows where anæmic hopes and charities froze in the chill November weather, and at the high altar. This last he knew for a relic of the ancient sacrificial stone whereon the priest was wont to sacrifice the victim, ripping open his stomach to read the portents in the entrails.

Standing waiting in the purple blur of music, he wondered what portents they would read of this marriage in the entrails of a sacrifice. Beside him, stout and preserved and clothed in fine raiment, his sister-in-law was unusually pale. Her flabby lips shook a little. He wondered if she were thinking better of it—if the prospective embraces of the groom were troubling her. Damned good job if he troubled her considerably—she's still young enough for it. A child a year in the good old fashion would give her something to do. But that was hardly to be expected these days when contraception allowed women to practise prostitution without paying the piper.

Ah! the groom. Weedy, but clean. Damned if I like the look of him even now. Something about the fellow that's dark—they have that tinge, some of those Dutchmen: the old Walloon taint. Borrowed the money for his clothes, I suppose. M'm. Has a sense of humour, at least. Fairly plainly regards Griselda as a mine of home comforts and not impressed with the figure she's managed to struggle into for the occasion. Wonder the damned woman doesn't burst her stays.

The Canon. The chill November light showed him for a tall, ascetic cleric with the face of a grave, cruel horse. In and out of church he propounded the belief that the creed of Christ was a disgusting proletarian superstition. He was an agnostic, but believed that a return to Mithraism, from which he traced all that was good in Christianity, alone could bring order and discipline to the countries of Western Europe. He attacked St. Paul and Dr. Marie Stopes in the monthly reviews, and declared that the true lot of labour was helotry and gang-servitude.

The ceremony began. Koupa and Mrs. Gayford knelt and rose and made responses, Koupa in a clear, mellow voice, Mrs. Gayford in nervous squeaks. And, by the saying of the ancient words they were married, and the man who had crossed the ice to fight for Kronstadt was given dominion over the body of a woman whom he called the fat sow.

By evening they were on the Dover train, en route for Calais and Greece, where the honeymoon was to be spent. Koupa walked the corridors of the train, smoking a cigar, fairly clad and washed, with his nails trimmed and his hair brushed. He put his head out of the window once.

"God mine, the smell of the good, wild wind!"

Then he closed the window and went to his wife.

CHAPTER THE NINTH

Wherein Christmas Eve, which Some say commemorates Christ and Some Charles Dickens, is celebrated without Plagiarism.

Subchapter Introductory

IT was Christmas Eve. Long sheets of rain fell on the London streets, washing westwards till over the suburbs and so by Middlesex and the West Counties it was an attenuated drizzle that passed in Cornwall and the Scilly Isles into a woolly fog. South, across the Channel, was frost and brightness, with a sinking sun that smouldered on the horizon of all France, but rose a little by Mentone and the Azure Coast, cleared and grew bright in Italy, lay warm and steaming over the gloaming of the Mediterranean. East and South Egypt lay cold and crisp, in the grip of even such frost as held France, but up the Syrian coast and over the mountains of Lebanon and Moab the rain fell steadily, windlessly, on red, churned earth.

So on all that stretch of the world where the ancient pre-humans first wandered and prowled and dreamed by shivering camp-fires, where first reason glimmered and smoked and died and grew to life again, where first the magic hopes and cults and revilements grew into chains of thought, into creeds and beliefs and the tissue of racial brainstuff, came Christmas Eve in its guises of hail and faint heat. Between the Little Bear and the Southern Cross, where the sparse hordes once followed the sun southwards from the last advances of the ice-caps, and so passed away as a dream in that dim morning of time, their descendants, peopling the western outjutment of Asia as thickly as the ants, walked and looked that evening with each behind his mind a giant Ghost of thought, pale and remote, infrequently glimpsed and remembered.

So it was in the lands that lie between and beneath the Bear and the Cross.

Ellen Ledgworth came out of the folding doors of Cocotte Sœurs at half-past five. She had been let off early, for she had worked overtime on the previous five nights. Edward was waiting for her, in the rain, with a steady drip of water from his hatbrim. He kissed her with frowsy lips, having first raised his hat in an ex-officer's gesture of greeting.

"You've been drinking beer, dear," said Ellen, placidly.

"Only a spot. Met some of the lads of the regiment. Ugh! It wasn't half so muggy on the Ypres Salient as here. By God, and there was some fun in life then!"

"Better where you are, dear," said Ellen, walking by his side. "Button your coat or you'll catch cold. Where shall we go for tea? I'm very hungry."

"That little Scotch place in the Circus is all right."

"That'll be nice."

Presently, sitting in front of a view of Edinburgh Castle, decorated with tartan, they ate home-made cakes from the restaurant's bakeries in Kennington. These they spread with Scotch butter from Denmark. Edward talked earnestly. He had been put up for an ex-officer's club, but had not at the moment sufficient money to pay down. In a month or so, when he got a rise . . . .

And, drinking tea, he held his head in three-quarters profile towards Ellen.

"Well, I'd like to help you, Edward, but I just can't. You know you never paid me back that loan of Thea Mayven's which I paid for you. And I've had to buy a lot of clothes lately. You haven't seen my new jumper yet, have you?"

"No."

"Awfully pretty, I think. I hope you'll like it. Where are we going after this?"

"How the devil should I know?"

"Ted, you mustn't talk to me like that."

"Oh, mustn't I?" He spoke with a sudden, savage contempt, lowering his voice to preserve appearances but with the

152

growing discontent of months overboiling in utterance. "Mustn't do this and mustn't do that. . . . Who the devil do you think you are? It comes a bit thick when a damned shop-girl says what I must and must not do."

"All right, Edward. If you feel like that the best thing we can do is to stop seeing each other."

"Don't worry, you won't see me again."

"All right," said Ellen placidly. "We needn't quarrel."

"Needn't quarrel? You—think you're a woman? God help anyone who ever tried to marry you. You've as much life in you as a suet pudding. There's any amount of girls know how to keep a man. You don't. I mean it this time."

Ellen's tears subsided placidly. "All right, Edward. Good-bye."

Snooks stood up, took his hat and coat and then stopped to search his pockets. His face was pale grey with rage. He was elaborately polite.

"I'm sorry I've got no change. Send me a note to my digs and let me know what the bill is."

"It's all right, Edward. I knew I'd have to pay, anyway." She considered him placidly, and then enunciated a shattering opinion. "And I don't think much of ex-officers if they're all like you."

In a moment she was left to herself, looking up at Edinburgh Castle. When the waitress next passed she ordered more scones and butter.

Subchapter ii

James Storman had been going over the membership lists of the Anarchocommunist Party and dictating letters to individuals with initial letters ranging from A to G. Above his desk hung a large map. On a ledge underneath this map reposed a little heap of red flags. As the answers came back from members he would place the flags in position around the districts where members resided.

Yearly, since the General Strike, a questionnaire had been sent out to each Communist. Had the member had any military training, could he ride a motor-cycle, did he possess a motor-car, had he the right of entry to any public building?

153

Yearly the answers grew in bulk. In backyards of slums and suburban houses, in colleges and casual wards, the five thousand Communists of Great Britain furbished up their motorcycles and knowledge of forming fours in order to be prepared for the next great struggle.

"Working out the population of Great Britain at forty-five million," said Storman to himself, "the odds will run something like 9,000 to every Communist."

Last to leave the Party offices that Christmas Eve, he walked down to the Strand and a bus. The vehicle was crowded inside, so he ascended to the top and in smeary darkness and rain rode home by winding miles of streetway to Peckham.

Below a dingy brick tenement let out in flats he stopped and looked up and saw in the third storey the dimness of a lighted window. He stood still in the rain, looking at it with a queer passion. Then he sighed, a long slow sigh.

Home.

All day Norah had been working in the flat, wearily, till her hands ached with scrubbing, with bed-making, with disinfecting the lavatory. Between whiles she had had to ponder the question of a dinner for Storman on his return. They had dinner each evening at seven o'clock. From dawn till dusk Storman was seldom at home, being occupied with the emancipation of the working-classes.

Twice that afternoon, going into the sitting-room, Norah had found the fire out, for the coals were poor and cheap. Relighting it, she had cried because she noted the roughened condition of her hands. Also, she had suddenly been sick.

So, day after day in the little Peckham flat, she was wearied and bored to the verge of madness. Hating housework, there were moments, scrubbing at greasy pots or excavating lumps of spilt suet from the choked jets of the gas stove, when she would put her knuckles to her mouth to prevent herself screaming. Once she had started a scream, but the sound of it had frightened her and she had left off. Far down the dreary corridor of the hours the event of Storman's return would each day lie in wait like a dim beast.

She raised a flushed face from the gas-stove as the thin face of her husband was obtruded round the kitchen door. He raised his eyebrows.

"Well, how's the housewife?"

He came in and put his arms around her, negligently, to give the appearance of hiding from her his tenderness. This was part of the game that he played with her—played unceasingly, so that its repetition grated on Norah's nerves as a gramophone needle on the edge of a disc.

In the month since their marriage she had grown to loathe and fear him—to detest him with a fierceness undiscoverable before in her nature. It was to her as if she had married a man and awakened on her wedding morn to find herself mated to a pompous, fussy hermaphrodite.

Of that passion of his that had at first terrified, then fascinated her, of that madness she had glimpsed and feared and finally loved, no trace was left. This she knew, not thinking it out in so many words, but with a wider vagueness. Selfish though the first object of trapping Storman into marriage had been—the purpose of fathering her bastard unborn child upon him—yet there had been other reasons. She had, all unconsciously, sought in his eyes that light that never was on land or sea. She had sought Romance. And, as a draught a candle, so marriage seemed to have quenched that light.

"What's for dinner? Warmed up that meat? Good girl. Shall I help you carry it in?" He smelt at the gas-stove, appreciatively. "Rice pudding? That's fine."

He helped to carry the dinner into the sitting-room, then went back to close the kitchen door and put out the gas. In the hall he called to her.

"I see the hat-rack is loose. Remind me to-morrow to nail it up. I'll tackle those bathroom pipes at the same time."

Norah said nothing. Storman came into the room, looked at her, sat down, and pulled his chair close up to the table.

"You look seedy. Nothing wrong with you or the General is there?"

"I'm all right. Pass the mustard, will you?"

Every reference he made to her unborn child caused a strange griping in her stomach. He was to be a Communist, of course, this boy which she was to bear after her body had grown gross and ungainly. Of course, he was to be a boy—a Communist, a leader of hosts, a General in the Army of the Dawn. Only when speaking of him in these words would the old, mad light return to the eyes of Storman, his great bull-laugh boom out as of yore. Then he would ask to see the account-book of household expenses, check it up for Norah, and make suggestions for the next day's purchases.

He had from the beginning shown a passion for the flat and its meagre furniture, for mending and pottering and the setting to right of things. Every penny possible must be saved. But they were to stint themselves of nothing needful. For lunch he carried sandwiches and a thermos flask to the office, and on evenings would take Norah out for long walks, which were good for her and inexpensive. There was no need to waste money on bus-fares.

He looked round the room as he ate. "Comfortable, this. It's good to be home, my dear."

Looking up at him, seeing his eyes passing over her, Norah knew herself included amongst the things which pleased him and gave him comfort. That was what she was—something to keep things clean and inexpensively polished, something to take for cheap walks and back home again to suppers rehashed from rehashed dinners.

Storman lit his pipe. He had given up cigarettes. He stood up and walked slowly round the room, stopping opposite the bookcase to push in the volumes so that they stood side by side, evenly. Then he straightened a picture and walked over to the writing-desk. There he picked up the account-book.

"Christmas puddings and a cake? What are they for? Any-how, we're hardly likely to want more than one pudding, are we?"

He looked over the table at Norah. She was finishing her plate of rice. Now she pushed it back and stood up.

"Do you grudge me that as well? I know you grudge me everything else. Now it's food."

"You're hysterical, Norah. We've got to save every copper we can. Anyhow, come to think of it, the Christmas puddings will keep. No need for us to gorge to-morrow. We're beyond that superstition. What did the laundry bill come to?"

"Three and tuppence."

He noted down the amount and added columns of figures, put his initials at the foot of the column, neatly, placed the book and some papers in order, closed the desk. There fell a little silence, broken only by the sound of the rain outside. Even as it had sounded—surely so long ago!—on the night when she had told him she was to have a baby. Norah had turned her chair away from the table and had sat down in it again. She stared into the fire. Last Christmas Eve? Where? Oh, yes. Crowds and streamers. Dancing. Billy had been there. Dancing till midnight. . . . A pretty dress, I wore, Billy said.

"We'll wash up now, shall we?" said Storman.

Subchapter iii

A woman in the uniform of the Salvation Army halted opposite a congestion of traffic in the Strand. The rain sheeted down whitely in the glare of the arclights. Policemen waved white-banded arms. Buses purred and coughed and long cars, driven by sheltered, well-groomed chauffeurs, shook impatiently under the beating of their engines. Above and around, on the cliff-edges of the street, great lighted signs changed and moved and mounted and drooped, cataracting messages of fire above the hastening, thinning, yet never-ceasing streams of pedestrians. They scoured the dim night like searchlights, those changing signs, mostly unheeded and unnoticed, unless through the giant telescopes of packed crystals with which Martian astronomers view the earth. Uplifted to the skies, they cried the message of humanity to the blotted out stars:

> "KOMFY KINKLESS KORSETS.
> THEY BRACE AND EMBRACE!"

> "OLD HAG WHISKY.
> THE SPIRIT OF SCOTLAND."

> "SLYMPER'S RIGHTEOUS RAZOR BLADES.
> A NEAR SHAVE, A CLEAR SHAVE."

Standing under one of the arclights, the woman gazed mistily from the signs to the congested traffic. Then she rubbed her chin and peered from one to another of the packed and parked cars in front of her. On mission work, she was engaged in trying to detect signs of the white slave traffic. More than half-drunk, figures and faces knotted themselves confusingly before

157

her eyes. She had shortly before called a friendly policeman a snorting old bastard, and so left him profoundly moved and astonished. Meeting a Salvation Army captain out on the same errand as herself, she had grimaced in his face and passed him by without a word. Now, waiting and looking and following out her mission with a drunken tenacity, she wished for an ending of the rain, to which she attributed the uncertainty of her vision.

She had spent the afternoon in her basement room in the company of a Sergeant of Marines who had pulled her chin, called her Susie, and left her asleep without paying the final ten shillings agreed on. Awaking with a bad headache, she had gone in mufti to a wineshop near at hand and had bought a bottle of brandy. Then she had put on her uniform and sallied out into the streets. But frequently she would return to the brandy bottle in her room, for the cold was biting. Besides, she was lonely in her life in that basement room, nowadays. Listlessly she spent the days, giving herself to casual visitors or to her usual customers. Not one of them had kick or flap about them. By this she meant they lacked poetry. They brought their grave lusts to her body as swine bring hunger to a trough.

Whoosht! The policeman had taken a quarter turn, his arms still upraised like one crucified on an invisible cross, but in profile now. Over the greasy street-blocks, the traffic began to move forward with minute skidding of rubber wheels. Splashed by a swaying Daimler in its starting, the woman in the uniform of the Salvation Army uniform shook her fist at it. Thereat its occupant, a man, raised his eyes so that they looked into hers.

She stared at him with mouth agape. He was a man in the prime of life, dark, cleanly, aristocratic, in evening dress. His studs winked in the soft electric lighting of the interior of the Daimler. One white, carefully tended hand held a cigarette to his lips. Behind these his polished teeth shone even as his studs.

"Cripes! It's Andy!"

The car stopped, the door opened. Andreas van Koupa thrust out his perfect hat and head into the rain. He grinned and seized the hands of the prostitute.

"God mine, is it you? I had not thought to see your face again. Come in, you so-little fool, damn you!"

158

She entered in a daze. The chauffeur, equally in a daze, leant from his seat to close the door behind her. What was the little runt up to now? Salvation Army tart? What next? Whoa! Old bus damned quavery to-night. . . .

The Daimler snaked out through the traffic. The gorgeous Koupa smelt at the prostitute.

"Brandy. Dear Christ, it is good to smell the vileness of you again. It gives the zest to this that I have become."

She looked at him foggily.

"Blime! Where'd you pinch the togs, Andy? An this car? Aven't seen yew fer a month ef Sundays."

"You exaggerate, my little. Only since November. I have married now, you must hear. I have a wife. I have honey-mooned to Greece and eaten pork pies in the Acropolis and listened to the opinions of my life-mate on the probability of her having been Aspasia in a previous incarnation. She has clothed me and fed me, recognizing my genius. I am out of the so-infernal cold, and comfortable."

"Wadja want wiv me, then?"

He put his arm around her waist. "It was an impulse so sudden. I wanted once again to smell and touch the good gutter—akh God! to speak and listen to one who thinks nothing of my genius, one who walks the streets selling her body in honest prostitution, one whose brain-tracks are uncorroded by the slimy, wriggling bugs of the New Thought. So I had you brought in." He expanded his chest, peered at her, touched her, then put his handkerchief to his nose. "The so-authentic whiff of the little kennels!" He picked up a tube, murmuring something through it. They were now in Westminster. The car slowed down. "Now get out."

In some area of her brandy-drugged mind she discovered indignation. "Well, I likes thet. Oodja think yer playin wiv, jest because yer a bleedin swank? An a bloody pimp, too. . . . Tike me back to the Strand; I never asked yew ter let me in. W'ere'm I to go to now?"

He opened the door and with a twist of his arm propelled her out to the pavement. "To the devil, I should think." He chuckled without mirth. "A Merry Christmas, Magdalene!"

The chauffeur drove off. Some impulse made him peer back into the Daimler. . . . B'Gob! The bleedin little runt was sniffling!

Robert Gayford knelt in the Church of the Sacred Heart. A smell of cheap incense filled the air. Elderly worshippers sneezed at intervals. The organ boomed and the choristers uplifted young voices. It was the preliminary Christmas Eve service.

Sincerely devout, Robert crossed his breast many times. The church was crowded and he had had to kneel far back, beyond the ordinary pews, just inside the door and on the cold flags. His knees developed a frozen painfulness and he rocked upon them reproachfully, with his mind half-withdrawn from the sacred mysteries of his Faith to the need for warning tardy worshippers of his proximity to the entrance.

A priest chanted with uplifted arms, then turned his back and interceded with God, in a privy but courageous manner. This priest had a fine voice, strong in the service of the Church. At intervals he slipped on his tongue a pastille from a small tin box and, reinvigorated, resumed.

Spiritually uplifted, Gayford, in consequence of the pain at his knees, had fallen to a rhythmic swaying to and fro. Forgotten now were his lusts and frettings. His brain, soothed as with a soporific, comprehended only the goodness of God. By God! go to Mass oftener; live a clean life; perhaps become a priest.

A sudden cold draught of air smote upon the back of his neck, the door of the Church of the Sacred Heart creaked open, prayer-book leaves fluttered and someone, entering, tripped headlong over Gayford and, falling upon him, levelled him with the floor.

Neither priest nor worshippers took any notice. Their minds uplifted, as they had been exhorted to uplift them, to the contemplation of the mysterious pregnancy of a virgin—a pregnancy achieved by a mysterious visitation, warm and delicious to think of, however sacredly—they were engaged in a vast, echoing chant of affirmation and response. Gayford struggled sideways from under the being who had fallen on him. It was a woman. Kneeling upright again, as she too knelt, he looked into her face.

It was Ellen Ledgworth.

"I'm sorry," she whispered, placidly. Then: "Oh, it's you. Did I hurt you?"

"No," he whispered. Then: "Hush!" And he trebled out a response.

But, while he did so, he found his clasped hands were shaking. He had found her again at last.

He had never forgotten her since that walk to Edgware. Memory of her placidity, her wide hips, her cowlike gaze had troubled him innumerable times. Often he had hung round his mother's house, hoping to see her visit it again. But she had never come, and, on his once attempting to gain admittance, he had been flung out by the footman with the soft corn. That had been only a short time before the bloody old fool had gone and married that Dutch outsider.

And now he had found her again. In church. She was close to him. He had lain beneath her for a moment. She was warm. She did not wear much clothes. By God, he would not lose her again.

A placid piety had directed Ellen to the church. When the service was over, she walked out, Gayford accompanying her. Under the street-lamp she looked at him consideringly.

"You've grown older. You don't look very well."

"I've a horribly bad cold. . . . I've been looking for you everywhere ever since last Spring. Why did you never send me your address?"

She smiled at him, maddeningly placid. "Well, you see, I've always been so busy. Besides, I had a boy of my own, then."

"Haven't you one now?"

"Oh, no."

He was shaking. "Look here, I don't know your name but I like you awfully. Will you let me take you somewhere for supper?"

"Don't mind if I do have some supper," said Ellen. "I'm fearfully hungry."

Leading her to a restaurant, his thoughts blurred warmly. He would have a woman at last!

A Christmas Eve ghost of memory flitted through his mind.

Perhaps she was even a virgin.

Subchapter v

She was haunted by a phrase she had once heard, long before, in Scotland. "The sound of the rain on the roof when the kye come hame."

161

Homely—God, how homely. . . . She found herself remembering long-forgotten words of the good Scots, canty, lightsome words and jingles, things with old laughter and the smell of the peats and sea in them; darksome old words like clamjamfried and glaur and greep, words wrought for the bitter winter nights by the plodding peasants of the Eastern sea-coast. . . . A winter night like tonight.

"The sound of the rain on the roof when the kye come hame."

Oh, often she'd lain and heard it, happed in the muckle bed under the riggin, with the whisp-whisp of the falling rain on the roofs of Cairndhu. Just at the closing of night-time, when the brown beasts came oozing through the midden glaur, into the misty byre, her father driving them, her mother clanking the milk-cogs in the dairy, she herself warm and happit and in bed early because of the miles across the dripping fields she'd have to walk next morning to school. . . .

But this was London rain.

She sat in the darkness listening to it. The fire in the grate, unheaped the past two hours, had died down to a smouldering fluff of grey. In the coalbox there still remained two lumps and a packet of firewood. Daren't burn them to-night. Much better go to bed.

Fool. Cry if you stay in the darkness longer.

She rose from her chair, sought for the box of matches on the mantelshelf, and lit the gas. It flared up brightly, dazzling her eyes, till she found the regulator and switched it low. The room was now mantled in a yellow dimness. Gas too dear to waste. Besides, should be in bed at this time.

She looked at the table, where the tea-things were still as she had finished with them. Ought to have washed up. Oh, what does it matter? Besides, I'd have to go through the room of the Stickellys to the kitchen, and it's cold there. . . . And they stare at me, at my figure. Think they know I'm going to have a baby. . . . She's hardly spoken all day. . . . Oh, damn her, my dear, and go to bed.

A knock sounded at the door. Thea raised her head and called, "Come in."

It was Mrs. Stickelly. She wore a blouse of hard, glittering blue. She smiled doubtfully, looking at Thea with one eye, the while the other examined the contents of the bookcase.

"Eh-h-h. Mrs. Garland, Mr. Stickelly would like you to come along and speak to him."

"All right, Mrs. Stickelly."

She followed the woman along the passage, past the down-curving stairway. The door was held open for her. Mr. Stickelly was sitting with his collar off, his feet extended to a great glaze of fire. He had just finished a supper of tripe and onions.

"Sit down, Mrs. Garland." He spoke heavily, for his stomach was twinging. And, passing his hand over it, he thought with pessimism of the three new remedies he had tried during the last few weeks. He cleared his throat and thought. Thea sat on the edge of her chair, calm, unflushed. What was she going to do? Two months now since she had been forced to leave the office. She had nineteen shillings in her bag. The allowance from John just paid the rent and left a little over. She had lived on tea and bread and margarine since the beginning of the week. What was she to do?

For she knew what he was going to say—this unhealthy looking, dustmanlike person. He was going to tell her that she must leave because she was going to have a baby.

Looking at him, she felt curious and detached in a breath. What was the cause of the dirty yellow of his complexion? Wasn't Mrs. Stickelly kind to him? (Did men get like that when their wives were unkind to them?)

She almost giggled. Mr. Stickelly cleared the unnecessarily sticky phlegm from his throat.

"Im-m. Mrs. Garland, I want to ask you a question. You won't be offended? Mind, I don't like asking it, but it's my duty. You won't be offended?"

"I don't know. Perhaps you'd better ask it, Mr. Stickelly."

"Well, before I do, I want you first of all to know who I am. Who I am." He nodded his chin at her and she had the idea that probably a large, bleached frog would have a face like that. He meditated a little heavily. Then: "Who I am."

"Yes?"

"I'm a detective, a C.I.D. man."

Since ushering Thea into the room, Mrs. Stickelly had remained standing. Now, smiling doubtfully, with one eye fixed on her husband and the other on the wireless receiving apparatus, she nodded confirmation. Mr. Stickelly pondered, then nodded again, as at a sudden thought. "Yes."

"I see, Mr. Stickelly. Well, what's the question you want to ask me?"

"Ah, yes, that's just it, Mrs. Garland. About three weeks ago you had two visitors—a man and a woman. Was the man James Storman, the Communist?"

Thea stared her surprise. Was that the question? She nodded.

"Yes, he was. Why?"

"Well, I'm very sorry to lose you, Mrs. Garland, to lose you, and so is Mrs. Stickelly. But I'm acting under orders from Headquarters. I can't harbour under my roof a Communist or a friend of Communists." He stared at her, his brows wrinkling in thought. "No."

"But—I'm not a Communist. What have I to do with Mr. Storman's politics? He's just an acquaintance of mine."

"I'm very sorry, but I can't have you here after the end of next week. Orders from Headquarters. Orders from Headquarters." He slowly looked aside at Mrs. Stickelly, then nodded, as if he had forgotten something. "Yes." Then he looked again at Thea, the while he slowly creaked his memory back to the talk the chief had had with him at lunch-time.

It had been a disturbing talk. The notorious Storman, expensively shadowed, as usual, had been followed and seen to enter Mr. Stickelly's house. The shadower had hung around and ascertained that Storman was not, however, visiting the Stickellys in connection with some Soviet plot, but was calling on the lodger. Promptly he had reported this to Headquarters and several investigators had at once been detailed to hunt down all that was known of Thea Garland. This was not much, but to the police mind the fact of her having once lived in the same flat as the present Mrs. Storman was proof additional and conclusive. Submitting reports to their departmental head, the detectives had simultaneously sent in their expenses accounts to the pay section. For a little over £50 they had succeeded in finding out that Thea Garland had once lived with Norah Storman.

The chief, examining their reports, had thought it worth while to lay them before a high Government official. By the latter it had been suggested that Stickelly himself might be a Communist agent, engaged in selling secrets to the Soviets. Stickelly's desk had accordingly been searched during one of his absences, without, however, anything more damning being found in it than a packet of picture postcards showing French prostitutes lying nude and in amorous attitudes, and a bottle of stomach-stirring acid. This, combined with the fact that he had a record of good and unimaginative service during the past twenty years, and further, that as he worked in a subdepartment unconcerned with affairs of international importance, saved Stickelly. Next day, in the lunch-hour, he was summoned into the office of the chief and told of the facts of the case. After the third telling he had absorbed them and, deeply shocked, had promised to have the woman Garland put out of his house.

These things he did not explain to Thea. Looking at her glassily, he wondered with a slow hunger at her good looks and the flush on her cheeks. Very slowly revolving the idea, he came to the conclusion that, undressed, she would be singularly like the French women in the postcards. Yes.

Which Mrs. Stickelly was decidedly not.

"So, Mrs. Garland, I'm afraid you'll have to leave at the end of next week."

"But—oh, very well." Thea stood up. With that singular tightening round her head, she could not argue. "Is that all?"

Mr. Stickelly looked at Mrs. Stickelly, smiling doubtfully, with one eye slowly veering from the wireless set to the coalbox and the other as slowly changing focus from the chair on which Thea had sat to the door at which she now stood. He nodded. "Yes. That's all. Yes."

"Good night."

She let herself out into the dark passage. A chill gust of wind slammed the door behind her. Standing in the draught she experienced a pleasure in its freezing touch. She could feel it drying the perspiration on her neck and breast. She groped for the door-handle of her own room, let herself in, and carefully closed the door behind her lest it, too, should bang.

The fire was quite dead.

She stood and stared at it in the dim, yellow light. Doing so, the belt of pain surrounding the patch of clearness, of unnatural

165

brightness, nestling in the centre of her brain, suddenly snapped. It broke and sprayed red-hot fragments across her mind.

She was to be turned out—not because of the baby that was coming, but because of Communism. Communism! She was to be turned out? Where?

"My God, girl, where? Where are you to go? You've no money—not sufficient to last the week and pay for moving. John's allowance doesn't come for another fortnight. What to do? What . . .

"Oh, God, be quiet. Be quiet. . . . You can't get work anywhere. You'd faint again. No one to take you in. Quiet. Don't, don't, you damned fool. Don't scream. Keep quiet, quiet. . . ."

Suddenly she gave a low cry, putting her hand out against the table and steadying herself. Within her body was a slow movement, infinitely intent and appalling. She put her hand to her side, and, beneath the hand, felt a rounded shape laboriously curve out and then flatten.

A sudden sweet dizziness shook her. Her lips strained apart into a smile that creased her face hideously.

"Merry Christmas, baby!"

Subchapter vi

It was Christmas Eve in Bethlehem.

All afternoon and evening pilgrims and visitors had been arriving at the little hillside town. The Pope's representative had arrived. Representatives from all Catholic countries had arrived. Many Americans had arrived, smoking cheroots and talking phrases out of Mr. Sinclair Lewis's latest novel. This was one of their obsessions. They believed that foreigners demanded in Americans idiosyncrasies according to the novelists. For this reason they wore horn-rimmed glasses and said Gee, uncertainly. They apostrophized the Mountains of Moab with many Gees, contemptuous and profane, but the Church of the Nativity they Geed reverently. In intervals they tramped through unsavoury reaches of muddy bazaar and odoriferous culs-de-sac, where small tobacconist's dukanin sold Gold Flake and Lucky Strike cigarettes, and itinerant vendors of toilet necessities ran after them, crying on them to buy Jibbs's toothpaste and Jillette razors.

166

Scores of peasants, folk from the Balkans and South Europe generally, had walked from Jerusalem. Undeterred by street vendors, they tramped through muddy lanes and kennels to the Church of the Nativity. Most of them were accompanied by their wives. An occasional priest marshalled and commanded them, separated them when they fought or beat their wives, and compelled them, when possible, to give up stray articles which they appropriated from stalls and fields on their pilgrimage. Simple, pious, the pilgrims had set out to visit the birthplace of the Saviour in order for ever after to boast of the achievement to their neighbours, to have their warts cured, to view with sacred interest the actual stone whereon the Holy Mother had been delivered of the Bambino, and to have their souls cleansed in the mercy of the compassionate saints.

And, chanting, they trampled on one another as they forced a way into the Church of the Nativity.

The rain, which had held off for the last hour or so, now began to fall again, straight downpouring, even, indifferent rain. A lorry containing eight aircraftmen had come from the Air Force wireless station at Jerusalem. It stood deserted in a back-street, for an elderly Copt in an opposing stall had promised to keep ze leedle eye on it, oh, yes, the while the Inglizi zoljers kissed the couch of Oily Virgin, yes?

"Oily Virgin be damned," said the driver of the lorry. "I'll give you a couple of piastres when I come back—if I find everything right. If I don't, I'll twist your black neck. . . . Look here, sport, where are the wazzas?"

He was directed to the wazzas. In groups the aircraftmen tramped away. Three of them went to the Church of the Nativity. One, who had drunk too much arrack before leaving Jerusalem, entered into an argument with a Pimp—a member of the Palestine Military Police, so called from the initials on his shoulders—and was knocked down in the gutter, where he lay temporarily forgotten and forgetting. Four went on and hunted out the wazzas and indignant matrons to stir girls to effort even on a night like this—blood of the virgin, these English were virile men!—and prepare for trade. Holding in their arms brown, apathetic prostitutes, the aircraftmen called to each other through partitions, asking to be awakened in order that they might not miss the midnight Mass in the Church of the Nativity.

The eighth member of the party did not at first walk forward into the village. Instead, he held back along the track covered by the lorry till he came out on the high shoulder of the hill whereon is Bethlehem built. There, he looked down and across a frowsy dimness of landscape—bleak, half-desert landscape, with the rain descending upon it in a windless extasy. Far away below, and on the horizon, against remote granitic ranges, gleamed an occasional light. Back in Bethlehem a starving pariah puppy was wailing in the wetness.

"The chances are a hundred to one that it rained just in this fashion nineteen hundred and twenty-nine years ago," said Garland.

He had been posted from Heliopolis to Jerusalem a month before, as clerk attached to the wireless station. With a typewriter once more available, he had worked ceaselessly on the revision of his novel. Of Jerusalem or the surrounding country he had so far seen little. This was his first excursion to Bethlehem, and it he had taken to verify details for a final chapter of his novel.

His hero also had visited Bethlehem on Christmas Eve.

A curious melancholy always came upon him, and amused him, looking over rain-drenched lands. Nineteen hundred and twenty-nine years ago—but wasn't there some fault in Bible chronology? Christ had really been born three years before the first Christmas. So, nineteen hundred and thirty-two years ago. . . .

What was Thea doing in Shepherd's Bush?

With a misty detachment, as though his mind had borrowed a garment from the landscape, he thought of her. Adorable Thea of the wine-red hair and wine-sweet body. Thea.

And in memory he recalled the delightfulness of that body of hers, the touch and sight of her skin, the curve of her bare shoulders and straight back, slim waist. (Almost with his two hands had he been able to span that waist of hers.) Thea. Thea Garland. (By the Lord!)

He forgot alike the rain and the landscape of Moab, for this thought that Thea was Thea Garland pleasured him. Only a few months before such realization of dreams would have been banished to the remoteness of the future. Why, but for . . ..

His pleasurable mist of thoughts cleared suddenly, leaving a

168

black space across which a question wrote itself in letters of red pain:

My God, what was happening to Thea?

Alone in that house, in that stinking little road. Alone. What's happening to her? You swine, you useless swine, what's happening to her?

And, held in a sudden agony, for he had received no letter from her for over three weeks, he turned back towards Bethlehem and fumbled for a cigarette, and lit it. Doing so, his thoughts sought to readjust themselves in comfort. . . . She must be all right. Still has her job, perhaps. Besides, she can always write to her people in Scotland if the worst comes to the worst. And those other girls in the flat, they'd stand a loan— only a temporary loan, wherever she gets it. Damn it, she's healthy and strong. Your novel's practically finished. If you send it off at the end of the week, you ought to have an acceptance for Spring publication. Perhaps fifty down and at least ten per cent. And fifty pounds'll pay for almost everything. . . .

He became conscious of music and subdued chanting. Before him was the Church of the Nativity, lighted and looming, a frenzy of architecture. The words of the subdued chant seemed to fit ill with the music. Standing by a little chapel, he stopped and strained his ears to listen. Then he saw, in the mirk, that three of the other aircraftmen were also standing near. They greeted him mirthfully.

"Ello, where in the ell 've you bin? . . . Sly bird! Pokin round the wazzas, I'll bet. Married man, too. They're always the worst. . . . Shh. Listen. 've missed the best of it, unless it happens again in the service."

"Missed what?" asked Garland.

They explained to him. In the church nearby a service was bein eld by the Greeks—some dago crowd that said Christmas wasn't at Christmas but a fortnight later. So they'd learned from an old bloke who spoke quite good English and said he was a Greek priest. . . . Them Greeks, seems, oldin a service just friendly-like with the real Christians. The old bloke extended invitations to see it. 'd gone in, found the place crowded and been forced to stay away at the rear, near the door. After a lot o marchin and formin fours, the igh cockalorum of the show ad mounted a platform and sung out—Godstreuth, e ad! . . ..

"I saw im first!"

And at that all the other dagoes ad flopped down on their knees and yelled:

"You're a liar!"

After the tenth chanted repetition of affirmation and denial, the three aircraftmen had crept out and exploded in the open air. But it appeared that, fascinated, hardly able to believe in the goodness of the joke, they still hung around the chapel, waiting for the chant to recur.

"Guess wot it is, y'know, some English bloke's made up the service for them and kidded them for a joke. Put in them words and told the dagoes they were real, honest-to-god prayer words."

"Shouldn't wonder," said Garland.

They stood listening in the rain, but the chant was not repeated. Damp and hilarious, they tramped round to the main entrance of the Nativity Church. Aside from this a long queue was slowly moving into a narrow opening and down steep stairs. Garland the last of them, the aircraftmen joined the queue.

The head of the queue vanished down the hole in the earth, like a black snake. Carried forward in its body, Garland and the others stumbled down steep steps into a dim, gigantic cellar. In front the queue of pilgrims wound past an open ledge, and, as each pilgrim came opposite this ledge, he fell on his knees and kissed it. It was the ledge whereon Christ had lain when adored by the wise men and the kings.

"Gawd'slife! what a guff!"

The air was sickening. Sweat-exuding and unwashed, the pilgrims swopped diseases on the stone where Christ had lain, and then, passing on and up into the rain, ate onions and pieces of bread which they drew from their garments, and commented on the Holy Birth shrewdly, agriculturally, wondering if the beasts down in the stable had been disturbed by the Virgin's screams, and how such beasts had ever been driven up and down the staircase daily. Debating this latter point, they were satisfied that such problem of live-stock transport must have been solved by a daily miracle wrought by the saints for the glorification of God and the Blessed Mother.

Garland turned away from the other aircraftmen and joined the upward-winding queue. Presently he was in the Church of the Nativity, passing through a dank corridor into a garish hall-space. This latter was decorated with paintings. Beneath these gilded inscriptions recorded the sayings of the Aramaic prophet in the language of the judges who had crucified him as a disturbing vagrant. In giant stained windows the Christ bore the Cross, supported by scores of volunteers, allegorical, terrestrial and celestial. But mostly he sat in strange attitudes on the knees of innumerable Virgins. These, proud and cold, disregarding the plaudits of the surrounding angels, stared stonily and forbiddingly across the great hall-space.

Great candelabra glowed their lights. An altar shone red with gold and jewelwork. Around it massed priests for the coming service. Gorgeously clad, they scratched themselves through their thick robes and, in a far corner, laughed over a funny story related by a visitor. Plump, smooth men, they believed in the divinity of the Christ, the efficacy of prayers to the saints and the remission of sins obtained by eating the body of the dead god and drinking his blood. Anti-Semites, they denounced the Balfour Promise and the efforts of American missionaries to upset the faith of the native Muslim population.

And Garland thought:

"It is extremely improbable that Christ ever existed. Most of his so-called sayings are second-hand, rehashes of the voiced altruism of long millennia. Even if he did live, he appears to have been only an illiterate agitator, drunk with a certain power of words and suffering from an inferiority complex which led him on occasion to denounce the well-to-do, and on other occasions to proclaim himself their superior, a king, and divine. He betrayed the mazed shiftlessness of the poet without education and without anything of any real importance to say. He was a Judean Bernard Shaw, seeking startling effects by denouncing his mother and family, asserting the equality of prostitutes, cursing where others blessed. All in order to surprise people. Probably he watched them askance, out of the corners of his eyes, to see how they took it. And throughout he was consumed with a vague anger and jealousy, especially regarding his birth, for his mother, Miriam, was notoriously free of her body, and the chances are ten to one that he was fathered from her by some Greek or Roman legionary. Reminder

171

of this probability constantly vexed him, and, aware that he possessed an intelligence above that of the dark-brained peasants and artisans amongst whom he moved, he convinced himself that his origin must really have been through the agency of an impalpable, divine spermatozoon—rather than from the lust-hungry bedding of Miriam with some unsavoury foreign mercenary.

"His life was an insane, planless failure. But, like most agitators loud-mouthed enough, and inconsistent enough to occasionally turn and attack those whom he ordinarily defended, he left behind him a memory of angry simplicity and kindliness which took by storm the slave populations of the Roman world. He appealed to the brainless proletariat as never had prophet appealed before. He offered freedom and comfort and full stomachs in the next world in exchange for suffering and stripes in this. To an audience accustomed to suffering and stripes, but unaccustomed to the promise, his appeal was irresistible. He offered something for nothing. That is still mainly his appeal.

"All over the world in the beginning of his era—the world of the Roman Empire, at least—religions and priesthoods were falling into decay. Children in the streets threw mud at solemn processions of priests. The gods had become conventions to the educated, just as atoms and electrons are conventions, with no real existence, to the modern chemist. Even the slaves, the freedmen, the serf-agriculturists sportively piled manure and excrement in front of the ancient shrines. It was the dawn of a universal disbelief in gods, a going out into the cold air and frozen spaces of atheism. Men were awakening from the fatuous dreams of the savage-barbarian. But, as ever before an awakening, their dawn-sleep was being troubled by innumerable nightmares. Multitudes of fake religions were springing up and dying amidst indifference and laughter. Mithras sacrificed insanely, imported Sivas devoured improbable universes, the heavy Isis mooned through Egyptian mummeries in a blasé Rome. It was the dawn of reason through the wrack of nightmare. Men were prepared for a world without gods. It was the dawn of hope.

"And then the idea of Christ came to the Western world and wiped reason from the slate.

"He appealed as did none of the gods of the other freak religions—first to the common herd, because he voiced their woes, secondly to the quick-minded of the old sacrificial priesthoods, because in him they saw their salvation. For, as a god, there was nothing new or fundamentally dangerous in him. Instead, he possessed a great asset never before held by any other god of the Western world—he appealed to the populace both as a god and as a man.

"And the twisted memory of this crucified, muddle-minded agitator had ever since lain across the centuries like a black shadow."

A great burst of music pealed out. The crowds inside the hall-space grew thicker. Garland was forced back against a wall. It was the entry of the Papal delegate.

And, suddenly, thunderous and sweet upon the air, clanged the bells of midnight.

It was Christmas Day.

Subchapter Retrospective

He had hung senseless only four short hours. Now it was nearly midnight. The dark air seemed to wind in stifling swathes up the long hillslopes. Casual sightseers lingered in gossip. A soldier rubbed the blade of his spear with a handful of sand, and, looking across the hill to the lights of Jerusalem, thought grumblingly of this his extra watch and the warm couch of the little Ionian slave at the prefect's house.

A dog howled.

Suddenly, in the darkness, the dim brown form of the dying malefactor, Jesus, twisted and bulged against its cross. From his lips came a moan, a shriek of gibberish:

"ELOI ELOI LAMA SABACHTHANI?"

His attention a moment attracted, the soldier looked up. The brown body had ceased to twist. The soldier laughed, indifferently, and flung his handful of sand, soft-swishing, into the night.

173

CHAPTER THE TENTH

Wherein a Long-neglected Character repairs a Longstanding Neglect, and Divers Other Happenings, of an Import to strain even the Happy and Able Invention of the Subchapter, are recorded.

Subchapter Interlude

ON the morning of the second of February Mrs. Streseman Mullins, of Cocotte Sœurs, sat in her private office. Under the powder her face was an unhealthy pinkish-yellow verging on gamboge. All night she had writhed in the agonies of pyorrhea and only by an effort was she able to concentrate on the work of her establishment. Presently she rang a bell and asked for Miss Ledgworth to be sent up to her.

Ellen had been rapidly promoted during the past two months. Before the previous Christmas she had shown no ability whatsoever outside routine matters, but, in the week leading up to the New Year, the entire staff had noted a change in her appearance and habits that amazed and stupefied. Placid as ever, she showed a vigour and initiative hitherto entirely absent from her efforts at salary-earning. One morning she summoned the manager and displayed for his inspection two models constructed by herself—each model with a twist of distinction and distinctiveness. The manager promptly reported the matter and showed the models to Mrs. Streseman Mullins. Gazing up into his face, the proprietrix of Cocotte Sœurs, her breath unpleasant from her chronic complaint, had discussed the matter and then, with a sigh, had allowed him to return to his duties. As a result, Ellen's models had been sold for twenty-five guineas each and she herself had been promoted to chief assistant in the designing-room, at a salary increased by ten shillings a week.

There, by all precedents, the matter should have ended. But

it did not. In the designing department Ellen daily worked miracles of draughtmanship and design. She blossomed forth fresh creations as the earth new life in Spring. She became a power with whom the staff reckoned. Finally, after the visit of a Royal patron who had a design in her mind which she was completely incapable of putting into practical being, Ellen was placed in charge of the designing-room. In a placid ten minutes' interview with the Royal patron she safely and brilliantly performed the surgical operation of extracting the idea, improving upon it and swamping the Royal patron under a thaumaturgic display of fabric-twisting. Within a space of six weeks she had made a reputation seldom achieved within a like number of years.

"You sent for me, madame?"

Surveyed by Mrs. Streseman Mullins, Ellen, placid, respectful, stood in the doorway. The proprietrix nodded to a chair.

"Yes. Sit down, Miss Ledgworth."

Ellen sat down and the light from the window fell full upon her face. It had undergone as marvellous a transformation as had apparently the creative powers of her mind. The cowlike expression had disappeared in a soft, yet strong, placidity. Her lips had reddened and now jutted out in a wide, sweet pout. Warm brown lights flickered in her eyes. Her figure, once compact and uninteresting, had acquired mysteriously a charm. The broad hips, swaying as she walked, were seductive and adorable; her breasts, flattened though they were in the prevailing mode, yet jutted forth a projection of each nipple beneath her jumper in a fashion that caused the sales-manager, fresh from a too-close interview with Mrs. Streseman Mullins, and forgetful of his passion to reform the Empire, to move warm fingers across a tingling palm.

"Whatever's happened to change you so, Miss Ledgworth?"

The question was wrung in sheer amazement from Mrs. Streseman Mullins's painted lips. As a rule she paid little heed to her staff, beyond seeing that they were properly dressed, were respectful to customers and the sales-manager, and washed low down the backs of their necks. This last she ascertained in frequent inspections of the work-rooms, gliding behind each girl's chair and acquiring information at first hand. But Ellen, not only by her elevation to control of the

176

designing department and her entitlement to the address of Miss, but by her changed physical appearance, had ceased, in the eyes of Mrs. Streseman Mullins, to be non-human, an employee, and suffered an anthropophuistic change.

Ellen showed no surprise at the question. It had been asked her, in varying degrees of intimacy and familiarity, too often of late. She regarded her employer with a shrewd placidity. A considering, pitying light came in her eyes.

"Change? Oh, there's been some alteration in my private life, madame. Perhaps it's done me good."

"Really?" Temporarily forgetting her affliction, or the reason for which she had originally summoned the head of her designing department, Mrs. Streseman Mullins stared at Ellen, rudely, undisguisedly, woman to woman. Ellen nodded, placidly.

"I have a lover, madame."

"You are engaged?"

Ellen shook her head. Sitting in comfort, she crossed her ankles.

"No, madame. I have no intention of marrying."

"Then . . . I don't understand." Mrs. Streseman Mullins gradually sat erect. "You mean, Miss Ledgworth . . .?"

Ellen elucidated further, placidly. "I have a lover, madame. I sleep with him, sometimes."

Mrs. Streseman Mullins gasped an expulsion of air which shot a fresh twinge of pain down each tooth.

Ellen spoke the truth. She had Robert Gayford for a lover. Since Christmas Eve they had frequently met by arrangement, and, a fortnight after falling over him in the Church of the Sacred Heart, she had allowed him to seduce her. Lonely herself, and filled with a placid maternal pity, she had on the afternoon of this occurrence refused his offer of marriage. He had thereon burst into tears of baffled desire and sex-cowardice. Ellen had looked at him, taken him home to his flat, and then, after taking due precautions, had, with a placid tenderness, allowed him to satisfy his long-thwarted virility.

The effect had been startling. The happening had horrified and abased Gayford; Ellen it had stirred and amazed and transformed. Her body, long awaiting the purpose of its design, sprang to a life that at first placidly shocked its owner.

177

Her mind reacted similarly. She was as one, long healthily asleep, awakened violently but pleasurably. In Gayford's embraces she discovered an ardour which staggered and terrified him. Then she would dress, placidly, and make coffee and saunter through his flat, searching among his books and borrowing copies of Phillips Oppenheim. Twice or thrice a week she went to his rooms, a white-bodied goddess, blossoming the more each time into womanhood and an ample, thrilling seductiveness. Placidly drowsy and contented, she would then walk home along the Embankment, refusing her lover's escort. Her womanhood discovered required meditation.

But meantime Robert Gayford, who had before held out the allure of marriage in order to trap her, now pressed it upon her because he was physically afraid of her and desired, completely possessing her, to be at liberty to possess her, yet not compelled to. For her strength and exhaustless energies terrified him, and, an unaccomplished lover who had imagined that Nature would teach him the way in all such matters, or that he would know by instinct, he was aghast to discover that it was an art that could apparently be acquired only painfully and with suffering. Further, he desired marriage because the consciousness of his sin weighed upon him as a good Catholic.

Meantime his uncle, looking up from Gibbon on his nephew's rare visits, wondered at the boy's thin face and undrained complexion, and, immersing himself in the footnotes on Zozimus, thought:

"Young skunk shows the bad blood of his mother. No guts. He wants a woman."

And he would glance up with contempt and aversion at the lounging Robert, listlessly recovering from the embraces of Ellen.

For a little, after hearing Ellen's placid disclosure, Mrs. Streseman Mullins sat with open mouth and fishlike eyes. Then, closing her mouth, she stood up and pointed coldly and uneasily at the door.

"Go out. You are discharged. Leave the building at once." She sat down, exhausted, scared. "The impudence of it! To tell me that you are a . . . .. Go at once."

Ellen arose unhurriedly. "Very well, madame. I merely answered the question you asked me. And I don't mind being discharged.

René Freres have already offered me double what I'm getting here. I thought of leaving at the end of the week, anyway."

"René Freres? Do you think they'll employ you when they know what your private life is? And I shall certainly make it my duty to inform them."

"Why shouldn't they? My private life's nothing to do with my work—except that recently it's improved it. And even if René Freres cancel their offer because of anything that you may tell them, I can find money to start on a business of my own." The ex-saleshand was placidly conscious of power. "I can make and sell better hats than anyone in London. My reputation won't worry customers. It'll help."

She left the room, her wide hips moving gracefully. Mrs. Streseman Mullins sat and looked at the door. Then she rang the bell again.

"Send Miss Ledgworth to me."

In a short time the door opened and Ellen reappeared. Mrs. Streseman Mullins spoke harshly, averting her eyes.

"Miss Ledgworth, I have reconsidered your case. If you will give your solemn promise to abandon the kind of life you have lately lived, I will withdraw your notice of discharge and say nothing more about your . . . revelation."

Ellen's brown, attractive eyes regarded her unwinkingly. "You mean give up my lover, madame? No. Why should I?"

Then she saw that Mrs. Streseman Mullins was amazed, almost frightened. "Then why did you tell me about—your lover? You do not tell everyone, do you?"

"No. I told you because you yourself want a lover. You're the same as I myself was before. . . . And, of course, you've been married, which makes it worse." She regarded the proprietrix with an energetic placidity. "Why don't you have your teeth seen to and stop powdering? You've ever such a nice face beneath that covering. . . . Madame, I'm sorry."

For the proprietrix of Cocotte Sœurs, her arms outspread upon the desk, was weeping noisily, flourily, scaredly.

Subchapter Interlude (continued)

A week later Mrs. Streseman Mullins, who had been absent from the millinery establishment owing to indisposition, appeared in her private office at nine o'clock in the morning. Her appearance electrified the staff. Her face was white and smooth and creamy, and appeared to have disdained the aid of powder; her mouth, when she spoke to the sales-manager as he brought in her letters, exuded a normal breath. Shaken out of his thoughts of Signor Mussolini and the Empire, the sales-manager almost dropped the sheaf of correspondence. Mrs. Streseman Mullins smiled at him, thereby disclosing an uneven gap, here and there, amidst her teeth.

"I'll attend to the letters later. Send in Miss Ledgworth, will you?"

When Ellen came in she gave a start of placid astonishment. Mrs. Streseman Mullins smiled at her, warmly, friendliwise.

"I'd have never had the courage to go to the dentist if you hadn't come with me."

The following Friday both Ellen and the sales-manager found two weeks' pay in their envelopes. Served out to them with those envelopes were type-written notifications that they were discharged from the service of Cocotte Sœurs without further notice.

Subchapter i

Storman was on the revolutionary tramp.

He had left London on a Wednesday, spoken at Plymouth the evening of that day, gone on to Bristol on the Thursday, addressed two meetings there, and, on the Friday afternoon when Ellen and the sales-manager were notified of their discharge, was scheduled to address a meeting of the South Wales Anarchocommunist Group.

The evening broke in sleet, but cleared by seven o'clock, when the meeting opened in the Masonic Hall. Storman arrived late, climbed to the platform, and sat listening to the chairman and surveying the audience.

Looking down so, he shivered, for it was draughty. Further, it was as though he looked from the ledge of a hunter's pit upon a collection of trapped, unclean animals, and knew that, but for care, he himself might lose foothold and fall into that festering no-life.

Dark, Welsh, excitable, miners crowded the hall. The stains

of coal-dust still lingered where the hair encroached on fore-head and neck. Finger-nails showed their black serrations against clenched fists. And a smell, a pit-reek, pervaded all the hall. Through this the miners peered and talked, energetically, in a cheechee swoop and fall of conversation. They were men brawny, eager, cowed and devout. Their eyes showed red rims and their teeth, yellow and unhealthy, gleamed in the reveal-ment of loud guffaws.

The meeting opened with a hymn in Welsh. The chairman stood up, Storman stood up. While the singing held, Storman mused. These folk he, a Leninist, should regard as mere instru-ments; once he would have so regarded them. But now he found himself looking upon them as badgered, beaten sub-humans, morlocks of the pits, each with a striving, pitiful, hopeless, individual existence. . . . Leninistic instruments? For what?

The closeness of the hall gave him a headache. Standing, his mind turned with relief to thought of his flat in Peckham. Was Norah being extravagant? And he thought carefully over the question of refurnishing the bedroom, of curtailing his own expenses during the tour, of negotiating an increase of salary from the Plenary Committee of the Party. Smoking he must cut out altogether.

He found the hymn finished. Sharp, on his mettle, he stood up to speak.

"Comrades, the Government is on its last legs."

This was a good opening, but, saying it, he knew that he lied. A year ago he would not have known this. Or would it merely have been that he would not have troubled to remind himself that he knew? The legs of the Government, though rheumaticky, were stout enough. Nothing would transpire to upset it. Like a dirtbug, it squatted athwart all England, and so would continue to squat. He was mouthing revolutionary bunkum, proletarian pap.

Behind his mind this causal commentary kept on during his speech. As a result, he was uninteresting. Speedily he lost grip of the audience. The miners' attention wandered. Groups began to converse in low tones. Presently many pipes were lit. The smoke grew thick. The hall became blue-hazed as an August moor.

When Storman finished, there was a low, half-hearted clapping. He had said nothing but what was new and startling. But he had not said it so that it could be believed. He had hardly finished when up from beside him rose the secretary of the local Minority Movement. He smelt of the pit. His accent was the volplaning whine of his country. He recounted an obscene jest in which a local coalowner was the butt. He spoke of Jesus, Buddha, St. David, Spartacus and Karl Marx as early Communists. He entered into questions of pay, shifts, coal seams.

The meeting awoke. It cheered and yelled encouragement and reminders of omitted details. The speaker accepted and absorbed the reminders. Remote, at the back of the hall, a policeman, a Londoner, stood large and contemptuous and faintly amused. Tears streamed down the speaker's cheeks.

"And, py God, when we fight next time, we fight to a finish! There'll pe no Paldwin, no landlords, no ploody coalowners left. Only the People. And we'll take what's ours, what we've made, what we've been ropped of through the centuries, and use it for ourselves alone. 'From each according to his apility, to each according to his needs.' Py God, we'll rememper that when we're on top. We'll rememper then what the capitalists thought were our needs. When the fatgutted swine work their share in the pits and their lily-fingered whores are wheeling parrows on the surface, we'll rememper. . . . We'll organize a decent State, where every man shall have justice and chance for self-improvement, where in time there shall pe no more weeping, neither shall there pe any tears, as the first Communist, Jesus of Nazareth, prophesied. . . . "

The meeting cheered, leapt to hobnailed bootsoles, swung, in a hysteric extasy of fine Welsh voices, into the chorus of the Internationale.

Across the swelling wave of song, from the rear of the hall to the platform, the eyes of the only two men left unstirred met in a glance of ironic amusement.

Subchapter ii

The annual musketry practice in the Palestine Command was being fired at Bir Salem, and the Air Force detachment at

182

Jerusalem was being sent down in relays of three to take part in it.

The ranges were in high bluffs beyond a creek. Already the sunshine was broiling in the plains about Ludd and Bir Salem. Each sunrise the fetid creeks shrouded themselves in malarial fogs, wherethrough unceasingly came the chorus of the frogs. Then these sounds would still as the first pappatapappat of firing broke out from the ranges.

Kneeling, standing, lying, the aircraftmen fired only a restricted table. Crouching in a trench below the butts, but in front of them, markers noted and signalled results. Each marker possessed a pole surmounted with a coloured disc. At the end of each round of firing he would cautiously elevate this pole, rotate it in various positions to apprise the rifleman of the species of hits made, and then withdraw again into shelter. Occasionally the poles would rapidly describe arcs against the skyline. Then the instructor would curse the rifleman concerned as clumsy bastard. For an arc indicated a complete miss.

Behind the riflemen each day, as the sun increased in strength, a native vendor of cooling drinks would approach with large, coloured bottles set about his person on an arrangement of trays. He had a brown, dried face, like that of a well-preserved mummy. He believed all English infidels would one day burn in hell, and have no cooling drinks provided. Walking behind a kneeling rifleman, he would interrupt a long and steady aim with his constant cry:

"Dringgs. Leemonade. Nice and cool. Lovely."

The last word he pronounced lovilly. Waddling uncertainly behind the belching rifles, under the burn of the sun, out over the sands to the pools of the quietened frogs, his voice would echo, plaintive, unceasing, a monosong:

"Lovilly."

In the second week of February John Garland came on the ranges. He had descended from Jerusalem by railway, together with two other aircraftmen. They were lodged the night in a hut and the following morning marched out to the ranges in a squad under a sergeant who held the M.C., had been an officer in the Canadian army, and was saving up money to buy himself out of the Air Force and purchase a garage in Jaffa. A pleasant man, he

183

was a convinced internationalist. Reading Mr. H. G. Wells, he believed in the Open Conspiracy of scientists and business men to seize control of the world which they already controlled. He hoped they would succeed in wresting power from themselves. His squad he regarded as being trained in murder.

As the party marched to the ranges, he walked by Garland and talked to him, for Garland's voice had seemed more cultured than that of the average aircraftman, who split infinitives and dropped aitches as regularly as he broke the Ten Commandments. Looking round the ranges as they approached, Garland answered the sergeant absently.

"But for the scientists, sergeant, you wouldn't have your present job. Fourteen million wouldn't have been killed or disabled in the late War. You wouldn't have your M.C. or I my D.C.M. The dream of salvation by science is on a par with the dream of salvation by incantation."

The rest of the squad, listening to Garland and the sergeant, guffawed, and remarked amongst themselves that this Garland must be a religious bloke.

Ten of them detailed to fire, and two to act as markers in the butts during the first practice, the squad under the command of the scientific sergeant took up a position at ten o'clock. Of the markers selected Garland found himself one. The firing opened. It came raggedly. Some of the aircraftmen poised long upon their triggers, some fired quickly, trusting to God. The markers, crouched in the trenches, listened to the whippoot-whippoot of the bullets overhead. Then, on the firing ceasing at the end of a round, they noted the results on each target, and, uplifting their poles above the trench parapet, signalled the results.

Occasionally a ricochet bullet would hum backwards towards the trench, always burying itself in the second bank of sandbags just below each target. At such occurrence the other aircraftman would throw himself flat on his face, cursing. Standing upright, Garland would look at the punctured sandbag meditatively.

Once, when a round had ceased and the other marker was signalling results over the parapet, he glanced at the religious bloke. His back resting against the trench-wall, Garland was reading a soiled letter.

"Oi, wike up, chiner. The bleedin instructor'll be after you."

"Go to hell," said Garland. He folded the letter and put it in his pocket. An afterthought:

"And take the bloody instructor with you."

Eyeing him, the other marker noted a white, set face and curiously dead eyes. Bloke looked as though he was going to be sick. Blast im.

Presently Garland picked up his pole, indifferently, and began to record the hits on his target.

An hour passed. The voice of the lemonade seller came occasionally to the markers in their trench. The riflemen were now firing from the standing position. A whistle blew shrilly. There came with it a hail in the voice of the scientific sergeant.

"You fellows, there! Time to fire your practice."

Garland and his companion climbed out of the trench and crossed the sand. They picked up their rifles, oiled and ready, were handed clips of cartridges, and instructed to give the bores a final pull-through. Two of those aircraftmen who had already fired crossed to the trench to record for the ex-markers. The others surrounded the lemonade seller.

"Lying position first," said the scientific sergeant. "Spread out that blanket a bit more, will you? Ready? Lying position, prepare!"

At this order Garland and his companion fell flat upon their stomachs, holding their rifles clear of the ground. The sergeant took out his watch.

"Load!"

The two aircraftmen clicked back the bolts of their rifles, placed each a clip in position, and with their thumbs forced five cartridges down into the magazine. Each then shot home the bolt and set the safety catch.

"Prepare to fire."

Garland's companion flung forward his rifle, brought the butt against his right shoulder, peered along the sights, altered the sighting gauge. The sergeant inspected. He looked down at Garland absently.

"Fire left-handed, do you?"

"Yes."

"Right. Five rounds deliberate: take your time. Fire!"

Crack! Psst! Crack! Psst! Crack! Psst! Crack! Psst! went Garland's rifle. The scientific sergeant called out to him.

"Here, not rapid firing. Deliberate, I said. . . . Want to start over again?"

Liking Garland's accent, he offered him this concession. Garland shook his head.

"No, thanks. I knew it was deliberate. . . . They think in the butts I've finished."

For the hidden marker for Garland's trench was showing the recording pole. Four times he elevated it. A buzz of excitement rose from the audience of aircraftmen. Bloody good shooting.

Garland had scored four bulls.

"Damned fool that marker," said the sergeant. Stentorian: "Hi! Didn't you hear me say wait for five rounds, blast you?"

The recording pole disappeared. Crack! Psst! went the rifle of Garland's companion. Garland clicked back his bolt, ejected a spent shell, jammed home the bolt again, and looked sideways. His audience had become spectators: their eyes were on the target. Garland set his teeth, swung his head aside, gripped a hand, suddenly sweat-ejecting, above the magazine feeder, and pressed the trigger with his little finger. . . .

"Christ!" said the scientific sergeant.

He jumped back. From Garland's rifle had come a sputter, a crackling backward ejection of gas, a flash of livid blue flame. Dropping the rifle, Garland rolled aside. The sergeant swore, ran forward, and leant over him.

"Hurt?"

"My hand."

The sergeant looked at Garland's left hand, tore out his packet of field dressing, shouted to one of the gaping aircraftmen to get water, and knelt down. . . . By God! grinning with his hand smashed!

"Keep it up. Plucky devil."

"Unscientific world, isn't it, sergeant?" grinned Garland, and fainted.

Subchapter iii

It was ten o'clock at night, and Andreas van Koupa was having his bath.

Bathing he made a lengthy process. His valet, personally selected from some seven applicants, was named Clelland. He was tall, spare, with weak eyes and a truculent manner. The manner had caused Koupa to engage him. He promised amusement. Finding that he had been baptized James, Koupa brooded upon the matter and then delivered a ukase.

"James will not do, my little. It is seemly for a valet to be called James. And a seemly valet I will not tolerate. I shall call you Sardanapalus."

"Very good, sir."

Clelland had been in service for twenty years and a valet for ten of these. Born in Dorset, he had been begot by a gardener upon a cook. From his earliest years he had looked upon service with the gentry as only technically inferior to the service of God. He liked being a servant. No man capable of paying him a salary could be of the same blood and flesh-texture as himself. He was convinced of hierarchy upon hierarchy of the divinely comfortable divinely ordained to that comfort. He was a fatalist in philosophy, and as a result stole as much as possible whenever opportunity offered. He seldom left a master but he was the richer in saleable studs and links. To rob his master he was as divinely appointed as was his master to have his face shaved and his bath prepared.

His truculent manner was due to a purely nervous weakness, and had misled Koupa. But the poet went in constant hope of provoking revolt in the heart of Clelland. Suspecting him of current proletarian superstitions, Koupa would talk scoffingly of Mr. Ramsay MacDonald, trades unions, and the *New Leader*. To all such remarks Clelland agreed with enthusiastic respect. Sighing, Koupa gave up his self-appointed task.

"He has the soul of the proverbial worm, this Sardanapalus. But its turning he will not emulate. He is an efficient blot upon my bedroom. I shall rename him Ashurbanipul."

When he could remember to do so, the poet worked his valet hard. He enjoyed being tended as though he were a paralytic. Examining his own soul in the early days after Clelland's engagement, he was delighted to find in it a certain shame of having his person tended and seen to and shaved by alien hands.

"God mine, but this is good. My soul, thou art bourgeois. Unless it be that thou art ultra-modern. Which is worse."

He lay in his bath, thinking of this. It was a wide, deep bath, sunken in the floor. It steamed pleasingly. Grateful odours floated over the head of the poet. About his body the water, softened by expensive bath-salts, had a caressing intimacy. Towels, in series for service, stood by the electrical warming apparatus. Great sponges of silky texture lay within reach.

"But it may be that all service of the individual master is shameful. It is a survival of the bullying with bone and sinew and club. Even before the day of the club was the day of the personal servant. Man's unfortunate gregariousness was the indirect cause of his appearance. The so-great he-ape sought companionship in his forest-wanderings, in his vermin-hunts, in his raids upon the screeching female group. He caused some lesser male to accompany him, to hand over the choicer vermin caught, to assist in the abduction of the female. Then he would sit, slow-dozing by the stagnant drinking-pool, the while the lesser ape assiduously picked the lice from his master's back and shoulders. Or licked his wounds. Or was killed and eaten when the hunger-time and famine came."

And the poet gently twiddled his toes, and, regarding his tended body, smiled.

He loved the life into which he had climbed through the affections and prestige of the one-time Mrs. Gayford. He drank of its comforts and luxuries, not sparingly, not ravenously, but slowly, as a gourmet at an exquisite banquet. At meals he ate much, but with deliberation. He had himself clad in costly and highly-coloured underwear at ten o'clock each morning. For twelve hours out of the twenty-four he slept in a large and expensive Empire bed, with rounded pillows and springs of ease and wonder, so that he would feel himself lying, already dead, in some Jehovian heaven. And, with this humour upon him, he had a barrel-organ come and play outside his bedroom window, two mornings in succession, in order that the illusion might be complete.

But his acts of eccentricity, outside the hiring of the barrel-organ and the naming of his valet, were few. With a grave appreciation he lived this new life. And he would think:

"Like my he-ape of the drinking-pools, I also am a cannibal. I live on food grown on sweating farms, by the toil of serf-like yokels. I go clad in silk from the men-manured fields of France. Like a vampire sucking blood I suck life and service from

Ashurbanipul and a so-great host of others. In return, I now and then write the so-little sonnet. I am one of the world's anointed. For this consummation dreamers have dreamt, inventors invented, rebels rebelled, kings have been kingly. For this they died at Marathon and were crucified along the Appian Way—that I might forget them and sleep."

He slept as one who had due to him long arrears of sleep. He slept luxuriously, frighteningly, so that even after twelve hours nightly his valet had to shake him awake. He slept with a vast, comfortable, impersonal weariness. He nightly sank himself in a tideless, dreamless sea of no-consciousness.

"And the so-fat sow would protest? God mine, have I not the long years to atone for? Has she slept upon the snows of Russia or in half the windy ditches of Europe, as I have? I could out-sleep Arthur in Avalon, and with better excuse."

Mrs. Koupa feared and admired him, nor yet saw any prospect of wearying of the novelty. It was as the mating of a middle-aged peacock to a sea-hawk, but the ex-Mrs. Gayford was unconscious of the fact. The hawk alternately thrilled and frightened her. Once, when she had protested against his refusal to attend a dinner owing to his affirmation that he needed sleep, Koupa had burst into a torrent of abuse. Who was she to criticize? Was he her paid servant? Could he not be master in his own house? And, grasping her shoulders cruelly with his long fingers, he had thrust blazing eyes within a few inches of her own. She had thereat soothed him and apologized, abjectly. Koupa, alone, had smiled at himself in a great mirror.

"God mine, I think she half-believes this house is verily mine."

The first issue of *The Lyre* had met with an excellent reception. By careful advertising and the employment of an expensive press-agency, it had achieved not only stimulating reviews but a surprising sale. Reviewers, praising Koupa's poems, which filled half the issue, had done so with sentences beginning: "The maturing of Mynheer Andreas van Koupa's verse since early days has been even and deliberate. . . . " "From a poet of promise, he has achieved genius. . . . " And the like.

Elected member of an exclusive literary club, Koupa had now arranged for the publication of his poems in three slim volumes. Less than a fourth had previously appeared in print, but they were to be published as reprints. Advance notices had already appeared in most journals. And Koupa thought:

"I wrote them ten, fifteen—so-long years ago. They refused, those English houses and publishers. Not one of them would usher my dream-children into the world. And now they praise with their so-buttered words. They speak of growing genius. . . . God mine! I could not now outsound the bullock-bleat of a Chesterton or the whip-whoo of a De la Mare. They praise and acclaim not me, but the scabby young pimp of the Montmartre brothels. . . . *Ave atque vale*: To you the so-good glory, O my youth; to me, the comforts. Had you not gone an-hungered how would I now be able to feast on the fruits of your so-tortured brain?"

And he would reflect:

"It was well that I was of the Keatsian, not the Shelleyan genius. Had I expressed my so-brave rebel philosophy in terms political, even now it would be looked coldly upon. But I swathed it in trees and streams and damp stars and the bedgowns of the ancient gods. Wherefore I am a poet."

Convinced that no good could come from the stirring of the gutters, he had dropped all relations with the Anarcho-communist Party. Both he and the ex-Mrs. Gayford had been blacklisted in an issue of *The Red Republican*. And, surveying his thoughts with that soundless mind-chuckle of the Other Self, the poet saw that he already looked upon his late associates not only with contempt, but with a certain cruel anger. These animals who sought to drag in the mire all the fair and sweet and lovely things of Life. . . .

"God mine!"

The poet ceased to float idly in his bath. He clasped his hands behind his head. His eyes shone with sudden resolution. Thought of a new act had come upon him—an act which would bow in weeping all the grey rebel shades in Hell.

"By the so-little Christ! I will join the Primrose League!"

CHAPTER THE ELEVENTH

Wherein Garland evolves a System of Religion and renounces the Belief that Life is due to a Faulty and Accidental Mixing of Chemicals.

Subchapter i

EARLY in March a young man descended from a tramcar in Clerkenwell and sought a side-street. Though it lay remote from the main thoroughfare, he found it without difficulty. Entering it; he was apprised of an unusual smell. This was caused by the upper half of the street being used as a stable for the horses of the London and Surrey Cartage Company. Through the white and blue of the March day arose the sound of iron-shod hoofs clumping on worn cobbles, the whoas of drivers, the lift and fall of stable effluvia. The young man paid no attention. With a letter in his hand he walked up the street, amidst disordered dustbins, seeking a certain number.

He found it on the doorway of a house, wedged sideways between two others and leaning crazily forward as if to peer round the shoulder of its neighbours upon the faces of the passers-by. The young man rang at a bell, and, obtaining no answer, beat upon the door with his stick. Doing this, he noted, detachedly, that the bellpush was green and that round its edges a minute fungoid growth flourished obscenely.

The door opened. A man, unshaved, wearing cloth slippers and carrying a copy of the *Daily Mail*, appeared. From his face exuded a smell of kippers. Upon his waistcoat were the miniature ribbons of three War-medals. He regarded the young man with large, fishy, grey eyes, the while he absorbed details of his appearance.

He saw before him one of middle height, stout, with a heavy face and sulky eyes. The young man was in Air Force uniform and carried one arm in a sling.

They spoke simultaneously:

"Are you Mr. Roupell?"

"Mr. Garland?"

The fish-eyed man stared at Garland queerly. A heavy redness uprose beneath his unshaven skin. "Mr. Garland? I eard you were in Egipp. Urt your and?"

"Smashed by a bursting rifle. I've been sent home, invalided out of the Service." Garland's eyes smouldered sulkily. The letter in his hand shook. "Is my wife in?"

Mr. Roupell backed away. "Ere, come in. In there. Sit down and I'll . . .."

The door closed behind him. The flap of his list slippers sounded remoter down a passage. Garland looked round, sat down. His heart was beating high in his throat. He loosened the neck of his tunic, stared at the door, looked away from it again. Thea . . ..

He became conscious of the letter still grasped in his hand. He read it, tiredly, looking up at the door uncertainly, once folding the pages and putting them in his breast pocket and then taking them out again.

He had received this letter in Jerusalem on the 15th of January. It showed creased and soiled with much re-reading.

> Dear Husband-lover,
>
> Thanks for your letter of the 29th. It came a week ago. You're a dear man. I wish I were with you, for you're a lucky one as well, and it must be a kind Air Force which organizes such Cook's tours.
>
> But I wish it was a little kinder to me. You'll see that I've changed my address. The Stickellys turned me out, and I know you wouldn't guess the reason though I gave you a hundred years to do it in. It was because James Storman—remember him? the Communist who was in love with Norah and is now married to her—paid me a visit. Dear, Stickelly was a detective, Storman was well known, and it was concluded that I was a Communist. So the Government instructed that I should be thrown out.
>
> I found this place without much trouble. It's cheap and quite comfortable. I have a bed-sitting-room, with a gas-ring on the landing to do my cooking. The people,

Roupell is the name, are not detectives. Mr. Roupell is a carter. He eats kippers at every meal, I think, and wears medals on Sunday. He's interested in you because he was a driver in the R.F.C. during the War.

I'll be all right, don't worry, though money's a devil of a nuisance.

This, in Thea's wide, easy scrawl, had ended page 2 of the letter. Each sheet was numbered, and page 3 resumed:

Been rotten weather this last week, but it should clear up soon. Haven't seen anything of Norah or Ellen since I moved here. Don't suppose they know my change of address. I'll have to write a note to Norah, anyway. At home I think they're still sulking over our hasty marriage, but they'll cure in time. Silly old geese!

That's about all at the moment, sweet heart. Do look after your dear self and don't go falling off pyramids or camels or anything. Write me often.

Yours,
THEA.

This ended page 3.

But there were four pages. The fourth was also numbered 3. It was a crumpled page, obviously inserted by mistake; written to ease the fear and loneliness of the writer, then thrown aside; picked up in the twilight of the bed-sitting-room and enveloped with the lighthearted other sheets.

Oh, my dear, my dear, God knows what I'll do. I could go mad when I sit thinking; I daren't sit thinking. I've no money—I've been without food, except for bread, for two days. Your allowance comes to-morrow but it'll hardly do more than pay off the rent. And so on it'll go for months, never ending. . . .

And the baby's coming. Soon be here. I've no clothes for it, no cot, nothing. Poor little kid! I can't afford to see a doctor, and I don't know anything about things, but I think it's a criminal offence not to notify a doctor. I should see a doctor, I know, and arrange to go

193

somewhere, or have a nurse, or something. But I can't I can't. I've no money, not even to pay for a bus-fare. And walking tires me so that I can hardly stand. My legs have swollen.

I'm afraid, God, I'm afraid. Not only of this but the pain and loneliness to come. In the darkness, nothing to hold on to. Oh, I'm a scared coward, but I can't, can't go on. . . .

John. Oh God God God God . . ..

Subchapter ii

It had brought him from Egypt, that blotted, hysterical page; it had led him to shatter his hand at Bir Salem by the old trick of disablement—firing a rifle with an unscrewed bolt; it had accomplished his invaliding to England and his pending discharge. Now he waited, hearing steps. The door opened.

It was not Thea, but a woman with great breasts and a red-scoured face. She held out a red, damp hand. There was about her the smell of soap and laundering.

"Mister Garlan? Sit doon. That fule o a man o mine is as fusionless as only a bairn or an Englishmin could be. . . . Och, I mind noo, you're English, though Mrs. Garlan's no. Where did ye come frae?"

"From hospital, Mrs. Roupell—isn't it?"

"Aye, I'm her. You maun be tired. Sit still an I'll mak a cup o tea. Would ye like an egg?"

"Mrs. Roupell, where's my wife?"

The woman's eyes winked together rapidly. "She's no in just noo. Sit doon an I'll bring ye a cup o tea."

Garland walked over to her at the door, looked into her eyes, saw the trembling of the heavy, kindly lips. He felt cool and undisturbed.

"Mrs. Roupell, where's my wife?"

She made a strange, helpless gesture, half-holding out her roughened hands.

"Sit doon, sit doon. Oh, Mr. Garlan, I dinna ken hoo to tell ye. . . . Puir young lassie. We havena slept for thinkin o her, me an my man, thinkin that maybe we were to blame. But we didna ken, we didna ken." A tear rolled down her face. "We didna ken."

"When did she die?"

"Die? I dinna think she's dead. The nurse told Roupell this mornin that she was sinkin fast. But she's no dead. Puir young lassie. I'll never forgie mysel . . .."

Garland sat down. He lit a cigarette. His calmness seemed undisturbed.

"Will you please tell me about it, Mrs. Roupell?"

And presently everything was told. Three days before his arrival Thea had been discovered lying in a dead faint on the landing outside her room. A doctor had been called in, and Mrs. Garland removed to the London General Hospital, suffering from undernourishment and certain complications of advanced pregnancy, culminating in eclampsy.

Subchapter iii

The doctor looked Garland over with critical, kindly eyes. He seemed to be harbouring some remote jest. He wore a white surtout, streakily stained.

"There's no change. She's still unconscious. Yes, you can see her. Nurse!"

Garland followed a nurse along corridors which rang under the steel of his feet. The nurse kept turning to address cheerful remarks to him. Cold weather. Looks like snow. No spring even after such a winter. Have you hurt your arm? Your hand? A rifle? My! you'll have to press for compensation. Just in here you'll find her. Oh, quite all right. You can move the screen. . . . Now I'll leave you. Quite safe. If you want anything press that bell. There's a chair over by the radiator.

Garland stood inside four walls of grey screen. He looked down on a bed and into a pair of very bright eyes.

Thea lay on her back, on a kind of rubber sheet. Her coppery hair was flung back from her brow. He had never before noticed the shape of her brow. She stared up at him, brightly, unseeingly. Her eyes wavered away from him, her lips moved as at the jerk of a string.

"Oh dear, oh dear."

He bent over her. For a full minute he failed to comprehend

195

that no mind of the Thea he had known functioned behind those bright eyes and moving lips. He kissed her and she moved her head aside in steady, unceasing rhythm.

"Oh dear, oh dear."

For sixty hours she had lain, singing underbreath that monotone. As he looked he saw the purpose of the rubber sheet. From Thea's lips a thin brown liquid oozed and fell. In its passage across her cheek it had already worn a trail of red, raw flesh.

"Oh dear, oh dear."

He sat down and looked at her. All the ward outside was very quiet. Surely listening to her. He picked up a cloth and wiped the brown acid from her lips. He placed his hand by the side of her cheek.

"Thea. You know me. Thea."

And, with the sound of his own voice, he realized with a dull amazement that he was weeping. In the restricted space left by his hand, Thea's head moved to and fro, ceaselessly, on the pillowless bed.

"Oh dear, oh dear."

He withdrew his hand. A memory of a day in the Zoo at Regent's Park came to him. Why? Oh, the pacing of the cats. . . . To and fro, endlessly, unwearyingly, seekers after an undespaired-for freedom. To and fro endlessly.

"Oh dear, oh dear."

He became aware of a horrifying change. Her lips had closed, were caving in, her eyes seemed gouging from their sockets. Upon the rubber sheet her body curved and twisted, white and bloated, scarred with giant sores upon the poison-laden flesh. He reached blindly for the bellpush.

"Nurse!"

A screen was quickly drawn aside. The nurse looked in, cheerfully. Immediately she entered, then turned back to the screen and thrust her head out.

"Sister."

Garland stood up and aside. Of a sudden his mangled hand began to throb. He would not look again. He looked.

Cheerful, deft, they were holding her down on the bed. The nurse had clamped an apparatus of metal and linen over the distorted face. The other uncorked a bottle and handed it to the nurse.

196

Thea suddenly shook and fell away from them and lay very still. Her head did not move now. Below her eyes gathered a strange bluishness.... The nurse turned cheerfully to Garland.

"Scared, were you? I don't think you should stay any longer. Go and have some tea, do. You'll feel better. No, there won't be any change for some hours yet."

Garland followed the nurse down the ringing corridor, to the hospital steps and a glimpse of the closing darkness of the London March.

"When shall I come back?"

She looked brightly from the clock to his face. "Well, any time. You can't do anything, you know. When would suit you best? Come at eight? The doctor'll be examining Mrs. Garland again."

"Nurse, is there any hope?"

"Why, of course. Going to snow, I'm sure. Now, do have a good tea. Good-bye."

Subchapter iv

He wondered how he would feel when Thea was dead.

Crossing the Hungerford footbridge, he brooded upon this, but impersonally, as though he were an observer on a ship at sea, knowing that a dim-seen island would shortly vanish in a submarine earthquake.

For all his senses seemed preternaturally sharpened. Never had he felt so alive. Except that something which was not his mind, something back of it and above it, was dead. Of that he was conscious, with a cool wonder, and knew that dead something for the real Garland. The thing within his brain with which he now thought and brooded was a false and alien self.

He passed through cold, ringing streets to the Union Jack Club, and booked a room there. Then he went out into the night again and became aware of something which he had surely never seen before. Under the electric lights was a drifting fall of whiteness, a magical, never-ceasing descent, a growing to being out of skyey darkness into terrestrial light. He stood on the steps of the Union Jack Club and held out his hand.

"Snowing."

Slowly, like a tame thing, a flake swung down to his hand. He stared at the marvel of it. Newsboys were shouting in the streets. Cabs rattled. He looked round him with a sharp surprise.

Didn't they know about Thea? Lying there on that rubber sheet, the brown acid dribbling from her lips? Didn't they know?

Something to read. Something to forget. Supper. Something to read.

He crossed the street and went up the stone stairs of the Waterloo Station to the bookstall. And, going, he read the advertisements, saw their value. They were extraordinarily bright and attractive. That whisky splendidly postered. A new magazine out since he had left England. Running a Tarzan serial. Good old Tarzan. Michael Arlen. Can't abide Michael.

He bought "When the World Shook" at the bookstall and took it with him up the Waterloo Road to a frowsty restaurant where the unemployed munched pieces of bread and drank coffee. He sat down at a small, marble-topped table. There was a warm fire in the room. Several men, drinking their coffee, were discussing the day's football. A cheerful waitress came to him.

"Two kippers, please, and tea and bread and butter."

"Large or small tea?"

"Large, please."

He opened "When the World Shook" and began to read it. Soon he was deep in it, enjoying it. The kippers were brought and he ate them, with mustard, and drank the large tea from a thick cup. Bread with butter. Good after Air Force margarine. Time to be going. A cigarette.

He bought a packet and lit one and sat smoking in the warmth. The waitress came and paid him his change in many coppers. She stoked the fire. Garland got up and buttoned his coat, pocketed "When the World Shook" carefully, and went out.

The snow fell steadily. But up the Waterloo Road the crowds merely thickened. Garland stopped often to look in shop windows, and now and then at his watch. Plenty of time.

But near Charing Cross, stopping, he knew he was in a nightmare. He had never married Thea Mayven. He had never gone to Palestine. Thea was not in hospital. He was mixed up with ironic happenings in his own novel. Presently he would wake up in Burford Camp.

He must awake. Else his brain would split in the glare of the lights. Else the crowds would know, as he had imagined he did. They would not run and loiter and shout and chatter if it were true. . . .

A girl with Thea's way of walking passed him. He followed after her, breathless, knowing that in a little she would turn her face towards him, halt with the old, glad cry, the amused lips, cry "John". In a moment.

She went into a shop, and so turned her face towards him, a peaked, red-nosed face, at sight of which he halted and stared till she had vanished and the crowds forced him on.

Snow fell steadily. Ravenously hungry, he stopped at a cof-fee-stall, and bought a cup of tea and sandwiches. The keeper of the coffee-stall talked to him of a man whom he knew in the Air Force. A sergeant pilot, and doing very well. Yes. And Garland found himself interested, and making authoritative statements on the Air Force, and feeling the copy of "When the World Shook" pressing comfortably against his hip.

Ever after he was to associate Rider Haggard's book with that night. Inextricably mixed with that night and the snow were Arbuthnot, Bastin, and Bickley. They swept across the southern seas in a typhoon that was a drifting snowstorm, they talked and wondered in the ruined ship, in low voices, because somewhere at the back of their minds, closed out, desperately forgotten, was the knowledge that Thea lay in a remote part of the ship, lay moaning, turning bright, glazed eyes to and fro, endlessly, whispering "Oh dear, oh dear." And then her mouth would cave in, her body twist.

Snow fell steadily. Garland climbed the hospital steps to the porter's lodge and was admitted. The porter's moustaches, curving and bovine, hung from his cheeks like creeper growths. Turning to guide Garland, he expectorated cracklingly into the night. Then the corridors rang again under the hobnails of Garland's boots.

The doctor, smiling at some cryptic jest. His hands bloody, his sleeves rolled up. "Mr. Garland? Come in here, will you?"

He led the way into a small room, the door of which was labelled "Store". There was a table, a chair, a bed. The electric light did not work and they stood in a glow from the corridor. A window was open and the snow drifted by, an unbroken curtain against the square of darkness.

The doctor stood with his bloody hands held away from his surtout. He was taller than Garland. His teeth glimmered as he spoke.

"There's a change, Mr. Garland. A quite unexpected change. Never encountered its like before. Your wife is in labour."

"In labour?"

"Yes. Yes. Distinct signs of it. Unexpected. Is there anyone who would look after the child for you, Mr. Garland?"

Look after the child. Look after the child. But the doctor did not wait for a reply. He moved towards the doorway in the bright-shining corridor. Somewhere, further along, a nurse was laughing. From a yet more distant place came a burst of cheering. In the doorway the doctor stood with his head turned in the direction of the cheering.

"Patients' concert." He smiled. His bright teeth glimmered. Recollected Garland. Moved to let him pass. "Yes. Distinct signs."

"Can I see her?"

"Don't think you should. Only upset you. They haven't cleared the mess up, yet. Best thing you can do is go and have some food and come back later. If you like. There'll be no change for some time. Not till morning, anyway."

"I'll come back at midnight."

"All right. If you want to. But get some food and sleep. Still snowing?"

A sudden scream rang out—a scream thin, horrible, animal, mounting chord upon chord up a quivering scale of agony. It died, then rose and fell again. Rose again, till the corridor rang with the peal of it. The doctor nodded to Garland.

"Get some food and sleep. There'll be no change till morning. Good night."

For a moment, lowering face frozen, Garland stood hesitant. Was that Thea? Impossible. Go now and come back at midnight. No change. . . .

The scream quavered up again from an underdrooling scarp of shrill agony. Garland nodded to the doctor.

"Right. Thanks very much. Good night."

It had been Thea. . . .

He became profoundly convinced of the existence of God. In the thinning and thickening snowfall as he walked the Victoria Embankment he knew that there was verily a Deity.

Only, God was a Devil.

All the legends and tales were true. Created not by their own forces, but by a reasoning mind, had been the universe, all the stars, life, movement, sensation. Created by a super-scientist eternally experimenting. And at the beginning he had set aside the earth for his experiment in organic life.

Sometimes, busied elsewhere amongst other jars in that giant laboratory, he forgot this planet, and the thing labelled Life mouldered forth unforeseen growths—pity and compassion and star-wonder, the adventure-soul, and love. Then, in the close heat of the laboratory, God would lift the lid off the jar and survey the new shape and form of his experiment. With cold, clear eyes he would look on it, then reach his hand into the midst of it, flick fingers here and there, withdraw them, stand watching. And where he had flicked a finger the crabs of writhing cancer would move in agonized stomach, great tumours would root and sprout in rotting brain-cells, viviparous organs would contract and close on unborn offspring. Then God would replace the lid, make notes, walk away, and stand watching through the star-studded windows a never-ending snow. . . .

And God himself was but a fleeting drift of atoms in an experiment by yet another super-scientist, who flicked his fingers in the brain of God to induce God to set the plagues and cancers in motion.

Oh, rot, man, rot. Step aside and laugh at it. Let the drums and the processioning go by, the tears, the love, the pain. Step out. You were never made for that march. Probe in their comical gestures and beliefs. Step aside and laugh at it all. Step aside. . . .

It was a voice that cried inside his head, and there was agony in the cry. Garland, the old Garland, fighting a last fight.

And, standing looking over the snow-sheeted River, he heard, as in a dream, the voice pass by and out of his life for ever.

Subchapter vi

He walked up from the Embankment towards Leicester Square, where the theatres blinked dead eyes. The snow ceased abruptly. Frost set in. Underfoot it was a soft carpeting of crispness. Garland walked like a ghost amidst deserted cañons of stone. The noise of a last office door closing re-echoed thunderously.

At a corner a man stood aside to let Garland pass. They looked in each other's faces.

"Garland, isn't it?"

"Eh?"

"Our meeting the time before last was in the National Strike. I was on a motor-cycle, and you threatened things with a rifle. I have often wondered if it was loaded."

The man pushed back his hat so that the light fell full on his face. It was Storman. Garland nodded, dully.

"Captain Storman, isn't it? No, the rifle wasn't loaded."

He passed on, but Storman walked beside him. "Thought you were abroad. How's Mrs. Garland?"

"She's been in hospital three days. She's not expected to live."

"Baby coming?"

"Yes."

They walked down the street together. Absently, Garland related the happenings to Thea since Storman had visited her in Shepherd's Bush. His face dim under his wide hat-brim, Storman listened in silence. He expressed neither sorrow nor regret.

"I'll call round to-morrow. So will Norah. How soon do you expect your discharge from the Air Force?"

"I don't know. In a fortnight or so."

"Work to go to?"

"No."

Storman walked in silence for a little, then:

"You'll need work soon. Especially with Mrs. Garland and a baby to keep."

202

But Garland was not listening. Storman brought a card out into the snowlight.

"Look here. This is Wednesday. There's a friend of mine who's manager of the Kyland Press. He wants a sub-editor or proof-reader. Go to him Saturday forenoon. I'll ring him up meanwhile. All right?"

"Eh?"

Storman looked into his face, nodded, and then put the card into his hand. "Put it into your pocket. Don't forget."

Garland was suddenly conscious. The thing dead in him since his first visit to hospital flamed raggedly alive.

"But why are you doing this for me? I thought Communists didn't believe in charity?"

"My wife has a baby coming."

They were at Charing Cross Underground. Storman stopped.

"Can I lend you some money?"

"I've plenty—for the time being. . . . Oh, you know what I feel like. Thanks awfully. I'll go on Saturday if . . . My God! My God!"

"Give Mrs. Garland my regards when she wakes. Hope it'll be a boy. Can't blame you for tramping the streets all night. I'll do the same myself. I'll be round to-morrow. Good night."

Garland stared after him. Hadn't he understood? God, hadn't he understood that Thea . . ..

Clear and sharp across snow-whitened London Big Ben began to strike twelve.

Subchapter vii

"Sit down in here, will you?" said a cheerful night nurse. "Matron'll be to see you in a minute."

Garland stood holding his cap and listening. The whole hospital was asleep. Surely more than asleep. It was deathly still.

The door opened. The matron stood looking at Garland. She was tall, with a harsh, businesslike face, and efficient, bony hands whereon gleamed expensive rings. She nodded to a chair.

"Sit down, Mr. Garland."

He sat down. The matron sat down beside a small table, picked up a quill pen, drew a sheet of paper towards her, meditated for a moment, then swung round in her swivel chair.

"Well, Mr. Garland, the baby's born. Dead. It hadn't a chance. Best thing. I think . . . "

"I thought . . .."

"Yes. Came quickly. Can't be helped. We did all we could. Like to see it?"

He felt sick as he looked at the woman. Thea's baby. Dead. Best thing. Thea's baby. That which had grown inside the body he had loved and desired. That which he had fathered. Warm and a miracle, that which Thea had yielded to him. Thea's baby. . . .

"No."

"All right. Best not to. Not pleasant to see. Blood poisoned. You'd better go back to bed."

"I want to see my wife."

"Well, can if you like. There's no change. You'll have to see about an undertaker in the morning for the baby. Yes. Leave your hat and stick here. Nurse!"

The night-nurse took him to the ward, pulled open the surrounding screens, motioned him in with a cheerful smile. A reek, strange and repugnant, hung above the bed.

Thea lay on her back, on a rubber sheet. She had no pillow. Her head moved continually from side to side, a low moan issued endlessly, in a sing-song from her swollen lips.

"Oh dear, oh dear."

She looked completely unchanged since last he had seen her. And suddenly he was conscious that of the happenings to her she knew nothing. She, who had suffered travail all the long months, the days of starvation, the sickening agony of the last few hours, knew nothing of her release. Prisoned still, a prisoner unconscious that the bars were down and the gaoler gone.

Pitifully prisoned in mist.

And then, of a sudden, her head ceased to move to and fro. Dark blood gushed from her lips. Her eyes seemed to start from her head. She writhed under the thin covering as he caught her and held her, and he saw . . ..

He pressed the bell-switch beside the bed.

Subchapter viii

The matron stood talking to the night-nurse. It was three

o'clock in the morning. Garland had gone. The matron and the nurse were drinking tea made from an electric kettle. On the stand in front of her the matron was inspecting a paper fashion plate advertised in the *Daily Express*.

"Yes. Neat thing. Have you sent for it?"

"No. I thought of it. But there's hardly any time here for making one's clothes. Now, if I were a matron . . . ."

The matron smiled. She and the nurse were old friends, and in moments such as these, in the stillness of the nights, they relaxed discipline, and were critical and friendly. The nurse yawned.

"Eaoww! Time I went the rounds again. That septic case in Ward 3 is having a tough time of it."

"Operate to-morrow, I should think," said the matron. "Time to, anyway. You'd better have a look at Mrs. Garland, first thing."

The nurse stood up, fastening her shoulder-straps. "Yes. I think she's going."

"Bound to. Linger a few hours, perhaps. Not much more. Best thing."

The nurse finished her tea. "Ugh! She's poisoned through and through. The worst case of eclampsy I've seen."

"Yes, it's her waist that caused the bother. Too narrow: pelvis undeveloped, kidneys strangled with the double work of the child and herself. Should never have married. . . . We'll want that bed of hers for the patient who's coming from Norwood to-morrow."

"That husband takes it cool enough."

"Yes. Heartless. Ah, well, she'll know nothing about it. Won't recover consciousness again. Best thing."

Subchapter ix

Until those days and nights, Garland had never realized the extent of London. Its multitudes of streets and alleys shocked him as might some obscene and unlooked-for country discovered as hinterland to a well-known coast. He wandered them at all hours, aimlessly, mile upon mile of them, so that he strayed far away into North London, east into the depths of Limehouse, lost himself amongst the innumerable by-ways of

Thames-side, came unexpectedly upon stretches of countryside, upon queer, old-time gardens lost in slopes of slums, upon houses of a strange beauty standing on high hills and overlooking all London. Especially at night-time was he astounded at the unknown beauty of London—beauty of the spirit, he told himself—and would wander in mazes of speculation as to the relation of beauty to the human mind, the while his feet trod the muddied mazes of the New Cut. He had never before realized London.

His wanderings focussed on the hospital. It was as though he were a laggard factory-hand bound there by necessities of life and bread. Rigidly, once every three hours, he turned back from far wanderings and made for the hospital. And always, as he turned back, the covered mind with which he had thought and speculated seemed to bare itself anew, as a festering wound, to the reality of things.

For Thea had not died. Day after day, night after night she lay, turning her head from side to side, ceaselessly, the while a little stream of brown-red acid bubbled from her lips, the while she intoned in plaintive sing-song the commonplace that had once expressed a day's weariness or the sum of a moment's mirth.

"Oh dear, oh dear."

He came to expect the sight of her, so. Under the glare of the unshaded electric light, in the chill of the March day, he would stand and look at her, once every three hours, with a feeling of detachment. Away from her, outside the hospital, when he allowed his mind to uncover her memory, it was a searing agony. In her unconscious presence, somehow, there was relief. It was not Thea who lay there.

And then, at seven o'clock one Saturday morning, bending to kiss her as on every visit he did, there happened that which caused the cheerful nurse who stood watching to open wide her eyes. For at Garland's kiss Thea ceased the endless movement of her head, enduring the kiss, staring up into the face bent over her. Her thin, scarred arms came up, tentatively. She put them around Garland's neck, held him so, for a moment, then released him. And, as he stared at this miracle, she suddenly yawned, deeply, as might a child, and knuckled her eyes.

"Thea."

Her hands came slowly from her face. Puzzled, she stared at him. Then a smile touched the corners of her lips.

"Poor old John."

Subchapter x

She came out of hospital a fortnight later, and Garland brought a taxi to take her away. He had had her clothes sent by the Roupells, and when he saw her coming down the corridor on the arm of a cheerful nurse, he stopped and stared. Her clothes hung about her as though made for someone twice her size. She laughed at him, lifted an unsteady foot, waggled its shoe.

"Look, John, it's too big."

They were in the taxi. It turned south, down to the River, crossed Battersea Bridge, was in the dinginess of Battersea, passed on, stopped in a quiet, dead road that looked upon the park. Garland got out, helped out Thea. She looked around her with knit brows.

"John, you're a miracle to have got a place here. How did you manage it?"

"Luck and the impudence of despair. . . . Shall I carry you up?"

"That would be nice—if you were a romantic hero, John, and I were a romantic heroine. Instead—Why, what's wrong?"

His face was moving strangely. He laughed at her.

"Instead of being only an ironist one? Oh, Thea."

He picked her up in his arms and carried her up two flights of stairs. Mid-way up he halted to kiss her and she kissed him back with soft, sweet lips. She hid her head against him. With a song in his heart he opened the door of the flat.

It was furnished on deferred payment. Its five poor, tawdry rooms were new and shone. And in the doorway of the sitting-room someone waited.

"Thea—you wonder!"

"Oh, Norah!"

Outside, as Garland turned to close the door, he heard slow and deliberate footsteps ascending the stairs. He opened the door. The postman was counting over his letters.

"Name of Garland?"

"Yes. Thanks."

He took the package in his hand. It had been readdressed from Shepherd's Bush, from Clerkenwell. He stood looking at it a moment, then closed the door and went into the kitchen. From the sitting-room he heard the voices of Thea and Norah. He half-undid the strings of the package, then, with a laugh, flung it into the coalbox.

His first publisher had rejected him.

"Thank God!" said Garland.

CHAPTER THE LAST

*Wherein the Author avoids the Gloomily Immoral
Ending of the Modern Realist, and closes with Three
Separate Accounts of Domestic Felicity, thus proving
himself worthy of his Literary Heritage and an
Upholder of the National Morale.*

Subchapter i

THE Central Executive,
   The Anarchocommunist Party of Great Britain.
   Dear Comrades,
   I beg to give notice that I am relinquishing the
secretaryship of the Party on the 20th of this month.

This step I have contemplated for some time, and in
fairness both to the Party and myself can no longer carry
out those duties which were once more than duties.

At the same time as I resign the secretaryship, I also
wish to resign my membership of the Party itself.

The events of the last twelve months have convinced
me alike of the hopelessness of Communism and its lack
of justification. In Russia, a Communist state, I saw the
same purposeless disorder as rules in capitalist England; I
saw the same aimless enslavement to an archaic economic
machine; I saw a ruling-class—the Communist Party—in
power—a class differing in no fundamentals from those
ruling elsewhere. I saw Communism in operation as
merely one more refutation of the belief that betterment
is a thing capable of achievement by any mass action.

For a time I withstood the logic of my observations,
telling myself that Communism in England need not be
the Communism of Russia. That is a futile illusion.
Communists in England are no better or worse than their
comrades abroad. A successful Revolution in England

209

would be destined to the same bitter quaffing of the cup of success as has poisoned the Revolution of Lenin.

I can no longer believe in the saving of the world through the sinking of individuality in a common cause. Mob salvation is a proven lie. I can no longer believe that the common good is greater than the good of the individual. There is no common good.

I have no counterbelief to set against Communism. I am not about to enter any other Party. I have finished with politics and parties.

These reasons are hardly likely to commend themselves to you. I will not expand them. No doubt I will seem to you either a renegade or a traitor, and will be blacklisted accordingly. Though I am neither, I can only express a perfect indifference to whatever opinions you entertain. Their very method of formation is no longer mine.

Finally, comrades, thank you for your friendship in the past.

Yours sincerely,
JAMES STORMAN.

So that was that.

It was April outside—the clear beginning of an April afternoon which had surely strayed from the calendar pages of July. But the April had hardly penetrated to Peckham. Grey pall of smoke drifted across the sky. Below the room in which Storman sat writing buses stopped, sending up whiffs of stale petrol. A barrel-organ was playing a faded rag-time—"Good-bye, Blackbirds".

So that was that.

Storman stood up and stretched, read over the letter he had written, walked to the window. A fire burned in the grate, the room was mellowly warm. Storman adjusted the curtains into symmetrical lines, then forgot them, standing with his hand upon them.

So that was that.

He was going over again the phrases indited in his letter of resignation. They had been cold, lifeless phrases, he realized, staring down at a bus. They had enshrined his thoughts and disbelief clumsily and inadequately. Yet there was no other way in which to write.

No reason why he should take any pains to write them more clearly.

Finished and past that phase. On the 22nd he was starting work as the Kyland's manager. Good salary and excellent chances of increasing it. Be able to move from Peckham. But go carefully, do nothing in a hurry. No money to be wasted. Besides, there'd be more furniture needed if they moved to a house in the suburbs. . . .

For a little while furniture and details of a campaign of house-hunting in Purley or Wallington occupied him, but a persistent other thought intruded. That letter . . . .

He walked across the room to the writing-desk, picked up the sheets again, read them. . . . What else was there to say? Communism was slavery, the tyranny of the mob-mind upon the individual. He had realized it at last. He had finished with it.

Yet something in it sounded most false and futile. He dropped the leaves on the table, impatiently, and, in the moment of his doing so, a door in the flat opened, a murmur of voices came to his ears. He stood listening.

Then, of the murmurs, but distinct from them, there came to his ears the thin wail he had listened for—a murmurous piping that was abruptly shut off as the door which had opened was closed again. Footsteps sounded along the corridor. Someone knocked.

"Come in."

The district nurse entered. She was tall, old, bony. "Mrs. Storman would like to see you."

"Right. How's . . .?"

"Quite nicely. Strong, healthy child."

"That's good." He stared through her absently.

"That's good. I'll be along in a moment."

The door closed behind her. He was alone.

Yet not alone. Never alone again.

There was his son!

His son. Now he knew that which his letter of resignation had lacked. Mention of his son. The days of mass-enthusiasms, mass-achievements, were indeed over for ever. Yet, through the individuals, here and there, by hands and means unguessed, might yet be laid the first, unguessable foundations of the City of the Sun.

His son—his immortality, blood of his blood, flesh of his flesh—for whom he would slave and toil—his son would carry him on. He would see to that. And not hopelessly, aimlessly.

His son would carry him on, would, in the years to come, presently bear out into the world a torch to add to that light that has so often flickered and seemed to fail, yet is inextinguishable—the Light that men call by many names, by the names of Freedom and Knowledge, of Anarchy, and of God.

And, as Storman stood dreaming, there again penetrated to his ears a sound as old in essence as the stones that paved the streets of Peckham—the thin, mammalian wail of Norah's bastard child seeking the breasts of its mother.

Subchapter ii

"Goddilmighty!" said John Garland, "a day like this makes me want to cry."

"Why?" asked Thea.

Her husband smelt at the air. He wore no hat. His head was thrown back. His sulkily eager face opened its thick lips.

"I don't know. It's an unbelievable day. It's a taste of magic from the never-never. It's no right to be here—a day from the dim millennium. But I won't cry, after all."

"Don't," said Thea. "Let's sit down instead. Grass may be damp, in spite of the sun. Spread out that paper you brought. Which is it?"

Garland spread out the paper, carefully, absently, and absently replied.

"*The Red Republican*," he said.

Thea squatted down, on her heels, and folded her arms, and peered up at him, quizzically, under the brim of her green hat. For a little they looked at each other happily, with a perfect peace upon them. For they were in love with each other, with a love that was at moments the crooning of a mother upon an infant, and at others a welling of blood-red indignation against the whole outer world. And this love perpetually amazed them, because from books they had believed it unbelievable.

Putney Heath was a vivid, artificial green under that unbelievable April sun. Never could Nature have produced such colours or day naturally, Garland had said. She had risen early and decked herself from innumerable jars and caskets, with innumerable scents and pomades. She was a gay harlot.

"My dear, you are lovely," said Garland to his wife, consideringly. "And your eyes are very deep. I don't think the sun has ever been right down into them."

"Shall I open them wider?"

"Do. . . . Listen to that bird."

There was a bird whistling in the tree above them. Garland saw it through the foliage and pointed to it with his left hand. And thereat Thea's eyes stared instead at that extended hand. And, staring, a redness came in the depths of the eyes that Garland said the sun had never quite entered.

For the hand with which Garland pointed was minus two fingers, a hand maimed, almost dead, with the remaining fingers upon it slow and faltering, half-paralysed. . . . They had done that in the Air Force. Those damned, damned swine had forced him to do that. John, John, you hero, you poor, badly treated, sulky boy hero. They made you do that, and you did it. For me. . . . The swine, the swine!

"Why, darling, you're crying," said Garland.

"Sit down. I'm not. It's the sun. Tried to let it down into the depths of my eyes. . . . Oh, damn, where's that handkerchief?"

She searched her handbag. Not there. Garland sat down beside her. And he felt a queer, precious glow of happy, foolish, married intimacy, as he made a suggestion.

"Try the knee-band of your knickers."

"So it is." Thea brought out the handkerchief, and applied it, unnecessarily, to her eyes. For by then the sun had dried them. Garland watched her wonderingly. Her hair had a colour it surely never had before her illness. She was as slim as a schoolgirl, but about her neck and shoulders were little hollows which had no need to be there. She called them salt-cellars of a night when she stood in the bedroom and dabbed at them with a powder puff. Funny thing.

So, inadequately, he thought of her, and thought of another matter, but the latter adequately enough. How Thea would take the communication was hard to say. Even yet there were wide stretches of her mind that he had not explored.

A woman passed down the footpath beside them. She was young, with a thin anxious face. She carried a child, warmly wrapped, with a pink face obtruding from a white fluffiness of garmenture. Its eyes looked in Garland's with a great intentness. It smiled.

"That might have been our baby. The baby they murdered," said Garland.

Thea made a face. "I hope not. It would have looked better—if babies *can* look good. Insanitary little things. . . . And really, I suppose I murdered it myself. My narrow waist, you know."

Garland sat up on the sheets of *The Red Republican*. The new livid flush of anger was upon his face. "Don't talk rot. *They* murdered it—the swine who had you turned away from the Stickellys, the spy-hunting half-wits who forced you into the slums and starvation, the shaved and slavering apes who rule England."

Her hand sought his maimed one. She laughed strainedly. "Oh, my dear, don't let's think about it. It's over and past. They can't harm us now."

"Can't they? I used to think they were only fools. I used to think the world was a boring joke. But they're not. It's not. We'll be starved and tortured and maimed again—senselessly, for no reason—if we allow ourselves to be caught."

"And what are you to do about—them?"

"I'll see to—*them*. By God, I can play their game myself."

Thea lay flat upon the sheets of *The Red Republican*. Beyond their cover, where she laid her head, the grass was soft and young and green. She closed her eyes. John was near. Dear crusader. Smashing the world with the club of his anger. And, lying, she pondered. He had changed. That old-time humour that found a pleasure in the absurd cruelties and contradictions of life had gone. She felt his hand touch her leg and lie there, and the pleasure of the touch was sweet upon her. Her man. Her husband. Oh! Funny thing, Life. . . .

"Thea, I'm leaving Kyland's on the 22nd."

She opened her eyes, stared up at him, and he saw her face grow white. The old starvation fear.

"Why? Are they reducing the staff?"

"Not that I know of. Thea, I've joined the Anarcho-communist Party."

"And because of that . . . . "

"Not exactly. It's known that Storman is following Koupa's example and is going to resign. Turning renegade. I've been offered the Party secretaryship in his place."

"But, John . . .."

"Yes, I've accepted. Oh, it's a living wage. Besides . . .."

"What?"

"It'll be a chance to pay back a little of what you and I have had to suffer."

The bird piped in the near-by tree. The colour of Putney Heath began to fade. Thea looked at Garland. He sat with his elbows upon his knees, his chin rested upon his fist. A crouched, strong figure reminding her of someone she'd once read about. . . . Who was that? Oh, the giant in the "Food of the Gods" who sat one afternoon and surveyed all London. . . . She had a vague feeling of pity and loss.

"But you've surely changed a lot? You used to detest the Communists. Remember? You're joining them—just in order to hit back?"

Garland laughed. "What else ? What else is there to do or believe in the stinks and treacheries of this rat-run we call the world? . . . Oh, I don't know. Perhaps, somehow, I'll help a little to change things, to clean and fumigate the rat-run. No individual can, but some brotherhood of the shamed and tortured may do it yet . . . unless that's a dreary illusion as well."

"You've grown bitter."

"I've eaten bitter things."

She had sat up. Her eyes lit on his maimed hand. She stared at it. She put her arms round his neck.

"I'll join the Communists as well."

"Eh?" He turned and stared, startled, into her face, saw the seriousness and purpose in her eyes where the sun had never penetrated. Suddenly he felt chilled, as though a breath of cold air had blown across the golden afternoon.

"Why not?" She looked away from him, into the West. "Oh, Garland, my dear, we're young yet, and bitter and hurt. Both of us. And we want to hurt the world as well. But there's more in life, there'll be more in our Communism than just that. . . . Sometime, when the last year's grown dim. We'll do great things yet. There's more than just hate and darkness and hopelessness. . . . "

215

Garland did not look at her. Brooding, he also peered into the West. The wind shook the tree-tops of the Heath. Then:

"There's to fight. Even though it's a hopeless fight against immortal evils. . . . There's to fight. That for you and I and the thousands of other fools, Thea." He was silent for a little. "Or perhaps it was God, not Satan, who in times long ago was overthrown, and we rebels against Life are the champions of the dethroned God."

"That's a fine thought," said Thea.

Garland laughed and sighed. Thea shivered. Her husband put his arm around her and held her fast. So, sitting together, the sunset waned behind them, and below, far and wide, the lights of the City sprang into being.

Subchapter iii

From his bath that evening, after a long immersion in scented water and dreamy thought, Andreas van Koupa slowly emerged and towelled himself, passing the hard and then the softer towels over his body with the motions of one performing a religious exercise. Finally, caressed to a warm, sweet dryness by cloths of silken web, he put on a dressing-gown, and entered his bedroom. His valet was waiting, standing at attention near the dressing-table. Koupa looked at him drowsily, head on one side, then pointed to the bed. Promptly Clelland stepped forward and turned back the counterpane and sheets, and felt the warmth of the sheet beneath. Then he took out two warming pans and laid them aside. Then he tested the temperature of the bed with a thermometer, and showed it to the poet.

It was exactly at blood heat.

"Excellent, Ashurbanipul. Now I will go to bed. My pyjamas."

The startling garments were handed to him, and he was assisted into the trousers of them, and then the jacket held out deferentially for him to place his arms in it. He did so, standing with dreamy eyes.

"Button it," he commanded.

Clelland fitted the buttons into their holes, and upon his skin the poet felt momentarily the dank fingers of his valet. This was distasteful. Motioning him aside, Koupa got into bed, slowly, sinking deep down. Clelland stood to attention.

"Anything else, sir?"

Koupa opened his eyes. A gleam came into them.

"I would ask you a question, Ashurbanipul."

"Sir?"

"Do you believe in birth control?"

"Birth control, sir?"

"Even so, my little. Not anthropophagy, or bimetallism, or tar macadam, or rice puddings, or divination by water. But birth control. The control of the arrival of offspring. The cheating of the so-lively spermatozoon. Birth control."

Clelland looked at him with meek, truculent eyes. In his waistcoat pocket reposed a stolen tiepin. He shook his head.

"No, sir."

"Why not? Have you any children?"

"I am not married, sir."

"Ah. But if you were you would reproduce yourself as endlessly as possible? Why? Do you not think the good detached billions of atoms preferable in their detachment to being agglomerated into young Clellands?"

"My brother, sir, a grocer in Bethnal Green, is married. He has three very nice children."

"The atoms are arranged nicely? And he proposes still to continue arranging more?"

"Sir?"

"There will be other offspring of this good grocer, you think?"

"His wife is a healthy woman, sir."

"Ah. That will do, then, Ashurbanipul. Awake me at noon tomorrow."

"Two hours later than usual, sir?"

"I will leave the calculation of the difference to you, my little. Put out the light."

When Clelland had gone, leaving the room in darkness, the poet sank into a light sleep. Not as usual did he immerse himself deeply, relaxing each limb, deliberately numbing each nerve. He slept like one floating on the top of a gentle sea. He slept awake, as often in the past necessity had compelled him to do.

217

It was after midnight when he awoke. Sounds of movement had come to him from his wife's bedroom. They were attenuated ghosts of sound, for the walls were thickly panelled and padded with tapestry to prevent his being disturbed. But his hearing had been keyed to receive these sounds. He opened his eyes, and put forth an arm from the warmth of the bed. The night air of the room struck chillily upon it. He withdrew the arm and lay in thought.

Suddenly he flung aside the blankets and got out of bed and padded across the soft rugs till he stood by the window.

Outside, all London lay in the grip of an iron frost. It held the skies and streets and the roof spaces in a web of steely, salted rime. The skies were burnished and garnished with stars. He looked up at a Milky Way that glimmered like a tiara. And all London was strangely silent. The end of the world might be come, life dead and frozen and forgotten, a thin twittering ended and foregone beneath the iceglow of the stars. So it would end, some time.

A sudden fear, a desolation, held his soul. Not for the first time had he visioned the end of the world and of life, but never as he did on this night, in the stark silence. An awful loneliness horrified him. . . . For *that* his days and nights. For that all the countless days and nights of humanity, the changings of the innumerable seasons, the burgeonings of the vernal Aprils, autumns with hands red from the winepress. For that the dream and the desire.

Life! a misarrangement of the electrons, a phantasy against the still splendour of the eternal whorls. . . .

He drew the curtains suddenly and blinded the room from that desolate splendour. Through his mind rang lines of Shelley, singing the wild vision of a dreamer dreaming beyond dreams and desires.

> Life, like a dome of many-coloured glass,
> Stains the white radiance of eternity.

Stains the white radiance of eternity. . . . God mine, great Shelley! You at least have looked upon the winter skies, and seen. . . . Seen, and the vision scared that so-sweet soul of yours that you turned from it to Italy and the sunshine, Prometheus and his fires, to your bird-eyed Mary and laughter and song, to the fathering of children and the boating on wild seas. . . . Akh God! Did ever again you behold that terror of the skies?. . .

He covered his eyes in a kind of agony. What purpose, what meaning, what hope—the Dome aflame in the wastes of time and space?—Aflare with millennium on millennium, generation after generation since that first amœba in the Arctic seas. . . . Sceptic, believer, fanatic, fool—they whoomed and shrivelled like calcined flies in the furnace-Dome of Life.

God mine, forget it as did Shelley. Thou livest. Life is yours, comfort, the padded belly. You are clad in purple and fine raiment. You may build you wall on wall till you shut out the radiance for ever, and in the end pass as a mindless beast through the suttee yourself, with the debt of your blood paid out in replenishing faggots. . . .

He chuckled, standing by the drawn curtains. God mine, if a Clelland adventured in arranging the so-little atoms, might not a Koupa? Even though on the so-fat sow. . . . She would object. She believed and practised the contraceptive methods that in a civilized society would have damned eternally her own chances of appearing on the earth. . . . But she would do as he said. God mine, he would see to that. . . .

And presently, with the humorous cruelty of a tiger and the wistfulness of a little child in his heart, Andreas van Koupa knocked upon the door of his wife's bedroom, and entered, and drew the long folds of heavy tapestry behind him.

THE END